LAST RIDE OF THE UMBRA FAE

MONICA AMORE

Published by Monica Amore

www.authormonicaamore.com
Cover designer by Clint A. @clintcreates

Developmental Edits: Rachel Bunner @rachel.top.edits
Line Edits: Chelsey Brand @refinedlinesedits
Proofreading: Caitlin Lengerich @chronicledbycait
Formatting: Jasmine McKie @faye_reads
Interior Artwork by Clint A. @clintcreates
Visit the author's website for more books, merch, character art prints & more.
Digital Edition ISBN: 979-8-9889334-4-1
Paperback Edition ISBN: 979-8-9889334-3-4

CONTENTS

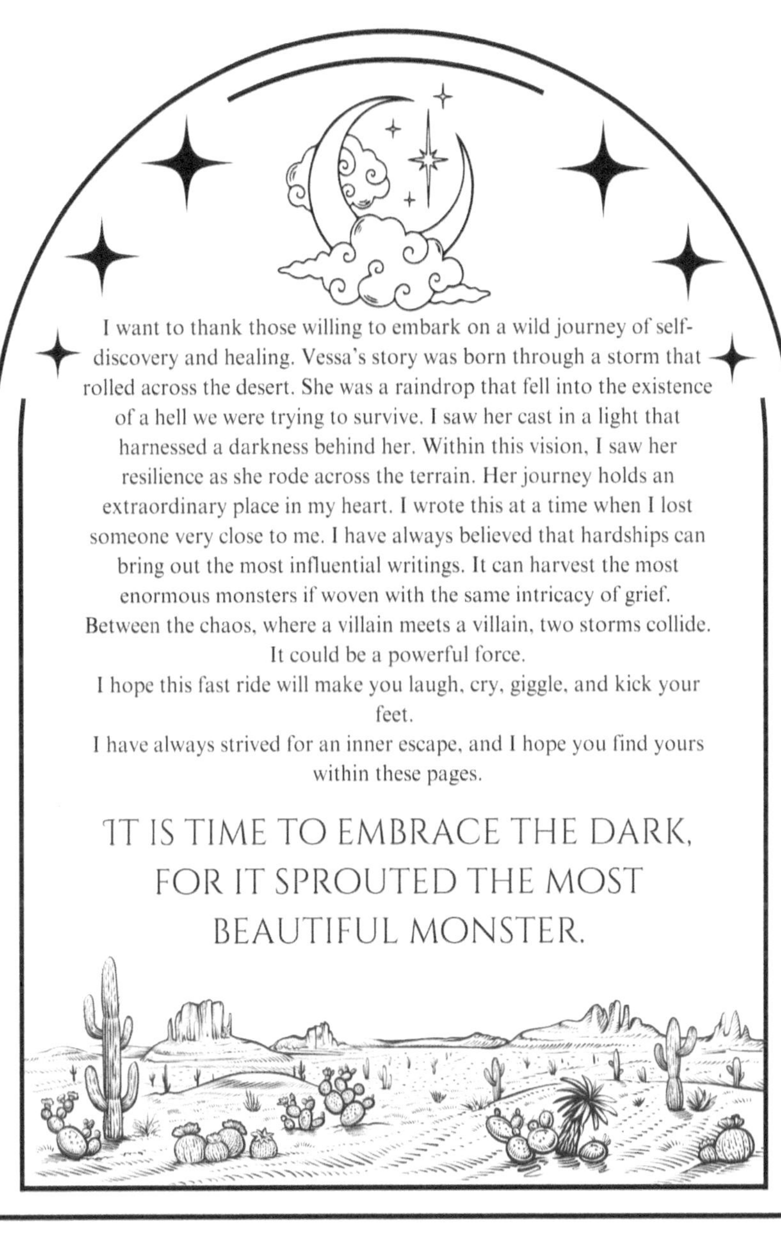

I want to thank those willing to embark on a wild journey of self-discovery and healing. Vessa's story was born through a storm that rolled across the desert. She was a raindrop that fell into the existence of a hell we were trying to survive. I saw her cast in a light that harnessed a darkness behind her. Within this vision, I saw her resilience as she rode across the terrain. Her journey holds an extraordinary place in my heart. I wrote this at a time when I lost someone very close to me. I have always believed that hardships can bring out the most influential writings. It can harvest the most enormous monsters if woven with the same intricacy of grief.

Between the chaos, where a villain meets a villain, two storms collide. It could be a powerful force.

I hope this fast ride will make you laugh, cry, giggle, and kick your feet.

I have always strived for an inner escape, and I hope you find yours within these pages.

IT IS TIME TO EMBRACE THE DARK, FOR IT SPROUTED THE MOST BEAUTIFUL MONSTER.

AUTHOR'S NOTE

This book contains mature language, graphic violence, explicit content, and subject material that may be disturbing or upsetting. It is intended for readers who are 18 and over. For an extended description for trigger warnings, please visit the author's website. Your mental health matters.

CONTENT & TRIGGER WARNING'S

Dark themes
Grief and heavy loss
Sexually explicit
Consensual sex
Death of a loved one
Dystopian
Explicit language
Gore & torture
Murder
Trauma
Isolation
Extreme violence
Verbal Abuse (not between MCs)
Assault (implied off page not between MCs)

This is your villain era. Ride the fuck out of it.

Names:
Vessa: VEH-suh
Ryder: RY-der
Pa: PAW
Raven: RAY-vin
Fang: FANG
Sergil: SIR-juhll

Places:
The City of Donia: DOH-nee-ya
Desert of Miera: MEER-uh
Emer Forest: EH-mer forest
Blightstone Hollow: BL-EYE-T-stone hollow

Power:
The Dark Side of the Moon:
Ama: AH-mah
The Light Side of the Moon:
Ano: AH-no
Wind
Nai: N-EYE
Fire
Lam: LAHM
Water
Ari: AR-ee
Earth
Nan: NAHN

I

VESSA

Sometimes I forgot the scent of rain, from the way it lifted the smell of upturned soil and dust to fill the air, to how the first drop always felt upon my skin. It was a call to cast our gaze to the skies and remember what was beyond the veil of clouds. The Vale was a beautiful place, so I'd heard; a place where all souls went to rest, to stake a claim upon their final destination, even if they didn't want to. It was an honor to be called back to the stars. The only thing was, I didn't believe in any of it.

All hope had been taken away from me the day our entire village had been destroyed and burned to the ground. The stories of the Vale were gifts, drifting down from the heavens by our ancestors to remind us of who we were. And while the rain offered a reprieve from the blazing hot sun, a peace offering from the gods, I saw none. And there would be no peace or acceptance from me. Where had the rain been to stop the embers from falling? Where had these gods been when everything around us had come crashing down? Children had run wild, wide-eyed, and barefoot onto roads full of smoldering remains.

I remembered that day like the scars that marred my arm; the smell of burning flesh as I'd stood outside my home, stunned and seized by fear as I'd waited. There had been no gods coming to save us, we'd been left behind to die. I'd screamed until I couldn't, praying until two strong, familiar arms came and pulled me off the ground, hauling me onto our horse with wings of shadow to carry me to safety. By the time I felt his grip, my lungs had succumbed to the thick clouds of smoke and whisked my breath away. Then, everything had gone black, and almost every familiar face I'd ever known had been gone with it.

That had been the last time I'd seen my home, my family and friends; the animals we'd tended had all vanished as hell rained down upon us. No power had been summoned as a last resort of magic, because death had already claimed them. Those names would die on our lips, never to be spoken again.

Pa was my savior, the man who now rode beside me with a sullen face and dark stare. His rare, simple, peek of a smile still reminded me of the sun. Though we thrived in the dark, it was his light that continued to remind me of home. He was my hope, he was resilient, and he was the last elder of our village. Though the memory of that fateful night was distant, it still tasted like ash on our tongues, so we rarely ever spoke of it or the scars it had left behind, inside and out. We were alone in this world, the last of the Umbra Fae, but at least we had each other in the hell we'd been forced to live in.

I'd like to remain what I am now, a shadow moving under the wing of night.

"Always so swift, not even the stars can keep you," Ma would say, and I didn't know why, but I'd always liked that.

The skies would never remind me of any peace coming for

us, only death chasing at our heels, promising great pain and suffering. All this for what? In hopes to go to a place we really didn't know existed? All because our ancestors had passed down stories from the stars to help us sleep at night? I would not wait on a whim nor fall victim to such a fantasy.

To hells with that.

I made my own fucking destiny.

I would ride into the dawn before I'd ever take a seat upon the stars. I'd earned my name, just as Pa had.

Hellions in the guise of cowboys riding into the dark.

We'd become the new stories humans told at night. We were the fear they invoked to whisk their children to bed.

They'd made us into monsters, but we just wanted to survive.

Somewhere inside this calloused heart lay the remnants of a female who still had dreams. But as long as humans ran this world and hid our healing source, our Eternal stone, there would never be any peace. They stood in the way of my freedom, and for that, I became the shadow that curled around their throats before claiming their lives.

They might have taken everything from us, but they would never lay a hand on me again without choking on their final breath soon after. If their faith was the same as ours, they'd better hope their souls embarked upon the stars, because I'd be keeping their seat warm, right next to me in hell. They wouldn't want to spend eternity with us, not the monsters we'd been forced to become.

Word had spread of what the humans had done to the Umbra Fae, and the Elemental Fae who had survived had disappeared as if wiping themselves off these lands. Our Eternal stone had been gone for quite some time, but something else had set us on this specific path as we embarked on a new vendetta.

It wasn't good to remain staring into the moment we'd lost ourselves, but I couldn't look away from it nor from the person I'd once been. It allowed the poison to make a home in my veins, and it was the reason I chose to take each breath as a promise. I would find who had sold us out to those humans and seek revenge for what they'd taken. I would burn every bridge until I faced the one who had betrayed us all.

We followed a lead south to a little town called Grand Dusk, which was more of a chasm beneath a mountain. A few small buildings led the way to an odd little place, as if it were something promising, something special. All I saw was a hole for men and women to merge together to get wasted. They claimed the whiskey was good, but humans were always so easily impressed. For a moment, it had piqued my interest. There'd been a small glimmer of hope I'd enjoy something for a mere moment, but once I downed my drink, the lack of burn I so desperately craved grew aggravating, which drew my attention to the doors. The bustle of life and bodies swayed to the music, but all I could see was the exit.

Dawn crept through the windows, casting rainbows around the entire room. Everyone continued to dance, not taking any notice of the array of lights shining in. I glanced down at the top of my hand, watching as one reflected off my dark leather glove, but the patrons' silhouettes were a constant eclipse of its luminosity.

Glaring at the windows once more, the light caught my eye as a searing memory took hold, one that clenched my heart so tight, I couldn't breathe. I swallowed the memory, catching sight of the one I was bound to weaving through the room in a darkened mist while Pa stood at the other end of the bar. The music was fast-paced and had an upbeat rhythm that would have made anyone want to dance; anyone except for Pa, myself … and him.

I stood idly among the crowd, observing the simple joys this place seemed to bring the humans, ignoring the vibrating hum of annoyance brushing up against my arm as Pa took the seat next to mine.

"This place is a shithole," he said beneath the brim of his black felt cowboy hat as he faced the bar. Which was his way of saying there were no leads, no remedy for me.

Drawing in a deep sigh, I dipped my chin and called to the shadows, begging for a release. I pulled it from the dark spaces of my mind until I felt its cold death grip wrapping around my throat. Gasps filled the room in unison as instruments fell from the hands of those who had played them. Only then, I caught sight of that rainbow one final time as it reflected off the window. Caught in a memory, I saw her chasing light through the forest, both of us barefoot as laughter filled the air. I gripped tighter, snuffing out her voice as everyone in the room continued gasping for air. Gritting my teeth, in one synchronous sound, they all fell to the ground.

"Just like that," Pa said in a deep tone that held no emotion.

Just like that …

They were gone.

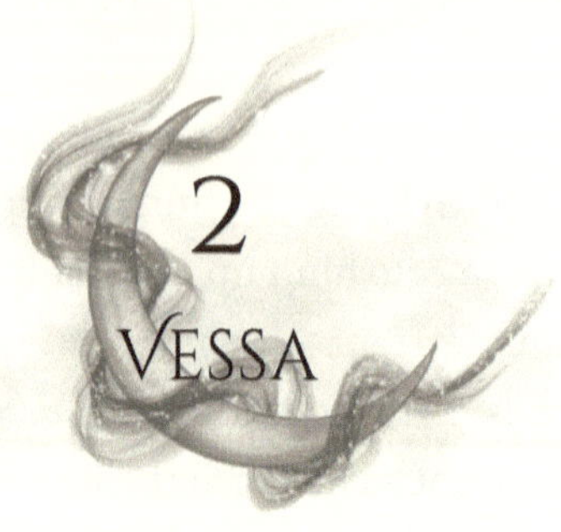

2

VESSA

The smell of heavy smoke clung to our clothes from the tavern we'd left to burn to ash. Dead bodies would have been gifts to those who pried, and we didn't need anyone on our tail for at least a few days.

There had been something hidden within the rain since we'd left that godsforsaken town hours ago, as if death had somehow found a way to break through the clouds casting light upon our course. Pa was in no rush to face whatever was lurking in that storm, he hadn't been in a while. He was waiting for whatever it was to catch up; a change since the day we'd lost my sister and Ma. It was like watching him dance with death on the crumbling edges of a cliff. Borderline reckless, if you asked me, always reveling in every life he took like a cowboy riding his way to hell.

In some fucked up way, I was just as reckless. If *that* was where we were heading, then at least I'd had a taste of it. I'd lived in it far too long to know a life outside of it. The only difference between Pa and myself was that I chased that high, riding so fast that not even the bird himself could keep up; with my arms stretched out astride my horse, open to whatever would catch me if I fell. If that was death, then so be it. The rush was always freeing, the danger compelling, lurking beyond the pall just to see what the fuck would be on the other side. Had I not been given the hand I'd been dealt, I might have cared about how hard I rode or how brutal I killed. But if the ancestors had been right and *they* were waiting for us, then I could see why Pa and I were in a hurry. I didn't fear death as I once had as a child. Grief had sprouted a grueling monster within, and we stoked it like a flame. I would watch this world burn until it turned to ash if it meant seeing their faces again.

As I looked deep into Pa's eyes, shadows lurking beyond his years, I saw we were the same.

We just had different ways of showing it.

I would have never guessed this was how the next chapter of our lives would have been, venturing out like this, but here it was, never-ending. Even after all these years, I didn't know how I was still holding on to the reins.

Pa's black stallion kept a slow trot as he looked up ahead. I caught sight of another storm thundering in the distance across the flat and desolate terrain. No doubt Mother Nature was boxing us in. She knew disease when she felt it littering the humans' soil, as if she, too, had already chosen a side.

Pa watched the birds give chase into the rain, hoping to find their own relief from this scorching heat. He was always hard to read, rigid and stone-cold, his expression void of most emotions. I didn't know why, but I still looked every day for something a little different.

"You won't find nothing here, Shadow. No matter how many times you look back," he said with a too-observant smirk that drew a huffed laugh from me. He had a way with words.

He could throw out a handful and each one would pack a punch to the soul. Pulling back on the reins, my mare slowed until we rode side by side, the last bit of heat against our backs. His voice was deep and raspy, one that held many years of smoked herbs and a special blend that he used to hide in his spruce box.

"I would kill a man or two just to have a hit." I smiled, thinking of the stone that would lift from my chest for a puff.

"Only two? You're just being coy now." He laughed gruffly, finding pride in the way I handled myself in every situation. "Here." He tossed something onto my lap. Looking down, a smile curled on my lips as I picked up and admired the rolled herb smoke between my index finger and thumb.

"How did you—"

"Don't thank me, thank *him*." He grinned, short and to the point, as he pointed toward the sky at the bird who'd been circling above us.

The bird and I were bound, not by fate, but by force, thanks to the elders of our village when I'd been a child—back when I'd been getting into too much trouble.

I looked up. "Thanks, asshole, but you forgot about Pa," I called out, only to get a cawed response.

"Oh, he took care of me," Pa said, finishing with a wink as he patted his chest, revealing an entire pouch of it. "You stay out of my pockets, and you'll be seeing more of these." The creases around his rich brown eyes deepened beneath the blazing sun. I loved it when he smiled. It was just as rewarding as the tonic he'd bring home to "keep my demons in check," as he'd say.

"Deal." I returned the smile, thankful he had sensed this coming before I had. This would have to do to ease the pain and the pounding of my heart until we could find more.

I'd been born with an illness that had almost killed me, and the scars that marred my arm from when we'd been attacked had led to a blood disease that manifested when the moon harnessed too much energy. The source of my power was a gravitational invitation for pure fuckery. I'd only experienced it a handful of times; the twisted, gut-wrenching pain so intense, I'd wanted to carve the damn marking right out of my chest.

The Eternal stone had once hidden within the Blightstone Hollow, a sacred forest southeast of where our ancestors foretold the path would be carved by the blood of fae. Within those crimson grounds of whispered tales and curses now lay the empty space that echoed its loss through the hollow.

Its presence was the only thing that could have created the remedy I needed. Looking at this rolled herb was better than staring down the bloodied beam from the gallows. "Hell's Mark" is what fae called that hellhole of a town where the others met their fate.

It wasn't long before I pulled out a flask of water, appreciating its stale taste as it went rolling down my throat. I removed my black felt cowboy hat, the wind cooling the sheen of sweat beading above my brows. As it blew through my hair, I was reminded of a time when it wasn't a sin to expose our ears or hands.

I took another long swig before pouring the remnants over my head, closing my eyes, and tilting my chin toward the sun as it dripped down my face and between my breasts. The breeze fluttered along my sternum against the symbol beautifully tattooed on my flesh.

Once in a blue moon. The power of Ano.

Ano was the goddess of half of the moon, and in the gods' ancient language, it meant light. I ran a finger over the slightly raised skin, tracing its circular shape. It was a fading reminder of the stories Ma had once told. It was a whimsical summon, calling upon the energy of the moon and harnessing the power it provided, for it was an echo of our past and a reminder of what the gods and goddesses had given us. Our ancestors had told a story about two star-born goddesses, one soul: *Ama* and *Ano*, the dark and light side of the moon, also called *half-lights*. Though I had the power of *Ano*, it wasn't always pretty when I summoned mine.

"A moon has many phases; do not sit on the dark side of it for too long, my moon."

Ignoring the hum in my chest, I ran my hand through my hair, allowing the pain of Ma's words to consume me by taking a deep puff of herbed smoke until the burn hit my lungs just right. Another hit to ease my mind. As soon as my ears felt the cool breeze, I knew it wouldn't be long until their star-like shimmer would reflect the sun, casting a bright enough glint to make Pa turn his head. It'd been a while since I'd exposed them during daylight. They had become a symbol of what we were hunted for. We were rare—barely seen.

With our black-tipped ears and onyx hands, the Umbra Fae were known as omens to the humans, our differences drawing the line between our two species as if they made us inherently bad.

The air felt like freedom. I missed the days when we didn't have to hide, but here I was, stealing a small moment of it before—

"Put your hat back on or you'll get yourself killed," Pa warned.

There it was. Fear. Not for himself, but for me.

"We are in the middle of a gods-damned desert. There isn't anyone for miles," I said, taking another puff of the herbed smoke, but my mind still reeled back to whatever was lurking in that storm.

"You don't know that," he sharply replied.

"Well, Pa, maybe I just don't give a shit anymore."

"You should."

"And what about you?" I pulled back on the reins until my horse came to a complete halt. "If you don't care, then why should I? Why keep fighting if it's just to survive?"

My heart pounded against my chest while he remained calm and calculated. You could cut the tension with a blade and it would still be potent. I stood my ground, hardening my gaze as his jaw began to flutter in aggravation. That had been too much truth for the old man as shadows stirred in his dark brown eyes. I gritted my teeth in challenge.

"You might be a grown woman, but you are still under my care."

Under his care.

I scoffed. "I am chained to a feathered bastard, who you so happen to like." I waited for a remark from the bird above us, but he was already flying away as I glanced up.

Clever bird. He hated when we argued.

The air remained charged as the two of us faced off, but a slight shift in the wind changed the entire atmosphere. My senses heightened as the energy hummed around us, but it wasn't from Pa nor me. With a brow raised, we stared in cutthroat silence until the feeling passed, but the inner cleave across my chest remained, because even now, I still couldn't get him to say how much I meant to him. Anger stung my eyes.

"I am a prisoner on open terrain. Fate be damned for you." I clicked my tongue and gently nudged my horse's sides with the heels of my boots, riding off before I could hear his retort.

I caught up to the bird, *my shadow*, and it wasn't long until we saw an outline of another shithole town off in the distance.

"Tell that stubborn old man there's a sight on the horizon." I opened the bond on my end so he could speak.

"He already knows," the bird said, coasting down to perch on my shoulder. Upon landing, he stretched his glossy feathers wide.

I huffed. "Of course he does."

Another land, another town. Another hellish place I could never claim as home for long. Nothing more than a bed to rest my head at night and maybe a man to fill it. Those nights rarely happened. Skies were endless and dreams were painless because sleep never came. All I had were living nightmares—ones I couldn't escape. By the looks of some of the people who roamed these dirt roads, they were living the same kind of hellish waking dream.

Pa's horse galloped in haste as he approached me. The tension had eased, but the way he tightened his grip on the reins told me some remained.

He'd get over it by tomorrow, but his leather gloves groaned and creaked, reminding me of his worked and calloused hands, strong enough to snap the neck of any fae or human alike. I knew my limits with the legend these lands feared, but I was still crazy enough to test him.

We seemed to draw every man and woman's gaze as we rode into town, pretending to be something we despised, like we were just some ordinary *human* folks. We had no choice but to stay hidden in a world where we were hunted.

Fear was a dreadful bitch, a disease that festered in the cracks of their morals.

This worthless town had no more than a dozen or so buildings, and we claimed it as ours for the night. All dirt paths led to some rundown places that not even the tumbleweeds wanted to bounce by. Luckily, the best-looking building was the saloon—most likely the only building that brought them any money.

They wouldn't know we were fae at first glance. Marked by darkness, or so the story went. Our markings depicted who we were. Black-tipped ears with hands that looked like they were dipped into the dark evoked fear in those who were not like us. But it was the rarity in the iridescent glow to mine that turned heads. The same star-like luminosity freckled across my face. They were beautiful when exposed, complementing my bronze skin. In the right light, they were what had made me stand out from the rest of the Umbra Fae—the shadow wielders. Ma had said I was marked by the goddesses of the moon and that's why I shone like a star beneath it.

We kept our ears hidden inside our cowboy hats. My dark hair cascaded down in soft waves, flowing to my hips with strokes of sun-kissed highlights. Pa's shoulder-length, salt-and-pepper hair had the perfect blend of dark leading to deep sideburns and a sharp jawline. For the most part, we appeared normal, but I couldn't let people get too close to me because, frankly, I was just too fucking shiny.

A man walked across the road, carrying a lantern to light his path. I caught sight of a faint, amber glow brimming out of his pocket. There was only one stone that harnessed that much healing.

Our Eternal.

The blightstone was a gaping reminder of the betrayal to all fae. It was a hybrid of amber and bloodstone. *When two worlds collide*, the ancestors had said of how the stone of Eternal was formed. Its never-ending glow would always light the way to those who needed healing.

The brute looked our way, dipping his worn hat in greeting as his leather chaps swayed from side to side, oblivious to who stared back. I felt the hum against my chest as the magic of Eternal cast its song, churning like thick honey, calling to salve the cracks in my soul and rebuild its crumbled foundation. My eyes stung as a deeper part of me summoned the shadows, which yearned to crawl their way out to make a home around his neck.

"Good evening, ma'am," he said.

I swallowed the lump in my throat, gritting my teeth and only sneering in response. I should kill the human and take back what was ours.

When he saw I offered no warm greeting, he looked to Pa. "Sir."

Pa tipped his hat, but beneath the brim, his side-eyed glare sent a warning strong enough to coil down my spine.

Not worth it.

My jaw tensed, reining back the recklessness that was brimming over.

He's right. We weren't here to take the morsel of the stone this human had somehow salvaged; we were here to find that tonic. But I knew, eventually, I'd be back, and I'd take the entire fucking realm of it.

Clicking my tongue against my cheek, I watched the man disappear inside his home as I rode on. In passing, I glanced inside a window where a hearth warmed their dinner. He was welcomed with a table full of food and a family that rushed him. Their muffled laughter from beyond their front door drew me to look away. Gunfire rang in the distance, but not many people ducked for cover. They weren't afraid to die here, not with the power of Eternal.

"*We will have our day,*" the bird said with a soft tone. He must have been truly hungry if he was being this kind to me.

"The hells are coming for them," I vowed, unable to stand how they clung to Eternal like their finest wine. He flew off my shoulder and disappeared out of sight.

We tied our horses to the hitching post near the water

trough outside the local saloon, hoping to get a room for the night. Two, if I could be particular. There was enough money, compliments of the man who had tried to cut off my ears a few nights ago once he discovered he'd been fucking a fae. I had warned him prior to keep his hands off my hair, but for some reason, the greedy fuck felt like being passionate, running his hand up the side of my face with fingers brushing against the tip of my ears. His end was met by the grip of my thighs straddling his head as shadows expelled his last breath. Now, examining the nice gold ring he'd left on my pinky finger, I considered it another parting gift.

Beside me was an untied black stallion with a calm and graceful demeanor. I briefly noticed the traveler's bags with the neck of a guitar sticking out. It struck me as odd anyone would leave something like that lying around.

Just as I was about to go inside, something else grabbed my attention. I felt like I was being watched, but when I turned, I noticed a piece of paper nailed to a post.

"'WANTED,'" I read aloud. My brows furrowed. "'For the murder of forty-five harmless civilians and counting at Grand Dusk's Tavern. Last seen heading west in the company of an old man and a pet *blue jay*.'" I snickered, ignoring the sharp pain in my right arm as I tore the sign off the post and handed it to Pa. He studied the paper, reading faster than I could with a twitch to his mouth. Somewhere behind that façade was a chuckle dying to escape, but his jaw was set tight; nothing pleasant would come out.

"You have a warrant out for your arrest. Two thousand nara coins to be exact," he warned, handing it back to me. "There will be more of these, with enough men looking to retire."

I brushed off what he said as I studied how they'd gotten my eyes just right. "I've never had my picture drawn before.

The bastard knows how to draw a nice cowboy hat. This one's cleaner than the real thing." I folded the paper and slipped it into an inner pocket of my trench coat. For a keepsake. "I wonder if this artist takes commissions."

"Your life ain't a game to play with. Stay in my line of sight," Pa said as a gang of men erupted in drunken laughter. He peered into the windows, getting a sense of what the patrons inside would be like, and then looked over his shoulder.

Giving one final tug on the reins tied to the post, I chuckled. "Whatever you say."

"I mean it."

Maybe one day he would be more direct. Tell me he sensed something following us and not just divert it toward these drunken men without any sense of their surroundings.

But realistically, that would never happen. His indirectness was a language only Ma, my sister, myself, and the bird understood.

Striding toward the swinging doors, his shadow gripped my arms.

"Vessa," he warned again. My eyes shot down to the dark swirls circling my bicep, not his usual stark black he summoned when killing. There was a softness to his shadows, one that matched his eyes, briefly exposing a flash of concern. Bold move, but as I looked around, night had already come, and we were cloaked by the blanket of its stars.

"You shouldn't worry about me. I can handle myself," I said, pressing a hand against the corner of the wooden door as I ignored the buzz of energy along my palm from whatever lay beyond it. I turned to him once more with a half smile. The motion released his soft grip. "Besides, I learned from the best." I smirked.

That's what I'm afraid of," is what Pa's face read, but he tipped his hat. I felt him watch me disappear into the crowd until the doors stopped swaying. Taking a look around, too many sets of eyes looked upon me from behind their decks of cards and the brims of their mugs. The gaggle of voices seized as I walked straight into the den of hungry wolves.

"KEEP to the shadows and low-lit taverns. There, your fate awaits."

3
RYDER

Nightlife had always been the same no matter how far I traveled. This was just another place men came to harbor their demons and nurse their liquor in hopes of wetting their dicks by the end of it. The same smells, the same racket of drunken men with roaming eyes looking for a pair of plump breasts to gawk at; this experience was a highlight of their poor existence. If they only knew they were no different from fae, but it wasn't my job to point that shit out. Inside a world where they were hunted, enslaved, and killed, hid a network of them harnessing a newfound magic to glamor their pointed ears and any other feature that distinguished them by sight. The convenience of the glamor didn't mean we could live a merry, fucking, little life together on this hell-wrecked land. I was here to do a job: to meet End's Wrath and his daughter and be their guide.

So he thought.

I was a job, a solution, a cure to what the humans felt was a disease spreading across their land. Tilting my head to the side, I watched the bubbles churn in my amber-filled glass.

Maybe I was a disease too. But I was considered special because I had a talent far exceeding basic human strength. I had no lines to draw. I only crossed them. I was death, kicking down their door, waiting to take a life to line my own pockets.

A bounty hunter's life had always been easy. The day my world ended, I faced this bold truth, sending me on an unexpected path.

Another sip to drown the memory. I always ordered the finest whiskey any shithole had to offer; it was a comfort in the dark. But I had something over this duo of Umbra Fae: more of the tonic End's Wrath's daughter needed. I had a few vials for now. Still, I had no fucking clue what it was for other than her body needed it—a "requirement" to take the job, one that would open a door to what I hoped would be the start to a wonderful relationship. I smirked, knowing I held the power over them, sway if need be, because these vials were hard to find. I've watched them kill the innocent for just a swig. The Eternal stone itself had the power of longevity, but once the blightstone was melted down, it was made into an elixir that offered healing. Not many fae were left that knew how to make this tonic, which was why the Umbra Fae were seeking a guide. They needed someone who knew the ins and outs of The City of Donia, a place far north and weeks away, and I happened to do business with one of the city's biggest suppliers.

While I sat here waiting for my next job to walk in, my eyes roamed the room, picking out each fae that hid among the crowd. There weren't many tonight. Far less these days, which told me our kind was burning out—down to the brink of extinction.

The hairs on the back of my neck rose as I instinctively turned my head toward the doors. The air was charged; the sudden shift in every shadow of the room seemed to shudder at whatever lay beyond the entrance.

A grin curved my lips. There was only one fae that could stir such a response. The moment those doors swung open, time slowed to a grinding halt.

"Fucking hells," I groaned under my breath, watching the shadow slinger herself stride into the saloon. The moment I laid eyes on her, I knew how everything was going to play out.

Arrogance emanated off her as she strode in with a vibrancy worthy of another glance. Not only by me, but by everyone else as well. She waltzed into a bar full of drunken swine with her hips swaying side to side, lulling us all into a dance we had no plans to partake in. For only a brief moment, the clamor of nightlife stopped then was resumed by the eager hands of a drunken bastard whose bravado extended to his fingertips. Rightfully so, the man eased into the seat by the piano, playing a harmonic tune that seemed to lull the drunken men back to their affairs. I had a feeling she knew she was a succubus in a crowd full of hungry men who would give their nextborn for a night with her. She would use that to her advantage. I'd seen it many times—a talent well-earned. But did they really know who she was?

I kept her in my line of sight as she weaved through the crowd—a calculated path. She brushed her dark hair behind her shoulders, eyes sweeping over the room while fixing the brim of her dust-covered hat, hiding those black-tipped ears. She must have abandoned her long dark coat, possibly leaving it on the saddle, but her gloves remained.

My eyes trailed up her arm; soft, bronze skin glowing beneath the candlelight, highlighting toned flesh, while the other hid inside a dark sleeve that reached her tricep.

Peering through the crowd, I caught another glimpse of her. Going up against the daughter of a legend would not be an easy feat. My eyes trailed down her body as a grin perked my lips. She was a storm I'd gladly trek four or five times—fucking hells, for eternity, maybe.

Gods-damn.

I downed my drink.

She stood between two stools, waving down the barmaid. The woman offered to remove her gloves and place them elsewhere, but the sneaky little fae declined. Imagine what they'd do to her if they saw her shadowed hands, the mark of her true identity. They would send her to the Scarlet Gallows northeast.

Do not worry, Desert Storm, your little secret is safe with me.

Something about her essence separated her from the rest of the fae, even from her father. I felt it now as we shared the air with sweaty, drunken swine. The more I looked, the more that thread of curiosity wanted to be strung. She pulled out a stool from the bar, sitting with her ass arched as if intentional, but I'd been watching her for weeks. Her body was a walking sin, built with curves carved by all the devils themselves for their perverse pleasures to tempt the foolhardy.

Foolish men, quite like myself. I almost fell out of my own seat stifling a self-deprecating laugh as I sat further back in my chair, crossing one ankle over the other. In another life, she would be a storm I'd love to get close to, but I had a job to do. I had to keep my focus and my cock in check.

I'd been sent to enter the eye of her storm, to rip apart every thread of magic that made her whole. She was a whisper in the dark. The rumored truth of her existence could mean the end of Fang's reign over The City of Donia. I'd been hired by him to learn why she was so fucking special. Why was she such a secret among the fae?

I knew something for certain, what made her whole and weak all at once.

Two things, actually.

The tonic her body depended on, and the tanned, salt-and-pepper-haired male who had just strolled in. I'd heard stories of who people called "the old specter who shifts into End's Wrath." A power harnessed by the dark side of the moon, which our ancestors called *ama*. He was ruthless and vile while he tore enemies to shreds. The kind of evil that kept his prey breathing long enough to feel themselves being filleted alive, carving them into nothing but a vessel of flesh and muscle. Seeing the legend himself before my eyes, this elder looked no more than a man in his mid-fifties. He would be the barrier to her.

I leaned into the crook of my corner, watching him from the shadows that stopped at the edge of where my shot of whiskey waited for me.

He didn't take the empty stool beside her. He sauntered over to a round table of drunken men who'd been gambling all night. I watched them deal him in. I tried to read his lips, but the old man barely had any words to say. Tilting my head, I studied how he took in the crowd, casually grazing over the bar where his precious daughter sat with her all too brazen appearance. You stare in the face of death long enough, and its flaws begin to surface.

Behind the hard lines of his chiseled face and days-old scruff held the eyes that softened *for her*.

I downed my drink as I took another glance at that empty stool on her right, signaling for the barmaid with two fingers.

Within a few quick strides, the voluptuous woman eyed me from the brim of her thick blonde lashes. Her breasts looked as though they needed air. Judging by the way her full lips gently fell open when she caught my stare, I knew she'd oblige. She smirked in response, but I bit down the temptation to invite her to air them out for me later.

"Another shot," I said coldly. She said nothing as she glanced at the collection of empty crystal glasses on the table.

Tempting—she truly was—but as my gaze drifted back to the fae sitting at the bar with windswept onyx hair, it would have to be a date with my hand tonight.

Something in the air shifted, a darkness that crept in on a breeze as every candle in the room flickered against the wisps of shadow. I kept my eyes trained on the opaque apparition moving past every drunken patron in the saloon.

"Luck's on my side tonight boys," her father said. The men at the table cast their sneers in his direction. A diversion as the shadow weaved unseen through the crowd.

Suddenly, a man appeared from the swells of darkness, taking the empty seat beside her. I lowered my gaze, eyes prowling over the man whose broad shoulders hunched. The fucker was too big for that stool. He stretched out a leg, running a hand through his short, dark, thick hair before putting his hat back on. A little too fancy to be a cowboy but too rugged to be a lawman. Pretty boy better be careful; if someone saw the iridescent shine to that all-too-perfect hair, they might view him as a prize. I understood who approved of the bond. If it were any other man, her father would have ended his life in a simple breath for getting that close.

Irritated by his presence, my eyes darted around the room. He was not like other fae. I realized he had the power of illusion, something I had never seen in all my years of living.

Who are you? I rubbed the scruff of my beard.

Aggravation fluttered my damn jaw as I clenched the glass of whiskey until it cracked; the sound reminding me to get a fucking grip.

Damn the hells.

How could I have missed this big fucking detail? One they'd kept so well hidden while riding into town. One I hadn't seen as I'd stalked their route from the mountain or when I'd watched them rest.

She gave him a knowing smile and eyes that might have lingered for far too long, stirring the urgency for me to see what shade of red this fucker bled. The soft sweep of her dark lashes sent an unexpected surge through me. The two Umbra Fae had always been alone. Whoever this bastard was, he was another barrier to her. I paused for a moment, looking at her father, who had just won another hand at poker, unaffected by the carcass that now warmed the empty seat beside her. As my eyes bounced back and forth between the two, I finally put it together. He was their sentinel, which meant he was a shadow shifter.

The raven.

With a simple wave of my hand, I summoned the power of *Nai* beneath my fingertips and blew into the air.

A soft light emerged from my palm, a faint wind swaying between the crowd. Within seconds, a bond appeared between them. My suspicions had been confirmed.

Interestingly, the bond had been forced and not bound by love.

This type of bond was a bodyguard, entrusted by their elders. I'd read about this after spending too many days in a library, back then, when I didn't have a home.

This raven was a complicated mass of annoyance to me.

She was her father's shadow, and this male of a bird was hers. But as I studied their connection through my own power, that *bond* was not well received on her end. I could tell in the speckle of stars woven through the magic that bound them. His was brighter, matching a star-filled sky, while hers ended in mute black, stark and void of any inkling of acceptance. She was a black hole, sucking up the life of those who had fallen by her beauty.

The raven followed her every step as if she were an extension of his heart. One I wished to sever if I could harness enough to expose the filth for what it truly was. If it weren't for the elders, she would have been easier to obtain.

I had to plan out my next move methodically. I was ready to ravage her and make her undone. I needed to get to her, really get inside the head of a hellion like herself and see what I could draw out.

4
VESSA

The saloon smelled of sweet bread and meats, coating the air to hide the stagnant stench of the sweaty bodies of brute men. My presence garnered some curious stares as their eyes lowered to the swells of my breasts. I remained calm, eyes forward, not even sparing any of these assholes a glance as I made my way toward the bar. There was a warrant out for my arrest, and I happened to have the pretty picture in my pocket. So far, this night was going pretty well.

I knew I was beautiful, and I'd used that to my advantage many times, but tonight, with my other pocket lined with nara coins, I could relax knowing what awaited me. A lady deserved a nice warm fucking bed once in a while. My shoulders slightly dropped, easing the tension from riding as I waited for my drink.

It wasn't long before I heard Pa's gruff voice as he settled into a poker game. A smile drew my lips, knowing he would end up robbing each fool blind.

Within minutes, I shuddered along the bond as the silhouette of a too-large asshole appeared beside me.

I turned my head and was met by a pair of dark and deep-set eyes, maybe charming on some days.

"Hello, bird," I coaxed, faintly smirking as I took in the sight of Raven to see where his emotions were drifting. The corner of his mouth quirked up, drawing out a dimple on the side of his face with only half a day's worth of scruff. Where he went to manicure himself was none of my fucking business. But when his stare seared down the side of my face, it became my problem.

"I don't need the bond to sense you're irritated that I'm at the bar having a drink," I said, taking a longer sip of my whiskey just to spite him. Had he forgotten fae could drink twice as much as humans and still only get a buzz?

He leaned in closer, a grinning acceptance to the silent challenge of who controlled who tonight. The ebb and flow of an unwanted relationship.

Though we were tethered, I couldn't feel a lot of things. His presence, yes—but anything that had to do with love or emotion, I gripped that part of the bond by the balls and castrated it. I was too powerful to fully accept it. A bond was supposed to connect a couple, body, mind and soul. I had the power to manipulate it, weave it into what I thought was acceptable. Which meant I was in control of how far it wove. We could speak to one another through this union, but only when *I* chose to. Which bothered him and was, in fact, the very reason he drifted into the saloon a heaving mess, because I had refused to answer him.

"You know, you're less of an asshole when you're a bird," I said.

"Raven," he corrected, unamused with how I had started this unwanted conversation. "I don't feel like babysitting you while you drink yourself into oblivion."

My head rolled in his direction. "You have to be kidding

me," I drawled. Apparently, the men in my life had forgotten I was seventy-five, though I looked to be in my late-twenties. I could have had a few dead husbands by now if this world hadn't been on the brink of destruction. "Is there somewhere else you would rather be? There's finally good liquor and a handsome chap that actually knows how to play piano, and you would rather roam the skies alone, throwing yourself a pity party?" I huffed, taking another sip.

"I don't have time for this." He deeply exhaled.

"You never do," I said, much softer than I'd anticipated. Between the two men in my life, I was always left with my own thoughts. Everyone was too damn depressed and sad to have a decent conversation these days. "You really should go sit next to that gentleman playing the piano. I know how much music soothes you." Anything to get my empty seat back. He thought about it for a moment. His eyes creased at the corner as he observed the pianist. He was just his type—elegant, suave, and talented, with veins full of sweet, tantalizing blood. Besides, birds always liked a good song. Unfortunately, his eyes were on me tonight.

Hells.

"You were supposed to get a room and wait upstairs when you walked in, not risk exposing yourself to these assholes. You're too obvious," he said.

I sighed, slowly lifting my gaze to catch him studying the freckles across my nose.

Too close, too intimate.

"It's not my fault I'm a shiny bitch. Besides. . ." I spun around in my stool to face the crowd. "I think I might want to dance tonight."

Raven ran a hand down his face, groaning.

"If you don't dance with me, someone else will," I teased. But as I turned to leave, he grabbed my wrist and yanked me against his hard, massive body, trapping me between his thighs.

"Sit the fuck down, Vessa. You're drunk."

Lies.

Maybe I was just tired of the same old routine. Maybe I just wanted to forget the pain my body was in and douse it with the best drinks stolen nara coins could buy so I could wake up regretting it tomorrow. Anything to feel alive, because the truth was, I was dying. Thankfully, the magic coursing through me was strong enough to sever a part of the connection to Raven, or else he would have known. I felt it in my blood, as if death itself was calling me from some distant place. I was gravitating toward it like a dying star.

Every. Single. Day.

Which was why I needed that fucking tonic.

I moved to take a step back. Another squeeze of his thighs anchored me where I stood.

Caged.

He pulled me closer to him, his minty breath huffed across the mark on my sternum. Ignoring what that might have done to me if I'd accepted the bond, I snuffed it out.

"Your hands are too clean to touch someone like me, bird," I hissed. "Besides, you didn't say please." With just a thought, a shadow lurched forward, wrapping around Raven's neck. "You look better collared," I said, allowing my inside thoughts to roam freely. I slightly pursed my lips, watching him exhale another deep breath at my words. He saw a flash of anger in my eyes, a mirror of his own deeply-rooted scar as he remembered how it had felt to be trapped and sold on the market as a young boy before Pa had saved him.

Trapped.

He had been tied to me without a choice. The silence was

choking him more. His grip loosened, jaw clenched. He hated feeling that way.

Raven's gaze flicked to mine. "Please," he growled through his teeth. "Sit down." The murmur was low enough for just the two of us to hear. Anger flushed his pale skin. With my free hand, I patted the side of his angled face before flicking away a strand of dark hair from his eyes. The shadow I held around his neck dissipated into the air. Another sigh, and he let go of my wrist and loosened the grip of his thighs. He looked around, but no one had seemed to notice our dispute.

"You will be my demise someday," Raven murmured again.

Unaffected by his words, I said, "You have always been mine."

A grin curved my lips as I rested both elbows against the bar, looking out at the crowd.

"See, humans are simple," I said, ignoring the tinge of hurt that I might have caused him internally. I cared about his stupid feelings, but mine would always be before his. Pa was getting up, making his way toward the end of the bar. Raven took that as his sign to leave. His job here was done. "Wasn't that a lot easier?" I asked, sitting back down on the stool. But he walked out the door without another word.

I heard Pa speaking to the lady, likely asking for two rooms. His gruff voice was always a low rumble, thundering beneath the clamor of the room. He carried on a straight-to-the-point conversation with the woman, who gave him a second glance as he strode away. Then she looked at me, smiling curtly as he disappeared into the crowd looking for another table to swindle.

A few moments passed. I was already on my second drink when another figure obscured the light beside me, taking a seat where Raven had been.

"Seat's taken," is all I said, shoulders hunched, leaning my elbows onto the hardened wood while I swiveled the ice in my glass. The sound brought comfort to my aching bones and encouragement to drink more.

"Judging by that interaction, I don't think your lover's coming back," he said. His words were enough to turn my head, my heart a pummeling beast against my chest.

"Don't worry, Desert Storm, your secret is safe with me." His whisper was a fearless gale sending a warning across my horizon. My ears grew hot as I flicked my gaze to his, finding a pair of pale-blue eyes peeking out from dark, tousled hair that framed his face. He sat facing the crowd with his elbows resting on the bar and one leg sprawled out as the bottom hem of his black coat brushed against the filthy saloon floor. Something caught in my breath as he continued to stare. A wave of mixed emotions swept down my spine in a frost-bitten shudder. Swallowing the lump in my throat, I only had a few seconds to decide if I should kill him; he'd seen who we were. And since he had called me a storm, I was suddenly in the mood for a knife fight. My mouth gaped open as the insult washed over me.

Before I could speak, Pa came up from behind. "I see you've met Vessa," he said to the man who had broad, wide shoulders and a look so penetrating, it held me beneath his stare. The bastard smirked, finding humor in my shock. I quickly closed my mouth, holding back the darkness coiling through me.

"I sure have," the asshole said, grinning ear to ear, a smile far too wide exposing pearly white teeth—diamonds in his rough appearance. Beneath his shadowed jawline, dark strands of hair brushed against the sharp edges. The jerk was a beautiful mess. With a slight tilt of his gambler-creased cowboy hat, I was ready to end this night and go to bed.

"Vessa, this is Ryder. He will be our guide in The City of Donia."

Ryder threw me a charming wink that sent my brows snapping together. With a slow turn of my head, I side-eyed Pa with a look.

What are you thinking?

There were many things he kept to himself—it was aggravating one hundred percent of the time—but this? Having a guide had not been in my plans. Nor had going to The City of Donia. Which meant my tonic was getting harder to find, something I knew he worried about. I held in my emotions, taking a deep breath as I felt pressure build behind my eyes and rolled my head around, easing the pain between my shoulders.

"Well I guess that's that then, isn't it?" I chided, but I knew Pa wouldn't have a response. He was three seconds from grunting as his way of saying, *"Yup."*

"Here." He tossed Ryder a skeleton key.

"And did you get me the best room this hellhole had to offer?" Ryder asked as they exchanged a look, one that forced me to believe they'd had quite a few discussions before this. How? When? I had no clue.

"Second," Pa corrected, holding out the other key in my direction as his eyes remained locked on the brute cowboy, eyes boring into Ryder's soul as if searching for something. Still not pleased about having to go this route, I held my hand out. As the key fell onto my palm, Pa said, "She always gets the best. Remember that. Be lucky your room came with a bath." With a quick once-over and a simple touch to the brim of his hat, he said, "You need it." He turned to leave, making his way up the wooden stairs to where I assumed the rooms were.

I remembered, long ago, when we'd stayed up all night as

he'd talked about memories of a haunting past that still hid in the shadows of his eyes. But he'd always felt better by the end of it, releasing whatever demons had been surfacing. It'd seemed to make his dreams better, less chaotic because we knew they were nightmares. Now things were vastly changing. As time went on, he turned in earlier and earlier, as if he were chasing something far better than this. I couldn't imagine what it was.

I felt Ryder's stare as I watched Pa leave, lifting his gaze above the brim of the glass as an uncomfortable silence hung between us. He threw two fingers into the air at the barmaid. I watched the flutter in his jaw as his attention was drawn toward her. A black bandana was tied at the base of his neck. But as he leaned into the weathered wood of the bar, I caught a glimpse above the cloth. The tips of his hair slightly brushed against the crook of his neck, a soft, thick, pulsing chord I'd like to sever.

The barmaid placed two glasses of smoky whiskey in front of him.

"Looks like you need a drink," Ryder said, sliding one my way. My eyes narrowed on the glass, the amber liquid sloshing around a few cubes of ice. My throat bobbed. The temptation was far too alluring.

I grabbed the drink off the counter and chugged it. He tilted his head to the side as he watched. When I was done, I slammed the glass down, causing a few heads to turn our way.

"He's right," I bit out. "You *do* need a bath."

He slid his tongue over a canine, watching me as if he were already naked in a bath full of warm water, and sucked in his tongue. This asshole was way too fucking confident and ornery.

Humored, he looked down at the room number etched into

the metal of his skeleton key. "Well, darlin', I'm in room twenty-six if you wanna watch."

I scoffed, leaning in a few more inches. His scent enveloped me—black licorice, spice, and heavens knew what he'd killed before coming here. "Fuck you, cowboy."

5
VESSA

Something tapped at my window before dawn broke across the sky. I pulled the duvet cover over my head, muffling the sound until it went away. It wasn't long until the rapid tapping came back. Growling, I threw the blankets off my body and flung myself out of bed. Raven appeared outside my window as a shadow cast in the luminescence of a fiery, crimson sky. He stretched his dark, silkened wings, as if he had been there all night. I never pried into where Raven went, but he was always waiting for me in the morning.

I slid the window up. "I'm shocked you didn't shift into my room," I said, yawning as he did just that in swirls of shadow, curling around my body in a familiar greeting before an apparition of a man appeared in a solid body on the edge of the bed. Now in fae form, Raven deeply yawned and stretched out his back.

"I have manners," he replied, rolling his broad shoulders. I knew by the way he cracked his back that phantom pains plagued him in the remnants of the shift—pain that often mirrored my own but in different ways—and I waited until he settled after some more groans and stretches.

Raven always slept in his bird form, but now, with his elbows leaning into the mattress, his stare was far too penetrating this early morning. For a moment, silence hung between us. My eyes lowered to his abdomen, a firm body I knew was hiding beneath that dark, tight-fitted cotton long-sleeve with suspenders that seemed glued to every muscle. I was glad he harnessed the power to shift with clothes on. Without any, it would have only made things awkward. He tilted his head, catching where my bright violet eyes were.

Clearing my throat, I briefly turned and pulled out my nicely drawn portrait from my coat pocket. "Apparently, your manners only extend to when I'm sleeping," I said, handing him the folded up piece of paper.

He watched me stride toward the washroom. With a wave of my hand, the wooden door slammed shut.

I heard him scoff. "A fucking blue jay? I'm a gods-damn rav—"

"A raven, I know." I couldn't stop myself from laughing.

"Well, hey, at least you look good," he said.

I summoned the door open just a crack. "Again, I know." I smirked before slamming it. "So did you know about the cocky cowboy Pa hired?" I called out.

"I'm just as shocked as you." His voice was smooth and airy —it always ended with a subtle rasp from sleep.

My brows hit my hairline as I blinked. "Huh," I whispered in sheer wonder. "You're off your game, bird." I'd thought he would have caught something, any information.

"And you were knocked off yours last night when you met our new guide," he prodded. The sound of his spine cracking sent a shudder down mine as he let out a groaning exhale.

"Stalking through the windows again?" I finished my

morning business, washed my hands in the wooden basin, and continued to get ready.

"I don't need the bond to know when your knees are ready to buckle," he mocked.

I abruptly yanked the door open and stuck my head out. "Lies."

He smirked, the corner of his mouth ticking up into a half grin. "He flustered you."

I ignored his words as I gathered my things, strapping my holster to my belt. A useless weapon for an Umbra Fae. Shadow wielders didn't need guns, but we had to pretend we did. Still, I knew how to use mine.

Raven held out my coat and draped it over my shoulders, his height eclipsing the sun that had barely started to filter in. There was an odd, slight chill in my room. I turned, eyes glancing up to find him still smirking while he straightened my collar and tucked the paper back inside the inner pocket. Sensing my aching muscles, his heavy palms squeezed my shoulders, ending with a few half circles of his thumbs. The gestures were too kind. I studied the way his jaw fluttered when we were close enough to share the same air. I wasn't interested in opening the bond to find out exactly what he was thinking, yet I always caught myself beneath his stare.

"Flustered," he whispered, low and soft, catching me off guard.

I cleared my throat, dipped below his arms, and grabbed my satchel off the dresser. Being five-four had its advantages. Without saying another word, I walked out the door.

)●(

I PAUSED at the top of the stairs, looking down into a room full of quiet conversations. The atmosphere was drab, a vast difference from the night before, while everyone nursed their hang-overs. Instantly, my eyes found Ryder leaning back in a chair facing the window with his hat hanging on the knob while Pa played a quiet round of solitaire across from him. The sound of shuffling cards brought comfort that I didn't often feel. It had been a while since I'd seen him at a table alone, finding his own moment of contentment with his cup of coffee. Steam curled and danced around the cards as he laid each one down. He'd always enjoyed his gritty black grounds after a big meal. He said it kept him from indulging in a long afternoon nap. The only thing in the way of my comfort was the cowboy sitting across from him—silent compared to the night before. The man talked too much for my liking, and he was flat-out rude. I sighed, debating if I should skip breakfast altogether and go straight to the stables. But my soul yearned for a quiet break-fast. We never spoke about our plans in any saloon, tavern, or parlor; we saved all our words for the road on open terrain, where the landscape could swallow us up without anyone in sight for miles.

Raven came up from behind me, the heat emanating off his body a reminder of the chill that had fluttered down my arms in the room. "I have a feeling I know which route we might take, and if my assumptions are right, you're going to wish you had that full breakfast," he observed.

I straightened my shoulders, rolling my neck. Before I knew it, I was moving toward them. Wooden legs scraped across the floor as Raven and I sat in the two empty chairs across from one another. There was a full house of silence at our table as I tipped my hat in greeting toward Pa, not giving any notice to Ryder's stare searing down the side of my face. Moments later, a young girl placed a breakfast plate before us. I couldn't remember the last time we had been in a room where we'd decided not to kill everyone in it. Judging by the amount of food on Raven's plate and his sullen eyes, he'd had his fix last night. I looked around the room for the handsome young pianist but found him at a table beside the piano. I hummed, causing Raven to look my way. We began to eat quietly.

This felt…normal, save for the bastard cowboy beside me. Thankfully, he smelled a lot cleaner than he had last night. He pulled out a black licorice from a cloth and took a bite. I gawked at him, wondering where he would have gotten something like that. I hadn't seen any sort of sweet candy since…

My mind reeled back to the times when Pa had taken me to the shores of our home in Black Water Woods. Back then, he had just begun trading with other fae, only allowing them to dock at our shores with enough time to do their exchange. Over time, more had come, but the masked man had always shown up with the best trades.

"Would you like a taste, darlin'?" Ryder grinned, offering me the piece that had already been in his mouth.

I scoffed, refusing to meet his stare. "Unless you have another piece, no. I don't know where your lips have been." Though I couldn't help feeling curious about how the licorice tasted. It had been far too long.

"You could have." He flashed me a wink as he took another bite, a sliver of a smile curving his lips. His scent surrounded me with a hint of the room's fresh floral soap.

Raven eyed me from across the table, and I could almost sense his mocking whisper to me.

Flustered.

He grinned, that dimple appearing as he speared his food onto the fork. I looked away with an eye roll, taking a sip of my coffee.

Ryder was walking a fine line, and he knew it; it was written all over his face. I could sense Raven's looming darkness growing aggravated. It was too tempting to remind Ryder of who we were, but seeing the content look on Pa's face as he dealt himself another round of solitaire forced me to save it for a later time. The old man deserved some happiness.

"I suggest you shut the fuck up. If you don't know how, you can kindly go fuck yourself and sit at the bar," Raven challenged.

So much for that. Here we go.

"Territorial much?" Ryder turned his head slowly. "Who pissed on your worms this morning, birdy?" This time, Ryder didn't grin as he glared at Raven. "Y'all act as if someone died."

Pa's eyes flicked up with venom coiling in his glare. In unison, the clamor of my fork reverberated around the room, causing surrounding patrons to look our way. My breathing stilled, and all I could see was darkness lurking at the corners of my eyes as they stung with vengeful spite.

I grabbed the ignorant cowboy by the bandana and yanked him close enough to smell the hint of licorice and spice on his breath. His eyes bore satisfaction at my reaction.

"You want to know who died, you fucking waste of life?" I said, voice shaking and gritting through my teeth as the horrors unexpectedly hit me like volcanic ash. "*Everyone,*" I whispered.

I released him, pushing him hard in the process, and made my way toward the exit. Behind me, I heard the remnants of their conversation fade out into the clamor of this dull small town as the sun warmed my face.

"I ain't paying you for company."

"No, End's Wrath. You're paying me for a whole lot more."

6
RYDER

Wrong move.

I had overshot it by fucking miles.

What was I thinking?

The anger looming in the irises of her purple eyes had been enough to cut me where I'd sat. I finished my coffee at the bar, facing the exit where she had stormed off. Her over-protective feathered pet followed seconds after.

I was off to a bad start.

While we saddled up at the hitching post, I caught her looking my way, a glower that had me thinking I needed to make some sort of peace offering to get off her bad side. However that would play out, I needed to be quick about it; being annoyed at my presence would have been far better than hating me. I thought about how I had dug my own grave as I watched the morning sun filter through her silky hair. The wind blew through every lighter strand in such an angelic way, as if she had the power of *Nai* at her fingertips. She was a dark angel beneath a blazing sun.

She paused when she heard my boots scraping across the gravel, saying nothing as I stood behind her.

"Here," I said, low and gruffly. Maybe I could have sounded more pleasant, but I didn't usually apologize.

She whirled around with a daggered stare but relented when she saw the cloth of licorice in my hand. "Candy?" She huffed a cocky laugh, but I caught a flash of excitement in her eyes.

A smile ticked the corner of my mouth. "Well, consider it a peace offering for me acting like a complete fucking idiot. I should have known." I paused. "Considering you are the last of the Umbra."

Her eyes hardened. "It's going to take a lot more than candy and a pearly smile to get on my good side, demon."

"Demon?" I questioned. A grin curved my lips. I kind of liked that. "Is that what you see me as?" One step forward, and I was in her range.

There was a long pause before she spoke, an observation as I felt her power, an unseen darkness curling around me. Deep violet eyes peeked out from under the brim of her cowboy hat. She smiled widely and ever so wickedly, like a mountain lion who had caught its prey. The tendrils of her *ano* crept inside my mind, like hands sifting deeper through my thoughts, trying to peel back all the complex layers that made me who I was.

I was a monster, a terrible one that would ruin and destroy her with a simple touch if I were to ever get that chance. But I also had a unique ability she had likely never experienced.

I was her equal in mind play.

I hid all of my not-so-flattering thoughts and memories but chose one to show her.

My thoughts wandered to the moment she had walked into the saloon last night so she could see how intoxicatingly beautiful she was through my eyes. The thought struck her back briefly.

Satisfied, she then yanked something out of the inside pocket of my coat, stifling the moment.

Fuck the hells.

"I see you are someone who doesn't play all his cards in the first round," she surmised as she held the *entire* hidden stash of my licorice in her greedy, gloved hands.

She took a bite of the flavored onyx rope, tearing a piece with a vengeance that unexpectedly made my cock twitch.

I was a demon, and I would be her demise.

END'S WRATH had beamed with pride seeing his daughter swindle the fuck out of me, getting exactly what she'd wanted. Though he looked content with the rope of licorice hanging from his mouth, his hands tightened on the reins. Gaze hardened, his eyes were now set on the terrain ahead—a brutal, grueling desert awaiting our arrival.

Vessa looked over her shoulder, flashing a venomous smirk my way. Her coat was tucked somewhere inside her bag, and her arms showed years of hard work, the sleeve going up her right arm hiding scars, burn marks. I felt a sharp twinge on the tops of my ears, phantom memories of the day the tips had been cut off by my mother's old lover, a man who was disgusted and jealous of me and the mark that had depicted who I was.

Fae.

The faint scars barely showed unless one were close enough to see where the knife had sliced through. Still so sensitive to the touch that, some days, it was painful to wear a hat.

Vessa and I had both been caught in a hail of storms the day the Eternal stone had been discovered by the humans. It had marked the beginning of an annihilation. That was when the old me still existed, the one who might have cared about the turn of events. Now, I was a mirage of a human disguising something far more powerful. I was, in my very own way, someone who could mix and blend with both worlds, moving around them in plain sight. No magic or power decorated my skin like some of the other fae. No tipped ears to depict if I lived or died.

I killed for a living, and my biggest payoff was riding on that mare. The silhouette of Vessa's feathered familiar flew above me, casting a shadow on my thoughts as my horse kept a steady gait. He dove down and flew beside me for a moment, analyzing me with a beady, black eye before croaking the equivalent of a "fuck you." He flew ahead, coasting on a gust of wind between End's Wrath and Vessa.

Clicking my tongue against my cheek, my dark stallion galloped alongside her. She eyed the neck of my guitar sticking out of my bag. I waited for her to ask about it, but she didn't. Silence hung in the air. It wasn't my job to tell her where we were going; I left that up to the old man, but the damn bastard barely spoke. So far, all she knew was that we were going north to The City of Donia in search of the one who knew how to make a plethora of her tonic. Those who knew the process had become a scarcity, and only I could get them in.

"We have a lot of terrain to cover. I suggest we ride until sundown."

Thank fuck, he finally spoke.

End's Wrath knew the bargain we had made. For a morsel of the tonic, a hefty payment every other night. I had just enough vials for the trip. I enjoyed the thrill of nara coins flowing into my pockets.

Taking them all at once took out the fun. He mutually agreed; it was a small comfort for him that I couldn't take off with his entire payment before my side of the deal was complete.

)●(

WE RODE UPHILL, the final trek that would be the beginning to their end.

Standing on the cliff, we took in the sight of an unforgiving desert that would soon be ours for the taking.

"There's no turning back now," End's Wrath said, his gloved hands tightening on the reins again.

Dusk began to break apart the horizon, swallowing the sun as the remnants of its light flared its desperate dance, drowning between the clouds. I turned to look at Vessa, a beauty so rough yet soft at the same time. As hues of orange light brushed across her face, something in me snagged. The look on her face told me she found beauty in this bleak moment. Most people feared this view, knowing the stories that had come out of this desert, as if it were the final nail in their coffin, but she seemed to grab it; held on as if it were the last time she would ever lay her pretty eyes on such a sight. There was something more than what met the eye with her. Eager for the danger she sought looking out into the horizon. She willed it; called upon her shadows as darkness filtered in faint stars across the sky.

She removed her cowboy hat, unveiling herself before me like the brightest of stars had somehow fallen and landed in this hellhole. The wind picked up, a perfect gale flowing through her hair. She took in a calming breath, a release I felt so intensely that, if I were standing, I might have fallen to my knees. The luminosity of her freckles peppered across her face.

Onyx- and magic-tipped ears shimmered as night fell over us. She tossed her hat and gloves to her father, wide-eyed and smiling. My gaze fell to her hands painted by the goddesses themselves. My breathing hitched. A tilt of his hat, and she tightened the grip on the reins. One simple glance my way was all it took for me to be undone. She winked, horse rearing up before she took off riding into the inky swells of darkness—a light storming into the mouth of the devil, with her shadow flying above her.

I could see why End's Wrath kept her hidden.

A light in the dark.

A fallen star.

We were to embark on a journey through the wild Desert of Miera—open game to those who sought the same path. Which meant open kill. Most counted their blessings if they made it through the day here and still breathed. The shadows acknowledged the Umbras' presence, kneeling, but it was the other monsters we'd need to be leery of. For it was likely I wasn't the only bounty hunter on their trail. If they only knew how valuable she *truly* was.

Tonight had solidified it. Damned be the ones who stood in my way. She was mine for the taking.

7

RYDER

We rode for another hour under the luminescence of the moon. Vessa had a never-ending glow to her, as if there was some sort of power she harnessed from the moon. Beneath the night sky, it illuminated her existence to the world; an essence I found hauntingly beautiful, ethereal perhaps. As End's Wrath's little spark of joy rode off into the dark, I realized why he was willing to do *anything* for her.

I didn't know much about the Umbra Fae other than that these two were living legends in my neck of the woods; the last vestiges. To see them in the flesh was like a mirage one couldn't help but curiously wander toward.

Long ago, they had dwelled somewhere in the west on an island called Black Water Woods, a land only accessible to their people, surrounded by bright, cerulean shores and obsidian sands and covered with a haze that had swayed the fearful humans from ever crossing it.

When we finally found a place to rest for the night, I

watched Vessa dismount. The curiosity and the allure remained tempting.

When she caught me in her line of sight, the threat of my imminent demise was written in her gaze.

I tipped my hat her way, but all I got in return was a scowl. Her bird stretched his wings wide, and they exchanged a look I couldn't translate. It made me think they must communicate through the bond. At least the prick was far more tolerable in this form, but his obligatory presence was getting in the way.

Her hat was already back on, hands gloved, her glow now dimmed and hidden beneath her dark brown coat. She removed her boots and massaged her feet and ankles before slipping them back on.

"A beauty like that will only burn you, boy. It's best you keep your distance," End's Wrath said, arching a salt-and-pepper brow my way before he went back to unstrapping two thick, wool blankets. I was far from a boy—although I appeared to be in my early thirties in human years, I was over one hundred years old—so I had an idea of what I wanted, but that was beside the point.

"Ain't she old enough to decide that for herself, End's Wrath?"

He paused briefly, then laughed darkly as he turned my way with a grin a little too wicked, even for him. "Fine," he drawled, tossing me what I assumed was her blanket. "It's your funeral."

8

VESSA

I felt Ryder's looming presence at my back, the darkness creeping in the shadows as he watched me. This beautiful and disastrous man seemed far too invested in everything I did.

"I don't trust him." I opened the bond, shuddering at the shame curling through me, desperate for a distraction.

"Not so flustered anymore, Vessa?" Raven's voice was a smooth salve to my discomfort. His chuckle was slightly flirtatious, sounding satisfied. I took a step back into the comfort of his wings. He stretched them wide and yawned. *"He is looking at you like a lion does a lambchop."*

I continued searching for the wool blanket I thought I had strapped to my mare. A chill swept down my spine at the sound of Ryder's heavy riding boots and the clashing of his spurs with every step he took toward me. With my back facing him, I smirked as I continued to unfasten the strap.

Raven cawed, his call of warning.

"A little slow on your game, bird."

"I believe this is yours," Ryder said, cool, deep, and

debonair. When I turned to meet his gaze, the stars hung in the irises of his pale-blue eyes as his dark hair flowed around his face. Feeling the night's cool air seeping into my coat, I grabbed the blanket without saying a word, unrolled it with a hard flick, and then wrapped myself in it.

I swore he laughed as I walked away.

We all settled for the night, taking spots around the fire. Pa had always been good at making them, keeping the flame low enough to keep us hidden from those who sought us out but warm enough to bring us comfort throughout the night. These lands were vastly different from what I was used to as the sun moved to make room for the moon. I'd imagined it would feel like living in some far-off place—on another planet, perhaps.

Darkness always had a way of bringing a barren cold and memories with it. As I lay with my gaze to the stars, I couldn't help but remember *them*...and how my sister and I would nestle on each side of Ma's arms.

"These are stories from the stars, my moon. I want you to always remember them, keep them here, in the same light you remember me." She would point to the space where my marking of the full moon was. *"Remember who you are when night falls, and let your power guide you."*

My eyes stung as the back of my throat swelled. Inhaling a deep breath, I turned away from the moon and looked toward the fire, watching the way its sharp edges violently flared and danced against the cool night air.

In my line of sight was Ryder, nestled up against a rock, eying me from under the brim of his hat, pulled down a little too low on his face, as if he sought privacy yet still kept an eye on who was around him.

I didn't trust him, but in the same notion, I couldn't stop looking at him as the flames flickered between us. He was a predator in our den. Every shadow cast by the glow of the fire highlighted his well-defined, chiseled face. I sensed the darkness in his eyes, possibly a mirror of my own. We all had tormented pasts, a shared one most of us never wanted to delve into.

There was nothing soft about Ryder; he was rugged and brash. But that sliver of a smile told me somewhere beneath his hard exterior was someone who had once been worthy of knowing, long before he had become whatever the fuck he was now.

A vessel. A ghost of the good man he used to be.

I felt the weight of Raven land on my hip, settling himself to perch for the night. I knew he would stay nearby with this ruthless cowboy around. Although my eyes began to drift shut, my gaze remained on Ryder.

"Good night, bird. Until dawn," I said through the bond.

"Good night, moon."

9

VESSA

I was jolted from sleep when a filthy, meaty hand cupped over my mouth. The taste of sweaty flesh dug into my teeth, and it was enough to make me want to hurl. The mark on my sternum burned as shadows wrung out in silence. An orange glow caught my eye as a man picked me up by the neck. Pain seared against my mark as sweat formed over my face. Looking down, I saw fire churning inches from me.

Fire Fae.

I desperately looked for Pa, but he was nowhere to be found.

"Raven!" A desperate call, but I was met with silence as I observed that Ryder was also gone.

I was dragged by my neck with a rope doused in fire magic. The more I moved, the hotter it grew. He was using the power of *Lam.*

Every time my shadow attempted to strike him, pain lanced through my body.

A struggle sparks the ring of fire, something in the cadence of the wind whispered to me—a faint call brushing against my mind as the moon's glow cast over us. The searing memory of burning flesh came flooding back. I did my best not to struggle.

At the other end of this rope was a masked bandit who smirked at my sneer. The creases between his eyes showed me he was grinning, taking pride in what he had caught.

"The legendary Umbra Fae is quite the little spitfire."

I spat on his boot, picturing a menacing smile on his face as pain swept through me at the sudden movement. "Fuck you, you traitorous scum."

"Your pretty little mouth has a lot of shit to say, doesn't it?" His voice was low and gritty—likely a smoker. He wore a dark, dirty vest with fancy buttons and a revolver with shiny grips in each holster. Not the typical dress of a fire wielder. He was working for the humans.

I carefully found my footing and growled as I fought against physically straining from the rope's intensifying heat.

Any other time of day, this could have kept me bound temporarily, but he'd only willed his death beneath the luminescence of the moon.

Suddenly, a wave of relief came over me, and my heart clenched as I unknowingly opened the bond, sensing Raven nearby.

"Such pretty freckles you have there," said the fire wielder, jerking the rope toward him, causing me to hiss.

I summoned the energy of the moon, a siphon to my shadows, as the surrounding air charged. An unseen force formed between my neck and the rope, relieving my skin from its touch. I grabbed the rope with both hands and yanked it from his grip. The fucking bastard dropped to his knees. With a whip of my own, a darkness unfurled, forming around his neck. I dragged him toward me, inch by inch, relishing the way he writhed like a worm stuck on a hook. I ungloved a hand, wrapping it tightly around his neck, squeezing his throat until he was gasping for air. The penumbra of my call was a whisper of death, and it seeped into his mouth until his very last breath was expelled into the night sky. With a hard shove, his body fell to the ground.

The air was knocked out of my lungs as another bandit came from the front, tackling me to the ground. I cursed as the back of my head slammed against the hardened soil. Dazed, I struggled under his excessive force as he tried grabbing my wrists. "My partner was right; you do have a pretty little mouth." He smirked.

Suddenly, a big, tanned hand wrapped around his throat.

Ryder leaned down to the shell of the bandit's dirt-crusted ear. "What about me, partner? Do I have a pretty mouth, too?" He flashed a wicked grin.

The man moved his hand down to his holster. That's all it took for Ryder to act, slicing his throat clean from one end to the other. Warm blood spilled in spurting waves, covering my chest and dousing my clothes, its iron-rich scent coating my mouth and neck.

I gasped at the sudden onslaught of hot blood as I pushed back until there was enough distance between Ryder, the carcass, and myself.

In one heavy gale of wind, Raven appeared behind me, landing with a slide that upturned the soil as he shifted forms; then a guttural wail sounded. He'd shifted way too fucking fast —his shoulders still bore silkened feathers. The sound reverberated down my body through the bond, and a new kind of worry for him was splayed all over amy face.

Raven helped me to my feet as I carefully inspected his shoulders, where remnants of his animal form still clung to his flesh, splattered with blood. At the sight of it, he paled.

"I'm fine," he huffed out. "I just needed a little more time to shift."

"No shit." I exhaled in relief, hearing the calm in his voice.

With a few strides, Ryder was at my back. "Are you alright?" He looked me over, brows tightly knit.

As I noticed my blood-soaked clothes, aggravation heated my cheeks. "Looks like you owe me some new clothes," I bit out, shoving my way past him.

I was running before I noticed the pain searing around my neck, the faint burn marks of the Fire Fae's rope. But I needed to find Pa. My heart wrenched in pure panic as I looked out into the desert—nothing but sand and random cacti, barren and desolate.

When I turned the bend of a small cliff, my jaw dropped when I found him heaving, clearly at the tail end of his wrath.

Bodies littered the ground around him.

No, not bodies, vessels of what they used to be. There were no clothes, no skin, just piles of muscle and organs.

Raven and Ryder came up behind me, and I felt the same shock roll through them.

"End's Wrath," Ryder whispered as Pa turned around, his moonlight-gray eyes meeting my stare.

End's Wrath indeed.

10
RYDER

The ambush had been a success, and I was a piece of shit for agreeing to it, but we'd had to make my identity believable. The first thing End's Wrath did afterward was stalk toward me, uncaring of the pile of bodies I'd had to kill to get to his daughter. He was heaving with menacing anger, the power of *Ama* still emanating off his body; in the gods' ancient language, *ama* meant "dark."

End's Wrath looked me up and down, trying to rip apart any walls I had built up, but they had been strengthened by decades of training—decades of being ripped down and torn apart myself. I stood my ground, cracked my neck, and squared my shoulders. Having a few inches of height on the old man was nice because I could still see Vessa staring at me over the top of his head. Blood caked her mouth, chest, and everything below. She was a beautiful mess.

"Find anything you like, End's Wrath?" I sneered, dropping my glare to his.

"Never have. Probably never will," was all he said before shoving past me.

Smart move, old man.

It wasn't long until dawn broke across the horizon and we were ready to leave. There was no reason to move the bodies; we left them as a sign of death for anyone who dared to follow.

We rode for hours in silence. I think the fire had done something to Vessa, unraveling a numbing darkness, sending her into some sort of daze—maybe a nightmare she couldn't escape. Whatever it was, she had been triggered. She glanced my way with a suspicious glower. I knew I had to make things right after showering her in death.

I rode up beside her, both our horses keeping a steady gait. The sound of their hooves had become soothing as gravel was crushed beneath them.

"Demons are a funny thing," I said, easing up on the reins as I leaned back slightly.

"So you consider yourself a funny guy?" She was vexed, refusing to look my way.

A low chuckle rumbled in my chest. Looking straight ahead, I caught her bird's silhouette flying half a mile ahead.

"Maybe."

There was a long pause before she hid a smirk, a comfortable silence; or I was just a horny, crazed idiot in the presence of a beautiful woman.

"They're unwanted guests. They show up whenever the fuck they want. Sometimes, it's hard to make them leave," I said, sneaking a glance from beneath the brim of my hat. I was a fool to allow my heart to jump like it did, already caught in her stare.

"How do you make them leave?" she asked, a tone less guarded than before as she rubbed her hand over the sore parts of her neck that bore dried, crusted blood.

"You don't. You just make friends with them," I said,

tossing her a vial of the only thing that might help at this moment.

She caught it in her gloved hands, looked down, and smiled.

Another glance from beneath her black cowboy hat, and I might just fucking perish.

"That should help with some of those *inner* demons."

II
VESSA

The tonic felt like an illusion as I rolled it between my fingers, its inky swells of dark magic glinting in the battering sun. I popped the cork off with my thumb, tipped my head back, and swallowed every last drop. I felt the power of the Eternal rush through my body, a welcome heat that coiled down my spine only to flush back up in a comforting, vibrational buzz. The pain had eased, and my eyes closed in a soft flutter as the sore flesh around my neck began to heal. I removed my hat and gloves to feel the full effect, freeing myself of any constricting material over the healing process. Hells, if I were under the moon, I would have stripped off all my clothes and doused myself in it.

The pleasant breeze was the calm to my storm. Every breath grew lighter, and the pounding of my heart slowed to a resting pulse. Looking ahead at Raven, I wished he could experience this type of healing. It had taken about an hour for the full shift to occur; his silkened, luminescent feathers had shrunk down to shoulders full of sharp thorns until they'd fully receded. I knew the poor bird would spend the rest of the evening sulking. I would have given him this tonic, but I already knew he would never take it.

I didn't expect Pa to say a damn word after what had happened. He was lost to his own thoughts, keeping his stare on the terrain ahead.

As silent as the dead.

I knew anything that came out of his mouth would end with a jab. The old man didn't mince his words for shit, especially when he was in a mood like this. I was lucky not to be the target of his ire because something loomed whenever he looked at Ryder.

As the cocky, invasive cowboy watched everything I did, every thought that flitted across my face, I used it to my advantage.

"What's your story?" I asked.

The question must have caught him off guard, because he looked insulted.

"There is none," he replied in a quick, muted tone, tightening his grip on the reins as he shifted in the saddle.

"Everyone has a story." I hummed.

"Well, mine isn't worth remembering."

I side-eyed him. "Why not?" I asked, putting my hat and gloves back on before leaning forward and reaching for my horse's reins, sensing his searing stare at the curve of my back. Sucking in a sharp breath, I continued, "Just because you're a cocky fucking bastard doesn't mean you should be forgotten."

The remark drew a laugh from him. A glint of a pearly smile peeked from his shadowed jawline, but I kept my poker face on.

"So what are you trying to tell me, Desert Storm? That after all this is over with, you'll want to remember me?" His tone was smooth and sultry. He caught something in my expression that made him ride slightly closer. I swallowed hard as his scent enveloped me. Somehow, even after all the bloodshed, he still managed to smell clean. I looked down at the bloodied mess I was covered in.

He must have had heat exhaustion, because he then said, "I can guarantee, after all this, I'd like to remember you. If I had to slice another man's throat to be in your orbit, I'd do it. I'd sever the chords of anyone who was ever tempted to touch you again."

Well fucking damn.

My breathing hitched. I wanted to look his way, but I was afraid if I did, it would be a one-way ticket inside his pants. My back stiffened. I couldn't lower my guard over a few heated words, but dammit, he made it easy. The air suddenly felt thin, and the space between us simmered with coiling heat. I needed to ride away before I became a moth dumb enough to fly into his flame.

FOR THE NEXT THREE DAYS, we managed to ride without another disruption as we closed in on Journey's Cliff, a resting place further north. After riding in silence for a few hours, I'd finally had enough. Though my veins felt like they were on fire, I made my next moments memorable.

"Let's place a bet," I said to Ryder, grinning. "I'll race you two miles out. If I win, you tell me a piece of your story."

The suggestion clearly piqued Ryder's interest.

"And what happens when you lose?" His smirk sent warmth pooling below my belly, as if I could see everything he'd like to do. He was looking at me like I was some sort of prize to be won, possibly a wild animal to tame, but there was no taming me.

"Trust me, asshole. I won't." With that, my mare reared, and I took off riding.

I heard his horse gallop behind me, but I left him in a cloud of dust. I felt the adrenaline wash over me as I rode faster across the desert beneath the hard and blazing sun. My horse's mane whipped against my face as I leaned into her lead.

When the timing was right, I felt no fear as I let go of the reins and held my arms out to the wind. I had no wings to catch me, but I rode as if I did, pretending my life wasn't in peril as I felt the dirt pelt harder against my face. I was dangerous when I didn't care. This was the side of me Pa and Raven feared, but to me, it was the best feeling in the world.

I heard the devil himself hoot and holler as a storm behind us rumbled, a thunderous warning growing across the terrain. He was gaining speed around every curve of the land, chasing at my heels like a disastrous nightmare. The hair rose on the back of my neck as a chill swept down my body. I felt the whisper of his power, like unseen tendrils reaching for me. Peering back, the ominous clouds were gaining speed. And so was Ryder.

I grinned.

Maybe I could finally wash some of this blood off me. Ryder's hat flew back, flicking rapidly like a trapped firefly caught on his drawstring.

Good. I hope that slows him down.

And it did. By the time I'd faced forward, I had hit the two-mile mark. Sensing it in my bones, I leaned back in the saddle and gave the reins a gentle pull for my mare to slow to a trot and then slowly came to a stop.

"Woo-hoo! You're *quite* the storm." His voice wrung out as he dismounted his stallion, still relishing the rush of adrenaline. The spurs on his boots chimed as he sauntered my way. With beads of sweat above his brow, he put his hands on my mare and stroked her mane. Surprisingly, she didn't pin her ears back, but I tried not to be disappointed; I wouldn't have been opposed to her kicking him.

"Well," he said with a labored breath, "looks like I owe you a story."

12
RYDER

The rain came pouring down in thick sheets, as if the Vale itself had opened up to wash away my sins. All in good nature though. I didn't blame the gods if they were really up there. I was going against everything that was ever spoken among the fae. Long ago, they had all been united—fae of fire, water, umbra, earth, and wind; the elements that unified these lands—until that peace had been stripped away. With the Eternal stone of longevity in the hands of humans, this entire planet was on the brink of destruction. Every day, I wished I could pull off a big enough heist to allow me to slip out and spend the rest of my days on a piece of land where none of this shit mattered. Being a killer would always be a darkness tainting the very blood in my veins.

I would get my prize eventually. Throwing out little things like tonic were the breadcrumbs that would lead Vessa to her fate and earn me enough nara coins to get the fuck off this continent. All her answers were held in The City of Donia, a sanctuary and a thriving city up north. With three days until Journey's Cliff and another short travel until we reached our destination, I had plenty of time to peel apart every layer that made Vessa who she was. By the time I placed her in Fang's path, we would know why her people had gone through such great lengths to keep her hidden.

As she began to unknowingly show me little pieces of herself, I was starting to see it. The power, the darkness coiling. Something inside her was rising. I didn't know if it was driven by grief, but I saw it every time she looked my way. She was dangerous and fragile at the same time. I wanted to break her and leave her undone, but I couldn't do it until we fit together all the missing pieces of the puzzle.

We rode hard through the rain for the next hour, stopping beneath the foot of a mountain next to a flowing stream where she finally washed the caked-on blood off her body. We gave her the privacy she needed to change into a fresh pair of clothes.

As she strode back toward her dark mare, the tight, little, buttoned-up top that highlighted the swells of her perfect breasts had her moon tattoo on full display. A deep shade of crimson that complemented her soft bronze skin and a dark, leather, corset-looking thing buckled across her torso at the same short height of that thin top I'd love to unbutton. A holster carrying her weapons was strapped to her side. Her beautiful onyx hands dripped with a power most men wished they could possess. She had it all. The way her tight leather pants fit like a glove made my cock twitch. Thank the gods I could hide it beneath my coat from where I stood. I leaned up against a tree to partially shelter from the drops of rain, now faint, but an annoyance nonetheless.

The burns spanned the entire length of her right arm, from above the wrists of her magic-honed hands to the curve of her shoulder. She flicked a daggered stare my way, brows furrowed with a look that said, *"Fuck you to every realm of hell,"* as she continued to search through her bags.

"Are you always such a nosy prick?" The sound of Raven's voice was jarring.

Gritting my teeth, I turned to find him sitting upon a massive rock on the other side of the giant oak tree, and noticed a few random palm trees beyond that. This part of the Miera Desert was a fuckery of confusion. Like Mother Nature had been indecisive and had just thrown out a bunch of random seeds to see what the hell would grow. Seeing Raven crouched on the top of that boulder in his fae form elicited a deep chuckle from me. The asshole resembled a bird perching.

"Raven, isn't it?" I felt like fucking with him.

His eyes darkened. "That is my given name," he replied with a steel expression.

How original.

"Cute name for a pet," I smoothly responded, hands clasped in front of myself as I kept my eyes on Vessa. Her head dipped back, exposing the column of her neck and that soft, tender flesh below her ear, massaging herself as she squeezed her right shoulder.

"Says the cowboy whose name was *carved* into existence."

A shudder went down my spine that had me moving for his throat. I closed the space in pure ferocity before I realized what I was doing, gripping him by the neck, squeezing every muscle I could grasp. He laughed as best he could within my grip.

"Tell me what you mean, little bird, before I decide to end your life." The scars on my body bore the very reason I got this name.

He smiled maliciously, as if a tendril of his power had latched on to something I'd never spoken of. What sort of fae was this feathered fuck anyway? I knew my damn history thanks to too much time hiding in libraries in The City of Donia when I'd had nowhere else to go.

Stabbing, sharp pain seared into the side of my abdomen. A blade ripped through my shirt and nicked the skin above my rib as a palm pressed against the opposite side. I looked down to see Vessa's soft, delicate hand on one side and a dagger in the other. Her touch was intoxicating, sending such a euphoric wave rushing through my body that I didn't care if she was dangerous.

"Are you teasing my bird?" she hissed, eyes glaring, perfect teeth bared, sending me into a sudden calm.

I let go. She released me from her grip while brushing her palm against the scar that formed the letter "R."

My eyes bored into hers. "No, we were just having a little chat," is all I said before I left to get my stallion ready for riding. As I walked away, I felt their glares searing into my back, but hers lingered far longer, sending that darkness swirling inside me into a frenzy, which spoke of the monster I truly was. No matter how many times I was beaten and bruised, I would always be one. I grinned beneath my hat as my horse veered. For the rest of the evening, not another word was spoken.

)●(

THERE WASN'T MUCH SAID over the next two days of travel either, just leering eyes, the mistrust palpable every time we turned our backs. It was three against one and us four against whatever the devil spurred from this desolate desert.

There were more bandits on our path in the distance. None of them were from Fang's gang, just a bunch of starved men banding together in the middle of nothing and nowhere.

There was a darkness that followed the Umbra; they were

the shadows looming over everyone's existence. If these prowling bandits knew what they were capable of, they would off themselves in fear of ever accidentally crossing paths with them. Even the coyotes stopped their howling as we passed. It only took one to send out its cry as the rest vanished. Maybe that was why we hadn't run into what lurked within the stories of these lands. Humans and fae be damned to ever step into the Umbra Faes' path. And somehow, I found excitement every time one particular little fae stole a glance or two or three my way. Her eyes sometimes said more than a "go to hell."

On nights when Vessa had been moments from drifting to sleep, her eyes lowered in a hooded gaze. I often wondered what she thought about before she closed them, if any of those floating thoughts were of me—thoughts that didn't involve holding a dagger to my throat or fantasizing about how she'd like End's Wrath to separate my flesh into piles of muscle and bone. Or did she have deep-rooted, lust-filled feelings for Raven, being as they had spent the entirety of their lives together?

I'd tried not to use the power of *Nai* to peek at their bond. It felt like an invasion, almost like peering through a window, watching a couple fucking on a bed, getting off on how hard the male would make his lover come. Being desperate enough to furiously jerk off to the sounds of her orgasm because, deep down, you're just angry it couldn't be you. But the one time I'd been stupid enough to give in, taking a glimpse at their bond, it was like watching a one-sided knife fight. It gave me satisfaction knowing she would be the one to hold the blade.

None of that mattered because Raven roamed her orbit nonetheless, like a lost pet, especially at night. But I'd watch him disappear once she fell asleep, doing whatever the hell it was birds do when the moon crept high. Raven always came back to her, as if he felt every breath she took as his own, knowing when her body was unsettled or restless. He would perch on her hip until her soft, faint breaths were a feathered sigh and she settled back into a deep sleep. Over the past few nights, he was always there the moment she opened her eyes to the break of day.

It was maddening to think of being that tied to someone. I would be more like Vessa and hold the noose by its end, knotting it so tight so nothing else would seep through. What they had wasn't love; it was a choice taken from them by End's Wrath.

I saw what her father's silence did to her, the days when his thoughts were too heavy for conversation. He was here but he wasn't—breathing but dreaming about something beyond what was right in front of him. I'd observed enough to know it bothered her. She only had Raven to talk to.

Still, she cared for the bastard bird.

Deeply.

From beneath the brim of my hat, I surveyed how they weaved around their bond as crackling fire filled the space.

I turned over some details.

End's Wrath's biggest weakness was in front of me, on full display.

I needed to work harder to pull Vessa out of her comfortable orbit and lull her into mine.

Luckily, by tomorrow night, we would arrive at Journey's Cliff. And I had a feeling by the time we walked out of that cave, she would be circling me. I knew exactly how to do it.

13

RYDER

The four of us reached Journey's Cliff, standing on the rise as we walked our horses up its rocky terrain. From this vantage point, the Desert of Miera was a breathtaking sight that reminded me of what a bird might see soaring in the sky. Maybe for a moment, I was jealous of Raven as he stood off to the side, looking southeast, where a canopy of crimson trees dotted the crest of the mountains.

"On the other side lies Blightstone Hollow," I confirmed. "And in the valley north of that"—I pointed further—"rests Crimson Valley."

"The Serpent's Path," Vessa replied, sounding haunted as the words left her. They were strong enough to drift my way, sending a shiver down my spine. End's Wrath tensed and looked away as Raven moved beside her, placing his hand on her shoulder. She reached up and gave a tight squeeze as if telling him, *"I'm okay."*

Vessa saw the confusion on my face and came to stand beside me, releasing herself from Raven's heavy palm. I was taken aback as she stood beneath my still-raised arm, our height difference prominent. She moved in front of me and held out her arm; the sudden brush of her protruding ass against my front nearly sent my heart hammering.

"See the path to Blightstone Hollow?" She pointed toward the distant trees that lined along the rivers. "Carved by the flood of fae."

The expanse of the forest seemed to be spreading beyond its own borders. *What the hell?* I squinted. "There is a town north of that called the Scarlet Gallows," I continued.

"Hell's Mark," Vessa finished.

"And that's where it all began. End of story," Raven interjected in a sharp tone as he stepped away from the cliffside.

End's Wrath seemed to share the same sentiment as he clicked his tongue against his cheek a few times and guided his stallion down the narrow path. "If you're as good of a guide as you say, *Ryder*, then that cave down there better be big enough to ensure we all aren't up each other's asses." His warning coaxed me to grin in response.

"Trust me, old man, those caves run deep into the mountain, like the devil's belly. Best you stick to the mouth of it or else you'll get eaten. I need you alive to give me my next payment."

Moments passed as he studied me with a hardened glare. He slammed one salt-and-pepper brow down so hard, to anyone else, it would have felt like a whip. He scratched the scruff of his short beard. "I'll give you your next payment come sunrise. If you're as dick-whipped by nara coins as I think you are, then it'll be in *your* best interest to keep watch tonight."

Grinning, I tilted my hat. "Sure thing, boss."

We led our horses down the steep path on the side of the mountain. It was so gods-damn narrow, the thought of slipping had my balls tightening. End's Wrath led the way with Vessa trailing him. I was next, then Raven walked the tail end.

To my surprise, he remained in his fae form. I felt the tall stalker's hostile stare on me the entire time.

When we reached the cave, nostalgia hit me all at once. This had been my home long ago, when I'd been no better than the bandits who roamed the desert. The cool air inside the stone walls instantly brought relief from the outside heat as faint gusts of wind blew from its depths. The same old musty smell and stale scent of water from the few hidden hot springs filled the air. Legend said this was the bathing chamber of the devil. I'd believed it for quite some time until I'd stayed long enough to find out the only devil that had resided here had been me.

As I unpacked my guitar, the three of them separated into their own corners within the expanse of this cave. Raven stood at the mouth, looking out into the horizon at the setting sun. As darkness began to settle across the terrain, tendrils of black shadow emanated off his body, as if the breeze itself were whisking him out. He dissipated into nothing but a dark onyx, emerging from the inky swells a raven. If I didn't hate him, I would have said he was an ethereal-looking fucker. Never seen a shifter like that before.

Vessa stripped down to her thin, dark crimson, cut-off top and tight leather pants. She even exposed her right arm that exposed the scars. I'd thought she would have kept that sleeve on. A small victory to claim; maybe she was letting her guard down around me.

End's Wrath started a fire, and the smell of burning wood filled my senses.

"He better bring us back enough kill to fill our bellies tonight," Vessa murmured, as if she was already tasting the flavors of whatever carcass he was hunting.

I pulled out a few apples from my bag and a slate of stone the size of a plate, then sat by the fire. I removed my long coat and hat, ran a hand through my hair, and relished the easing tension and the diminishing headache that had been forming in the back of my skull. I could feel Vessa's stare, knowing she could see every corded muscle on my arms.

I was a pretty bastard, that I knew.

I pulled the knife from its sheath and began slicing the apples. Judging by the juice that dripped down the blade, I knew they were good and ready to be eaten. The fire was at perfect distance for me to reach out and cook them. With a jab against the slate of stone, the sound reverberated down the cave. I speared a slice and held it up to the fire for a few minutes. Once it was hot enough, I set it back down and went for the next. Vessa watched with such a curious little stare, it had me grinning.

With a darkened brow raised, she asked, "What are you doing?"

"Ever had a baked apple before?"

She looked as though I'd just insulted her. The bob in her throat was subtle and delicate, lickable, if she'd ever let me get that close.

"No."

I dipped my chin and chuckled. "Would you like to try it?"

A smile curved her full lips as she came to sit beside me.

I heard End's Wrath's irritable sigh. From my peripheral, I saw him lean back onto his rolled-up wool blanket and cover half his face with his hat. My eyes must have lingered on Vessa's lips for far too long, because she cleared her throat wryly, causing me to blink. Another chuckle escaped me as I shyly looked down. Damn the hells. What was she doing to me?

"Well, Desert Storm, my knife or yours?"

With a hooded gaze, she smiled as she took mine, a gentle brush along my skin strong enough to flutter up my arm. Every touch, even a subtle one, was fucking magic, and she had no idea.

She speared a slice of apple and tasted it. The moan that escaped her was pure ecstasy, and my heart nearly lurched when she unexpectedly snorted as a sliver of apple smudged around her mouth. I kept one arm resting on a bent knee. It took everything in me not to lean in and kiss her, wanting to take the other end of that slice. Her head tipped back, and with her tongue, she licked the remaining portion into her mouth. She laughed some more.

When her eyes found mine, her gaze softened. Her freckles reminded me of uncharted constellations I wanted to explore, shimmering and perfectly placed across her nose. In a gentle wisp, they fanned out beneath her eyes, ending at her hairline.

I nearly lost my breath, and possibly my life, just looking at her.

"Gods-damn, woman." I exhaled.

"What?" She giggled. Her eyes twinkled mischievously.

For the first time, she smiled, really smiled. So wide, I could feel that part of her she kept sealed away, open up.

"You make everything beautiful."

Her chest sharply rose as her breathing hitched.

Something raw and tantalizing cracked between us, and suddenly, it was really hot.

She opened her mouth to speak but fell silent. She quickly closed it, lashes softly fluttering down as she gave the knife back. "Here." She sighed, placing it in my hand.

There was no denying the moment we'd shared, but she was holding back, and maybe I was too. It wasn't the ideal situation, given End's Wrath was on the other side of this fire. She brought her knees to her chest and wrapped her arms around them. I speared another slice into my mouth.

"It tastes just like apple pie," she finally said. "It's been a long time since I've had any of that." There was a sadness to her, one that I could only surmise was because she was always on the run. I couldn't understand how something so beautiful could be so devastating at the same time. And here she was, inches from me, not knowing the price so many would pay for her head while she sat and smiled at me. She reached down for another piece and popped it into her mouth. Another hum beneath her breath.

"Same here. I suppose that's why I prefer to eat my apples this way," was all I said. I could understand how she felt, how such a simple thing like this could bring so much joy and pain all at once, a reminder of what had been lost.

"Next man I see holding an apple pie, I'll make sure I put a knife to his gut and take it," she said, chuckling as she turned her head toward me.

"Well"—I leaned in a little closer—"I'll keep my eyes peeled for you." I winked.

"Such a violent man." She hummed, grabbed a handful of the apple slices with a smirk, and stood. "Violent, violent man." With a slight shake to her head, she wandered to the mouth of the cave, her ears and hands illuminated beneath the moonlight. As she stood there, eating the remaining pieces, a part of me wondered if she was waiting for Raven to return. I hung my head in irritation as I stood and pulled out my guitar —the only thing that had managed to survive longer than I had—disappearing into the depths of the cave to find a quiet place.

14

VESSA

Everything was going fine until it'd hit me like a wave. I was angry. For the first time, I was in the presence of someone who didn't make me feel like I was vacant. Ryder was there, in the flesh, laughing and smiling with me. He was in the moment, enjoying the simplicities this fucked-up world had to offer, and he managed to somehow smile through the darkness. It was a side of him I hadn't expected to see. The radiance in his eyes and how that arrogant cowboy looked at me made me feel...*good*.

Damn him to hells. I tossed another slice into my mouth.

In my mind, I was soaring above the clouds, looking down at an ominous ocean, glad I wasn't beneath the waves...until I was, and I crashed through them hard. I was so gods-damn angry about how something so simple could rip open the memories of *her*. Ma always made the best apple pie, and I hated the feeling of missing her. The undertow of grief swept me away to this cliffside as I silently held back my sobs, and tried to enjoy the delicious apple. I was losing the fight against my own tears as the Desert of Miera became a blur. My sister's excited nudge carved a phantom pain across my heart, remembering how she would stir me awake to say Ma had been making our favorite.

Fuck the hells.

I'd sensed the fall the moment my knees were brought to my chest—a kick to the gut once the flavors had settled in.

I couldn't risk Ryder seeing me break, nor Pa hearing any muffled sobs. I looked over my shoulder to the empty space where Ryder had been, then to Pa. He hated seeing me cry. He didn't want to see it at all, actually. I had to lock away my pain and release it anywhere I could. All this time, I'd fed these lands nothing but death, relishing in taking lives along with their coins and watering its soil with their blood. Maybe that's why I had always been a wreck and a monster. Because he'd forced me to become one.

At least my stomach wasn't growling anymore. Who knew when Raven would be back?

Every breath I took burned the muscles in my body. Another inconvenience, stroking its reminder that I was completely screwed. I needed more tonic, but I was too prideful to ask.

Sighing, I wiped my cheeks and walked back into the cave, staring at the empty space again. With Raven gone and Pa asleep, despite feeling fatigued, I decided to find Ryder. Maybe he could help me forget again, even if it was for a short while.

I walked deeper inside the cave in complete darkness, allowing my memory to guide me. The air grew thicker, the scent muskier as I ran my fingers along its walls. When the condensation dampened my fingertips, I knew when to take a right. A few more left turns, and I would have complete privacy. I had once read bats navigated through the dark by echolocation, so I hummed a little tune and plucked my guitar, testing to hear how far the sound went. Though others had deemed that kind of literature useless, I preferred to weave the knowledge into my own. Sure, I could use my wind, the power of *Nai*, but it was the challenge I sought most. I was close enough to a hot spring to dull any sound, the stone walls so thick, my voice was now a prisoner in its confinements. As my eyes adjusted, I took notice of the few glowworms emitting a dim light above, faint but enough to see where the trickle of water was coming from. I watched it drip into a large puddle on the other side.

I stood in place for a moment longer before waving my hand to summon someone who made my damn skin crawl.

The magic slowly churned, its cerulean glow beaming across my face.

"So, what's the news?" A deep, throaty rasp rumbled beneath a mouth full of meat. Fang sounded like I was interrupting something because it ended with a grunt.

"The ambush went as planned, and we are now on Journey's Cliff," I said.

"A small sacrifice for the greater good, rest those poor souls." No remorse in his words. There was a long pause.

The way he slopped over his mug of wine made me want to puke. When a woman's soft moan invaded the meeting, a shiver went down my back. I saw a hand move up his chest and link around his neck. Gross.

"And the girl?"

"She's coming around."

"How long until you're in Donia?"

Trying to hide my disgust, I tilted my head from side to side and shrugged. "Less than a week."

The asshole finally turned his head my way, and those beady little eyes bored into mine.

"Good. I can't wait to get my hands on her."

Before he could say another word, I willed the connection to sever, wishing it was the chords to his neck. Within a few breaths, his silhouette wavered into thin air.

"Ryder?" Vessa called, sending another chill down my back, but it swept through my veins like lava.

I played a few downward strokes, plucking each one as if I were tuning the guitar until I gently strummed up.

She walked through the passage faster than I'd expected, and I could see why when she found me standing in the middle of this cavern. The luminance of her ears, freckles, and hands radiated a glow. Not as bright as beneath the moon, but enough for her to quickly stride through. I inhaled a deep breath. That had been too fucking close.

"What are you doing way back here?" Her brow slightly arched.

"Well, ain't it obvious?" I slyly grinned, emphasizing the next chord.

She laughed, but something caught my eye as it danced across her face. I looked up to find the glowworms casting a brighter light. She tilted her head back, gasping in sheer wonder.

"What are those?" She went into the center of the cavern and covered her mouth with her hands.

They were...gathering on the ceiling right above her head.

"Those are glowworms. Oddly, I think they're attracted to you," I observed.

She held her arms out, as if the light itself would wrap around her. She smiled as it danced along her skin like shimmering stars and her body was enveloped in it. Something in her must have seized because her breathing hitched.

"I've never seen anything like this. It's...beautiful," she said.

"It truly is." I stood basking in her aura.

She caught my gaze. "Come on. You owe me a story."

)●(

"You won the race. You get to decide whose story will be told. It doesn't have to be mine if that's not what you're after," I said. We sat in another part of the cave, in a cavern that gave us enough privacy from End's Wrath. This was the perfect space to see how far I could unravel her.

"A choice?" I saw her chin lift in excitement. It seemed like letting her choose was a good start.

"I heard what Raven said, how your name was carved." She

observed me through a hooded look of curiosity. "Tell me what he meant."

I scratched the back of my neck. Raven's knowledge was considerably accurate. I suddenly felt like a mouse in a snake's den, and the snake was staring right at me.

"You go straight for the punch, don't you?" An uncomfortable and unexpected laugh escaped me. But I'd give her what she wanted. If telling her my story would pull her under my arm, it was a small sacrifice I could make.

I removed my hat to ease the tension off my ears and set it on a boulder nearby. With one motion, I reached behind me, tugged my cotton shirt off, and tossed it somewhere. Her body went rigid, and those violet eyes widened as they roamed shamelessly down every divot of my abs. I combed through my locks and tilted my chin up, pretending to fix my hair so she could steal a few more glances.

With my legs crossed, I leaned back and lifted my arm to expose the jagged, raised letter on the side of my ribs. Again, Vessa's eyes widened, but this time, with shock. She said nothing as she took up the space beside me, much closer than I had expected.

Her fingers were cool to the touch, soft and feather-light as they followed the half-circle of the "R" down to its straight ridge, trailing further. She realized where her fingers were wandering, tensed, and withdrew them. The motion tugged a smile from me. Suddenly, I didn't mind sharing a piece of my past with her. Whatever lies I'd been about to say evaded me in the confinement of this space. Any words spoken would remain here. She was deathly silent, waiting for me to speak.

"I knew nothing of my father other than that he was a Wind Fae, and my mother was human. She loved me, but being in the company of bad men was her vice, and I often paid the price for that. She had a lover once, one she was keen on. She kept him around for some unknown reason, but he despised me, knowing I was half fae. I bore the brunt of all their fights. He was a jealous asshole who wanted me out of the picture. One day, things got bad…" I paused, taking a deep breath. "She ended it with him, and he lost his fucking mind. He grabbed a knife and held me down. To this day, I remember the blood-curdling scream my mother expelled as she watched him carve the first letter of his name onto my side. He said he wanted her to remember that I was the reason they weren't together."

Then I tucked my hair behind my ears, exposing another harsh truth about how evil humans could be. Vessa gasped as she took in the sight of the scars marring the tops of my ears. Her hand reached out, the pad of her fingers touching the now hardened and calloused tips.

"He removed the part that identifies you as fae." Her voice shook in anger and sadness at how anyone could be so cruel to a child. My body hummed in response as she touched them again. "Does that hurt?" she questioned after a grunt rumbled in my chest.

"They're…a little sensitive." My voice was low and husky. The fire crackled and popped as flames flickered and danced in the irises of her eyes. Something bloomed inside my rotten, filthy heart the longer we shared the same air, the same breath. "But with the right person, I feel more." She didn't withdraw at my words; she hung on every one. "So much more, Vessa."

Her name was dark honey on my lips, a venom I wanted to taste. Her hands tucked the hair behind my ears as she examined them, tilting her head from side to side. I watched the rise and fall of her chest as she explored the jagged flesh, the thrumming pulse in the crook of her neck. Her heart pounded just as hard as mine. A few moments passed before I spoke again, savoring how it felt to have her hands roam.

"My mother's lover went for her, and in her last breath, she screamed for me to take our horse and ride her until I couldn't run from darkness no more, and then I would find that light. *'Ride her,'* she said."

In this moment, we both slipped into the dark, and Vessa lifted her scarred arm and brushed her palm against my face. I closed my eyes as her thumb trailed across my cheek. I'd expected her to see me for the monster I had become, but her eyes softened, an unspoken understanding as she studied me.

"*'Ride her,'*" she repeated a few times. The more she said it, the more the meaning behind these two words sunk in. And with it, my desire for her.

"*Ryder.*" Her whisper was an unveiling to my soul, as dark and tarnished as it was, and even then, it wasn't enough. Hunger burned in her eyes; she wanted more. I succumbed beneath her touch. It should have been me doing all the unraveling. We were gravitating closer, a breath away from a kiss until something caught her eye over my shoulder and she frowned.

Fuck. I knew exactly who it was.

As I turned around, I saw Raven bite into some cooked meat with an obviously irritated glare.

"Sorry to interrupt whatever the fuck this is, but dinner is ready," he said.

Vessa sighed, glancing down at me, the moment definitely gone as she stormed past Raven, shoving him in the process.

16

VESSA

The cold sweat embedded in my bones was enough to pull me from sleep. I thanked the frigid morning and its unrelenting wind for saving me from the same recurring dream. I often stayed awake at night, hoping one day I'd feel a sudden poke at my side and find my sister beside me. That one day she would just show up and we would get to spend the rest of eternity catching up on everything we'd missed. I thought about what she would have looked like if she had survived. Every time, the same ache in my chest returned. Would she have resembled Pa or looked more like Ma and me with high, regal cheekbones? Every time I slipped too far, I ended up dreaming of the shores of home, of the onyx sand wedged between my toes, but this time, it was also of that masked man.

Pain pierced through me from the lack of tonic, causing me to moan as I lazily opened my eyes to Ryder scowling while he carved a piece of wood with his knife far too aggressively. I had spent too many nights with both my body and mind unsettled, so I refused to let the pangs annoy me. I glanced downward to find Pa standing outside the cave, sun filtering through his strands of salt-and-pepper hair. Another gust of wind swept down my front; the breeze was not coming from the outside but from within. As if the belly of the devil himself was telling us to fuck off. But the unexpected warmth at my back had my mind reeling. I recognized that thick, heavy arm draped over my body. I knew the rise and fall of that chest, the way his deep breaths fanned the top of my head, always ending with a slight shudder, as if wherever he was while dreaming was somewhere terrifying. My body went rigid as my cheeks turned hot, my backside fully enveloped in his unexpected warmth, nearly causing me to stop breathing.

Raven was *not* in his bird form.

There were no little claws perched and gripping at my hip. No little beady eyes waiting to purr a hello when I woke up. Raven's body nearly swallowed me whole, his firm arm over my waist and linked it across my chest. His pale skin had a luminous glow in the morning light. Apparently, I had been using him as a pillow and a blanket.

I swallowed.

"Raven," I whispered, shaking his arm.

He moaned in response, grabbing the blanket that must have been tossed behind him while sleeping and draping it around us. My eyes widened as I was cloaked by the wool and canopied in complete darkness, his thick, strong legs entangled in mine as he pulled me closer. The clasps of his suspenders pressed against my back. We were too close. I sucked in a sharp breath. The man was gripping me like I was *his*. It did something to me, tugging on the frayed edges of a forced bond. One that was always desperately trying to keep itself tethered to me. I slightly curled my fingers into his grip as my pulse thrummed in my ears, but then stopped and exhaled roughly.

I belong to no one.

I turned to face him as darkness surrounded us. Entirely doused in his heat as we shared the same air.

"Raven, wake up," I said hastefully into the confinements of the blanket, pressing my palm against his hardened chest, the black fabric soft beneath my touch. Another deep breath fanned down my face. I sighed, tossing the top portion of the blanket off us.

His eyes slowly opened. In the same motion, the sun crept in, casting light upon us, filtering through the strands of hair brushing across his face. I resisted the urge to pluck a thick lock away from his eyes.

"Tell me why I should allow you to keep breathing," I quietly hissed, trying not to let Ryder or Pa hear us. There was a flash of concern in Raven's eyes.

"You were shivering in your sleep last night, so I covered you. But then that didn't work. So here I am, in the flesh, beside you," he said in a low, raspy tone that sent another wave of heat down my body.

"Lies," I teased. The threat in my eyes diminished. His little sliver of a dimple raised up in a smirk, causing my shoulders to loosen.

He rested on one elbow and leaned into the shell of my ear, his lips but a breath away from me. "One thing about me is that I don't lie, Vessa."

When I glanced at him, his eyes bored over my shoulder in Ryder's direction before he got up. He took his hat from the ground and stood over the ledge outside the cave. Misted shadows curled around his boots until he was enveloped in darkness. Before he disappeared, he turned back and tipped his hat toward me as a satisfied smirk curved his lips. His body fell away into onyx clouds, and when he emerged, he was in the form of a raven.

)●(

Both last night and this morning were a continual shit show. I gazed at the golden band on my finger, and a wicked grin widened, remembering many of my one-night stands. Raven had never given a damn about any of them, so why was it different with Ryder? We might be bound, but we were not tied to one another romantically. His constant influx of men and women didn't affect me, and I had never cared to ask where he went in the middle of the night. We minded our own damn business.

Now, he was nowhere in sight. He hadn't been with us for most of the day, flying miles ahead as if he couldn't stand to be in my proximity.

"He'll get over it," Pa said, breaking the silence as we rode side by side with Ryder far behind us.

"If what I do plagues him that bad, I'll hear it one way or another. So I guess we'll just have to see."

Pa responded with a nod. Truth was, we wouldn't have been in this situation if it weren't for the old man. He had damned our entire existence.

Moments with Ryder came and went throughout the day, thinking about what he'd shared last night, but I had to cut off those thoughts.

All I cared about now was the smoked herb in this pipe, hoping it would chase away those looming thoughts. Pa had given me more of his special blend than usual, enough to pack another for this evening.

"Looks like you need it," he had said.

We continued north as the sun beamed down upon us. It wouldn't be long until we would see Ash Dunes on the horizon. It was hard to miss. A pain tinged my chest thinking of the stories that had come out of it. Those dunes had been built on top of the bones of fae, a place to dispose the remnants of their burnt bodies. A shudder swept down my spine as anger and vengeance coiled through me.

"We are riding into the beginning of their end," Ryder called out as if sensing my thoughts. He clicked his tongue as he rode alongside me and jerked his chin forward. Calloused to what lay ahead, he flashed a pearly yet mischievous smile. I looked ahead and squinted my eyes, and all I could see were the peaks of that hellish place cresting the expanse of the desert.

"The sands are white." I surveyed, bringing the pipe to my lips. I needed to feel that burn, anything to evade thinking of how those dunes had been made.

"That's an interesting-looking pipe you have there," Ryder stated.

I lifted my chin. "Oh yeah, cowboy? Here, take a puff if you fancy."

His fingertips gently brushed the top of my hand as he took it.

He held the ivory pipe close to his face and to the side, upside down, and all around. The fool was immersed in its design.

He huffed out a laugh, astonished while taking a hit, coughing and laughing at the same time with a cloud of smoke puffing out as he handed it back to me.

"Is that pipe made out of bone?"

"Sure is," I boasted. "Let it be a warning. If you ever decide to cross us, I'll be smoking out of your bones too. Maybe make a few necklaces out of them, who knows." I smirked. "Depends how creative I feel at the moment."

"Well, gods-damn woman." Ryder grinned from ear to ear.

I let the threat ride, keeping eye contact, and smiled with a shrug. "Fuck around and you'll find out."

There was an ache in the depths of my mind trying to take root as a silhouette cast between us.

I peered up to find Raven coasting on a gust of wind.

"Just in time." I opened the bond. *"I thought you were going to miss our run."*

"Now why would I do that?" he asked.

I hesitated for a moment. Silence filled that awkward space. Like Pa, I didn't want to talk about it.

He gently glided down and perched on my arm, his claws digging into the coat. Thank goodness there was another layer of cloth to cover my scars. It was my strongest arm of the two, shockingly.

Pa sighed.

"What am I missing here?" Ryder said.

"You'll see." Pa dipped his chin.

It was our ride into town that I enjoyed the most.

It was freeing.

Releasing.

It was our small tradition—Raven riding on my arm was his way of riding a horse.

I knew if he had a choice, a real choice, that is, one where he wasn't tied to the fucking mess I was, then maybe in another lifetime, he would have wanted to be a rancher. Maybe a farmer, anything other than the life he'd been given now. If freedom ever had a name, it wouldn't be Raven. The boy he'd been before had died the day he'd been tied to me. And yet, fae or bird, he still couldn't keep those eyes off me. I would always be in his line of sight.

)●(

As we crested the top of the wind-sculpted dunes, I dismounted, ignoring the pain that swept up my legs upon landing. I kneeled down, pinching the grains of sand between my fingers. The soft, white grains were mixed with smooth, ivory pieces.

"These aren't from stones," I said, confirming my own suspicions as I grabbed a handful and sifted more of it into my palm. They had once been skulls, crushed and redacted to nothing but sand. A thick, heavy cloud of ash drifted up from the motion, causing me to cough.

"Careful darlin'. You'll want to wear this while you ride into town," Ryder said, tossing me a black bandana. I covered my nose and mouth, leaving my eyes exposed.

When I mounted my mare, I glanced at Ryder, who lifted the cloth over his face.

"Best you keep it on, even when we stop," he said with his voice slightly muffled. Those piercing blue eyes roamed over my face, studying the luminance of my freckles before that penetrating gaze flicked to mine. "These people are very leery of newcomers. If they see how bright you shine, they might want to cut out that pretty little heart of yours."

Tightening the cloth at the back of my head, I grinned. "I'd like to see those fuckers try." They'd be lucky if I left any of them alive come sunrise tomorrow.

The creases in his eyes hid a smirk. He nodded at Pa, who already wore a gray bandana.

The thrumming against the mark on my sternum pulsed, an echo of a memory only my soul could recognize as we rode into town.

"This place is a tomb," I murmured, suddenly feeling a chill sweep down my spine as I thought about standing on the graves of fae.

Ash Dunes was the final town before we reached The City of Donia. It would be less than a week before we stood on the other side of those walls, in the middle of an entire civilization who would kill us on a whim. It was tempting not to just storm their sanctuary and end every last one of them. The power of *Ano* coursed through me, and for the first time, I felt a threat of something on the rise.

I wanted to leave the moment we arrived, but the closer we got to The City of Donia, the closer I felt more of the tonic. I found myself imagining what it would be like to have enough, to wake up and not feel like my entire body was on fire. Give me a chest full, and I would never have to ask for it again. But then, a part of my mind danced on the edges of temptation; what if I never took it at all? Would I suddenly ignite and burn to ash? Would I die a painful death? Or simply just perish in the most basic way possible? All of those felt better than living in the current condition of this body.

As we continued our ride into town, I realized karma sometimes had a way of coming back to haunt you. The people who lived in this town wore bandanas over their mouths as they hastily walked from building to building. Some disguised the necessity with decorative cloth, but they had no choice but to live in the hell they'd created. By the looks of some of them, they didn't seem to care either.

This was by far the biggest town we had ever been in, with rows upon rows of homes and small businesses bustling with life beyond their doors. I was surprised Ash Dunes held a town like this.

We would use this time to wind down, kick up our boots, have a few good drinks, and wash any remnants of travel off our bodies. Fill our bellies to the brim and go through our plans. It struck me as odd that Pa wanted to discuss them once we settled into our rooms, but then again, with how he'd been acting on the whim lately, it wasn't too big of a surprise.

Somewhere in this tomb of a town, I would find my bearings. I couldn't change what had happened to them. But it sparked something inside me—maybe I could prevent this from happening again so there would be no more towns made by the bones and ash of fae or rivers staining the forests with their blood.

)●(

I PULLED down my bandana as we walked into the finest hotel Ash Dunes had to offer. I did my usual: pulled the brim of my hat lower and waited by the bar while Pa talked to the lady of the house. Only this time, it was a young boy. His golden skin glowed against the lighting. He had light brown hair that brushed against the tips of his ears, but something caught me off-guard. As I hung out by the bar, swishing my drink, I could have sworn I saw pointed ears.

"That little boy right there is fae," Ryder said. I looked again, but his ears were round like a human's.

I blinked back. *What did I just see?*

"What do you mean?" I asked.

"Most of the fae in these towns work for the humans. They use a glamor to hide their pointed ears."

I gasped. "A glamor?"

"Desert Storm, you're surprised?" He curled a thick brow in observation. The scent of licorice and spice filled the air as he leaned closer. "Fae nowadays use glamor to hide their ears, but it seems like your Pa there has always remained too far off the grid to know what the rest of the fucking world is doing. It's new and still experimental."

He sounded annoyed, as if irritated I was so misinformed about the world around me. He didn't need to take pity on me or be angry at the choices Pa had made.

"He has good reason." My jaw tensed, wondering how I could see the glamor now but not before, as if something in me had suddenly changed. Too many questions I had no answers to.

Whatever flashed in my eyes, he wanted to grab on to it and rein in it.

"Secrets?" Ryder purred, swishing the ice in his drink. "I'd love to know why he keeps you so close." He tilted his head slightly with curious eyes glowing against his tan skin from above the bandana, trailing over the curves of my face.

I yanked his bandana down. "When all you have left is each other, the normal thing to do is hold on to one another a little tighter." My brows furrowed. "But you wouldn't know anything about that, would you, cowboy?" I poked the hard plain of his chest, ignoring how firm he felt beneath my touch.

He immediately tensed, and his calloused hands tightened into fists. He knew how to push, and I knew how deep to cut, so I smiled wickedly in response.

Then I continued, "My thoughts exactly. Do not judge or cast pity my way. I will squash you, ruin you, maybe." I closed the space between us so only he and I could see my tendrils of shadows unfurling as they snaked up his body between his pecs. "I'm known for ruining everything I touch, so I'd be careful where you pry."

Moments passed, and the tension was palpable. When Ryder smiled, it was like looking into a mirror. I felt something rough move around my waist, but before I could react, whatever the hells it was tugged me into his space. I gasped at the motion.

He leaned forward, whispering into my ear. "Why does that sound so tempting coming from you, Desert Storm?"

My eyes darted down to a wispy, ebony rope tightening around my waist.

"What the hell is this?" My fingertips roam over the lasso.

He took a bite of his black licorice, grinning. "I have secrets too."

Over my shoulder, Ryder caught sight of what I assumed was Pa. He gave a knowing tilt of his hat before slowly moving his eyes back to me.

"I guess we will have to play tie-up later."

17

RYDER

essa was playing this game where she couldn't decide if she wanted to hate me or fuck me. I was a greedy bastard for wanting both. Just tolerating my existence was driving her mad, and I knew I had the lead the moment she blushed, making her bronze skin rosy. Honey and vanilla filled the air in her absence, her breath a phantom caress across my lips. The swell of her breasts had done that little shake when I'd tugged her with my rope and left me with a swelling cock. Her threats were like honey on my lips, and I wanted more.

Seeing her reaction washed away the image of Raven sleeping beside her. Waking up to find his arm wrapped around her body had been enough for me to want him dead. He was a constant plague swirling around her.

I watched Vessa stride away, moving through the room like she owned it. She would always belong in any crowd she waltzed into. She was the kind of woman who would make men bend a knee if they felt otherwise.

Call her a demon, hellion, or whatever the fuck else people

said about the Umbra Fae, but deep down inside, I had a feeling she was good. It was intriguing to see behind Vessa's hardened gaze, witnessing her in those moments we'd shared inside a quiet existence.

She was reckless and untamed in a world where most fae were either dead or bent at the knee by the threat of Fang, who had the source of their Eternal. Once she discovered what Fang had been doing with the Elemental Fae and the Eternal stone, she might change her course of action.

Through the crowded tavern, I watched her speak with End's Wrath as her dark hair and sun-kissed highlights swayed back and forth. I studied his face for a reaction to see what sort of conversation they were having. As promised, he reached into his coat pocket, handing her the tonic and what I assumed was the key to her room. I took that as my sign to leave to see what this apocalyptic piece-of-shit town had to offer. I was suddenly in the mood for something sweet.

18

VESSA

Tonight was different. I felt a sense of freedom as I roamed through the crowd. Maybe it was the confinement of a mask and the relief that hit once I pulled it down. Everyone seemed pleasantly engaged with one another. I dragged my gaze away from a man and woman, who were nothing but clashing mouths and roaming hands as I squeezed past them, smiling in passing. There were candlelit alcoves lining the wall and deep crimson wallpaper with a dark damask design sprawling across the entire room, giving the whole tavern an elegant appearance in its own ominous way. A vast difference from the other taverns I had been to. There weren't any windows, which explained the overuse of candles.

"Not a shithole this time, Shadow," Pa said, sipping on his drink as he took in the crowd. The amber liquid reminded me of shimmering gold as it peeked through his gloved fingers. "Shithole," was usually our way of indicating if there were any leads to the tonic or not, but tonight, he really just meant this place was nice. A memory of him and Ma pushed to the front of my mind. They'd always ended their day by the fire with a drink in their hands, quietly talking beneath the stars.

His gray bandana hung low upon his neck, and when he smiled, the creases in his eyes overlapped just a little. He looked...happy for once.

"Definitely not. You did good this time," I said, patting his arm.

He chuckled. "The whiskey goes down just right," he said, facing the bar as he waved the boy down for another.

Shortly after, he reached for the inside of his pocket and pulled out a vial of tonic. I quickly slipped it into my pocket. Then he handed me a key. "Let me show you where we will be staying tonight."

I nodded. I could only imagine how elaborate the rooms would be if the tavern looked like this. My body ached for a bath, a nice hot one with steam curling into the air and a cup of coffee on a table nearby.

I had felt Ryder's stare the whole time as I walked away, and I let the bastard have his fill. But I didn't need to look behind me to know he had already left.

Pa grabbed his drink, and I followed him down a poorly lit corridor, save for the few sconces in need of new candles. For a second, I thought our luck had run out. The smoke-filled hall had a musky scent that made me want to pinch my nose, but when he led me up the stairs, it smelled like roses. It was a whole other atmosphere up here.

Golden sconces lined the corridor, and an antique table with a few old books stood every ten feet or so. One in particular stuck out: a royal blue book gilt with a golden spine with two clashing swords above the title. I slowed my pace to observe the cover, a picture of a woman with long, flowing hair holding two moons facing opposite directions. I couldn't read very well, but I still found comfort between the pages. Maybe tonight, I would try to read it. I quickly opened my coat and slipped it beneath my arm. Pa snuck a glance my way and smiled.

The walls were a deep turquoise with ornate crown molding and an intricate trim carved out of mahogany wood.

"I'll be here." He pointed to room thirty-seven. Then at the end of the hall, he pointed to Ryder's. "That's his, and up those stairs are yours. I got you the suite."

Of course he did.

"Why do you always do this?" I asked, smiling faintly, even though I felt I didn't deserve any of it.

"Because, you deserve it," he replied as if sensing my own thoughts.

"Are my eyes that readable?" I smirked.

"Too readable." He tilted his hat. "If looks could kill, Raven and Ryder be damned." With that, he winked.

I swallowed hard and blinked back.

Yup, his words were like a punch to the gut.

I watched him disappear into his room as I was left standing in the corridor with flushed cheeks and a thrumming pulse. *I belong to no one.*

My eyes widened as I entered my room—a large space that had an already lit hearth off to the side next to a plum purple settee with a rolled and tufted back. I sat down on the plush cushion, running both hands down the fabric.

Velvet.

On the other side of this area were a set of chairs and a table leading to a private washroom with mahogany sliding doors. Against the half wall was a king-sized bed and a side table full of fresh pastries. A welcoming pot of coffee greeted me, steaming into the air.

No matter what Pa thought, I didn't deserve any of this.

I spent the next hour scrubbing my skin raw and dousing my hair with the floral liquid, massaging it until I felt no more speckles of dirt. I enjoyed my warm cup of coffee, occasionally reaching out of the clawed tub for a sip, uncaring if I was being messy.

I put on a clean button-up top, leaving the last few buttons undone, and slipped on a pair of black cotton pants that fit me like a glove and hugged just above my navel. I sighed in delight as I slipped on a fresh pair of socks. The relief was short-lived as I immediately put my boots back on. I could never fully sleep without them, always feeling like I had to be ready to go if need be.

I pulled back the curtain by the table and looked out into the sandy, ivory roads. The sun was setting, casting a fiery glow over the entire town.

There was a knock at my door—four quick taps. Keeping tendrils of magic at my fingertips, I quickly strode over and opened it.

"Hello, Desert Storm." Ryder stood in the hall with something behind his back and a smirk that had my brow curling. I quickly observed that he too was in fresh clothes, hair still slightly damp, wet tips brushing against the black, sleeveless shirt that clung to his body. He looked and smelled divine. "Well, aren't you going to invite me in?"

My heart unexpectedly sped up.

I crossed my arms and shifted a hip to the side. There was an odd, mischievous glint to his blue eyes.

"I'm too tired to give you a rope-tying lesson," I said face-tiously.

He grunted and, in the same breath, held out a freshly baked pie between us.

My brows knit in confusion as I slowly read the tag aloud. "For...Molly. Who's Molly?" I said, looking up at him. No matter who she was, it was enough to let him enter. I stepped to the side.

He smirked as he walked through the doorway, looking around to find the table, the spurs to his cowboy boots clanking with every stride.

"Some sad little widow, I guess." The cadence of his voice had a wicked smile curving my lips.

"Well, I guess I'm not the only evildoer around here."

"You know what they said back in the good ol' days: every evil queen needs a consort." He pulled out a chair and playfully dusted off the seat as if shining it for me.

I scoffed. "Are you trying to butter me up?" I arched my brow.

"Yes." He did not hesitate. It caught me off guard so much that it was likely obvious I was blushing.

"Your knife or mine?" He wiggled his brows in a way that had me giggling.

I pulled out my knife and served us a slice. I was just finishing my second piece when I bit something hard that nearly cracked my tooth. "What the fuck?" I rushed into the washroom, spitting out what was left in my mouth and immersing my hand into a small basin of water. I swished it around until something solid struck the bottom.

"You have to be kidding me," I paused. My jaw hung open as the water revealed a ring; a silver band with a piece of our Eternal stone smoothed into the shape of a circle, its swirls of amber and bloodstone glinting in the light.

I walked out in pure silence.

"What is it?" Ryder slowly stood and walked toward me.

"I don't think Molly was a widow. She was about to be *proposed to*."

"Well I guess that explains why he was all fancied up," Ryder said. A laugh rumbled in his chest as we stood outside the washroom, staring at each other wide-eyed. He cupped a tanned hand over his mouth and then combed it through his hair. In unison, we erupted in laughter. My brows hit my hairline, still in disbelief.

"You are quite evil, Ryder." I sat in the chair, eyeing the circular stone. As I looked, something started to take shape. The amber formed a crescent moon while the bloodstone emulated the dark side of it.

I hummed.

"Wait here," I said. I felt his curious stare as I rummaged through my bag. When I sat in front of him, his eyes remained on the thin leather string I held in my hands, still following my every move. I hung it over his neck, measuring out the length until it stopped at the center of his chest, right between those sinful, hardened pecs. I ignored what the sight did to me as I pulled my knife out and cut the string, threading it through the band.

"Can I?"

"Now you suddenly have manners?" he playfully asked. "You may do anything you want to me, Desert Storm. Your imagination is the limit." His husky voice sent my pulse thrumming. Again, he'd caught me off guard.

The ends of his dark, tousled hair gently brushed against the side of his neck as his head tipped back, watching me slowly rise with a lust-filled gaze. Licking my lower lip, I leaned closer. He tensed as I stood caged between his muscled thighs, the slight motion sending my heart fluttering.

I swallowed.

His thighs brushed against my hips, hard and sturdy from years of riding.

His fists clenched, the rough skin squeezing together as if he was stopping his hands from roaming. His breath fanned across my chest, dangerously close to where my heart lay. With very little effort, he slipped through the cracks while a warmth ignited deep below my belly, eliciting an ache between my thighs. As I tied the new necklace around his neck, I felt the cords in his muscles tighten and flex some more.

He looked down at the ring and held it in his hand.

"A little something to remember me by when your job is done."

His smile waned into something unreadable—maybe sadness?

"Thank you," was all he said. Words that sounded foreign on his lips.

"Since when are you a polite gentleman?" It was a loaded question.

"Who said I am?" His voice was sultry and full of smoke.

I leaned back slightly so our eyes met. My gaze swept across his beautiful face and that half grin. I finished tying the string, now hyperaware of what I had elicited within him. There was no time to hesitate; the flames were already ablaze in his eyes. I became the moth, drawn to him, wanting to lose myself in the entirety of who he was. To push aside the resistance I held between us. I wanted to know what it felt like to have his tongue trace the seam of my lips, to know if he would be rough, or soft and gentle. Maybe this whole tough-guy appearance was a façade. I wanted to break through because the curiosity was stronger than the desire to keep him at a distance.

The urgency for his embrace was like stepping into an overturned hourglass. Time was running out. I couldn't place these emotions surging through me as I stared into his pale-blue eyes, watching the shadows lurking beneath his own hidden past. We were always on some sort of borrowed time. In this moment, I didn't want to think about it any longer. I swung my leg over his hip, then the other, straddling him like I was ready to ride as the anticipation sent my body thrumming.

"Have you ever kissed the devil?" Ryder said, tilting his head back to meet my gaze.

The center of my chest skittered at his words, like the end of a blade along my mark, eliciting the umbra in challenge.

"Sweetheart, I *am* the devil."

A low growl rumbled in his chest. The moment he released his fists, he wasted no time as he cupped my ass and jerked me forward. He was a man who knew exactly what he wanted.

As we shared the same breath, his hand roamed up my back.

He stared at me, long and hard. For a brief moment, I thought maybe he'd changed his mind, that maybe I wasn't his type. But he trailed his hand along the scars of my arm, the flesh that often reminded me of everything I had lost. The same scars that made me feel less alive because I'd always thought, for some damn reason, I was cursed. Maybe I was, but he did not shudder away. His hand slid up to my face, eyes holding a lustful gaze.

His chest rose and fell as he cupped the back of my head, a firm grip because he knew I was not delicate. He crashed his lips into mine, kissing me, deep and claiming, sending an awareness up and down my body, savoring every moment. He was rough as he pressed against me, and with a stroke of his tongue, I opened to him, moaning against his mouth. He tasted like spearmint, a hint of licorice, and whiskey. It was a welcoming coolness against my heated flesh.

Then he pulled away, leaving us in a heaving mess, as if he

couldn't believe what was happening. As if what he was entangled with wasn't real.

"You are quite the dream," he whispered before claiming my lips again. My head fell back as he kissed up and down the side of my neck, licking just below the soft part of my ear. I moaned in response as his length pressed against my very center, the precision too fucking accurate.

Gods-damn, has he been hard this entire time?

The magic coursing through him was a call to my own as it lingered, waiting in the middle of the room for a dance. The sensation hummed against my chest as tiny orbs of light moved around us. Ryder filled my head with the most tangible, indecent thoughts. I gave him a small thread of my magic, allowing his to brush against mine. That little tendril was enough to make my heart skip a beat, and then another. It was a light shrouded by a darkness, memories he kept alive by stoking the flame. A fire he never wanted to burn out. It willed him to keep moving forward, pushing those boundaries to the brink. I didn't want to open my eyes or lose sight. I wanted to see and feel everything, but then he closed the connection, drawing back as I wanted to push forward.

"Who are you?" I whispered, my chest tightening. He mulled over the question with another bruising kiss.

"I'm just yours, for now."

I laughed softly against his mouth.

"As I said before, darlin', I am far from a gentleman," he said in a husky voice, rising to his feet while still keeping my center aligned with his. The motion made him exhale into the crook of my neck as he nibbled on my flesh.

"You shouldn't have opened that door," he warned, "because I'm about to lose all manners and ravish you wholly. And when I'm done with you, you might consider being mine for a while longer. Or you might see me for the devil I truly am."

I dragged my gaze to meet his stare, grinning at his swollen and red lips, which likely matched my own. "You can call me yours all you want, demon, but I belong to no one," I said, combing my fingers through his hair. It was thick and soft, just like I had imagined.

Ryder growled in response, taking it as a challenge as he carried me over to the bed and brought me down onto the mattress. My back was enveloped in a soft duvet blanket as he pressed his hard body against me. He chuckled darkly. "You will return to me, you'll see." His mouth clashed with mine.

The necklace I'd given him fell against my chest. I looked down to find it resting right where my mark was, then looked back up at him. I whispered against his lips. "Is this how you usually thank someone when they give you something?" I teased, tugging on the thin, black, leather thread.

He stilled as he caged me between his arms, his long hair showering over us. My fingers traced every curve of his muscles, running along his shoulders, gripping his biceps. He watched me explore as I kissed the inner part of his arm, fully acknowledging this was a choice that I could finally make. One that had no ties. Whatever this was, whoever he was going to be, for now, this was mine, and it was here for the taking.

He rolled his hips, pressing his length against my very center as I brought him down for another kiss. I enjoyed the feeling of his scruff rubbing my face. He was the perfect blend of rough and soft. It was maddening. His lips brushed across my skin as he moved lower on the bed. He kissed the swells of my breasts, licking the flesh between them in long, languid strokes. My body trembled beneath his touch. He cupped his mouth over the thin fabric of my top, right over my nipple, drawing out another moan that made his gaze flick to mine.

His eyes reminded me of cerulean flames, and again I was that moth.

The fist that pounded at the door sent my heart slamming against my chest.

I growled in response, but Ryder kept going as if the knocking didn't phase him. I think he knew from the annoyed look in my eyes who was on the other side of that door. He pulled down my top, exposing a breast to the night air, and cupped his mouth over my nipple, flicking his tongue as a distraction. My head tilted back as my hips thrust against the bulge of his cock. He was big, so fucking big, the pulse between my thighs grew to an agonizing ache. Ryder's eyes bore through me, finding pleasure in watching how I reacted to his every touch. He chuckled darkly, a groan full of satisfaction as his lips ghosted over my nipple once more, finishing with another tantalizing lick.

The knocks ascended to an aggressive banging.

"Fuck off! I'm busy!" I yelled, but I had to roll Ryder off me.

"Fuck indeed," he growled.

I fixed my top as I darted for the door with tendrils of darkness coiling around my hips and arms. With extra force, I swung the door wide open.

Raven stood in the doorway, jaw fluttering as if he'd been grinding his teeth this entire time. "We are ready to discuss our plans."

"Well, I'm not," I hissed. I went to slam the door, but he stopped it midway.

"*He* is."

"I don't give a *fuck*."

"Well maybe you should, *Vessa*."

By then, Ryder was already standing behind me with heat and lust still radiating off his body. I glanced over my shoulder, observing the sheer mess, and the realization of what we'd been doing was written all over Raven's face.

"Read between the lines, asshole. She said fuck off." Ryder's eyes were bloodshot, possibly seconds from tearing Raven's head off with his teeth. He pressed his body against my back and leaned an arm against the doorframe. My heart fluttered at the motion.

"You don't want to fight someone like me, cowboy. I will end you where you stand," Raven warned with a darkness coating his words, one I didn't often see.

"We might be bound, Raven, but you do not own my life. Neither does Pa. Tell that old man that if he bought me the best room this place had to offer, then he should let me fucking enjoy it for once. I'll come out when I'm ready."

The tension was suddenly broken by the shrill cries of a woman. It was common for towns to have distant gunshots, showdowns, and fist fights in the middle of the road, but her cries pulled me away. I rushed over to the window, hearing a man yelling right outside the tavern. When I peered out, tears were streaming down her kohl-stained face. "You're my wife, *woman*. Do as I fucking say."

For a moment, I wanted to help. The adrenaline from watching two brute men argue kept the shadows curling around my wrists, but when I sensed no glamor on her ears, I sighed and took a step back, closing the curtains in the process.

My eyes briefly shut as a pang of guilt tried to take root. Humans did not deserve remorse.

The mood was gone.

Especially as Raven stood in the doorway, waiting to see what I would do.

While the bird and the cowboy played their game of death glares, I stepped in front of Ryder, peering up into Raven's eyes, noticing the satisfaction, because in some fucked up way, he knew he'd won.

"I'm walking out the door because it is *my* choice to make." I pointed a finger at him, but I went back for my pie, aggressively grabbing it off the table. No matter what Pa had to say, he had to know that asking and telling were two completely different things. I would not bend to the whim of anyone, but I was also a sucker, because this pie was so gods-damn good and I knew he'd love it. It would smooth over any growing tension. I pushed past Raven and went to room thirty-seven.

19

VESSA

Fuck manners. I stormed through Pa's door, preferring to bring hell with me. He did not even flinch when I slammed down the half-eaten apple pie. He continued to play the last hand of his deck. I knew he wouldn't say a damn word until he won the game or not.

Pa's room had the same structure as mine, only smaller, simpler for a man like him. I'd known the door would be unlocked. I remembered a long time ago, I had asked him why he never locked them. His response should have been carved into stone.

"My door is an open invitation for anyone seeking death."

He sat by the window, hat off, his onyx, pointed ears exposed. He was dressed down to nothing but a loose-fitted, gray, long-sleeve shirt, unbuttoned at the top, along with thermals and boots. The man looked ready for bed.

"Your mind is messy, Shadow. Better sort out your thoughts. See which cards you want to play."

"I thought I was doing just that until you decided to let Raven cockblock me."

He flashed a thick, salt-and-pepper brow my way, one that felt like a whip. A look that would have worked back in the day, but I was a woman now.

Hard on the reins, just like Ma, is what his face read.

"Since we are being bold and boundless tonight, yeah, I said it," I sneered.

"My gods, your mouth spits fire."

"Then don't poke the dragon."

Raven and Ryder walked in, their boots thudding against the ground like wild buffalo. I could pick out Ryder's footsteps by the spurs because Raven loved his steel-capped boots. I glanced over my shoulder to find Ryder taking a space against the wall, knee bent as his boot rested against it. His tousled hair and swollen lips gave away what we had just been doing. Pa set his hand down, cards thumping against the table with extra emphasis, and sighed.

"We are about to enter The City of Donia. There are things there that you will not be able to unsee nor will you understand. It's nothing like the wild out here. The humans here are spread out, but lump them in a city full of Elemental Fae where fear binds them, you'll truly see the animals they've become in order to survive."

"I don't see much of a difference between them and us. We've been teetering on survival for years—what difference does a wall make?"

He looked at me. "*We are free.* Ain't nothing better, no matter how monstrous we are. But we are going there for a purpose, and that's to meet the person who makes your tonic. I hate to break it to you, Shadow, but you need more."

"No shit." I swung one leg over the other and crossed my arms, bouncing my foot. "What happens if I don't take it?"

"Don't start this bullshit, Vessa." Raven moved toward us but kept his distance from me as he stood by the window.

I quickly uncrossed my legs and leaned forward, ignoring the phantom pain pulsing up my arm. "I'm not starting any bullshit. What happens if I don't take it?"

"Shadow, you will be in so much pain by the end of it, you won't even survive long enough to find out." Pa loomed closer with a warning that sent a shiver down my spine.

Rein in your shit is what his look said.

I knew what he meant.

"Why do you guys get to decide what she puts in her mouth?" Ryder chimed in as he kept Raven in his line of sight. Taking the bait, Raven's eyes darkened, rolling his head from side to side and straightening his shoulders. The grin on Ryder's face displayed enough satisfaction to last him a lifetime.

"If you two idiots want to sword fight with your cocks, take that shit outside." Pa's shadows spread out, curling and seeping into the room.

Ryder withdrew, holding his hands out in surrender. "Alright, End's Wrath, but you need to keep a tighter leash on that bird of yours. His feathers are too easily ruffled."

"He ain't my bird, boy. He's Vessa's."

I slouched in my chair, bringing a hand to my forehead, soothing out the sudden pain they all invoked in me. Everyone in this room wanted to dig each other's graves.

"It's obvious the man who makes these tonics is working for the humans now. Why let him breathe? He doesn't deserve to hone and share a gift so ancient with those who aren't fae. He is going against every word spoken by the elders of Blightstone Hollow and the true meaning of our Eternal." I felt like I was preaching for a second. It made my skin crawl, but the humans had taken too much from us.

"Ryder is going to sneak us in, we will meet with the maker of these tonics, and then we're out."

As soon as Pa started shuffling his cards, I knew this conversation was over. He silently set up a new game of solitaire, and I felt my stomach clinch; the realization hit me so hard in the chest that my eyes burned. A sense of foreboding hung in the air.

Pa could keep his plans all he wanted, but by the end of it, we all had minds of our own. I could leave that city in ruins and walk away knowing I'd sleep just fine, leaving every human and Elemental Fae to burn to ash.

He would not dare stand in my way.

"We ride at dawn," Pa said.

And that was that. I glanced over my shoulder to find Ryder already gone. Silence hung in the air, but there was a constant darkness looming over me, and I knew it was his.

I knew by the time I saw Pa tomorrow, that sweet apple pie would have washed away any anger and frustration he had because of me. It didn't stop my thoughts from whirling—his words remained echoing in the back of my mind, telling me to stick to the plan. Words had a way of creating monsters just as quickly as grief.

20

VESSA

There was no way in hell I could have slept after that. I went back to my room, slipped on the sleeve that hid my scars, put on my gloves, secured my hat, and threw on my holster before I slipped out the door to have a drink downstairs.

As the bubbles churned in the fancy wine glass, I realized I was going to need a whole lot more. I waved down one of the two boys behind the bar, who looked like they could be brothers. The oldest one came over this time. He was maybe around fifteen, if I was taking a wild guess.

"Whatever is left in that bottle of wine, I'll take it all."

"Yes, ma'am," he said in haste, sounding like a little perfectly-trained fae. This place was molding him to grow up too fast.

"That will be five nara coins, please." He held out his hand with a bright smile that didn't quite look right.

I leaned in. "Do you ever get a cut of what you sell, kid?" I asked casually.

"Pardon?"

I huffed out a laugh. His manners were too cute. "You know, selling all this booze and wine, do you earn a keep from it?"

His eyebrows rose in shock as he looked from side to side. I hadn't known asking questions was a sin. He immediately shook his head.

"Here," I said, giving him five pieces of nara coins and another small pouch just for him, enough to bring him happiness for weeks. "This pouch is special," I whispered, drawing his attention back toward me.

"You mean, special like you?" The boy's professionalism melted away as he leaned in to take a closer look at my face. He closely examined my sparkling freckles beneath the brim of my hat. He gasped, eyes widening as if he saw something else. "You're fae, just like I was, but there's something different about you," he observed, studying me as if he might see it if he squinted hard enough.

Such a smart little boy. The back of my throat burned as tears stung my eyes. I looked at the tops of his ears where his tips used to be, and I knew he was using a glamor to hide the jagged scars, but somehow, I could see them. Something inside me broke. I lifted my sleeve to expose the scars on my forearm. His eyes widened again when he saw how bad they were.

"No matter what they try to take from us, we are still fae. Don't let anyone tell you differently."

"Why do you hide them?" he asked. The question took me back.

"Well, it's not that I'm ashamed. People just ask too many questions. I'm not one to draw attention to myself. I prefer to be—"

"Like a shadow?" he guessed.

I smiled faintly. "Yeah, kind of like that."

He nodded.

"And don't worry, your secret is safe with me," I said, my eyes flashing to his ears. He shyly brushed a few golden locks away from his face.

"I know. That's why I told you." He smiled with more confidence this time.

I didn't want to draw out this conversation in fear someone might notice. "This pouch has enough for you to buy anything you like. A man like you has to start somewhere. You know, establish yourself. Who knows, maybe one day, you'll own this damn joint."

His chest puffed out a little with pride as the pouch disappeared inside his pocket. "Thank you."

I watched him walk off.

"Well look at you being all sensitive and shit."

I spun on my stool to meet the eyes of Ryder, who was casually leaning against the bar.

"Not exactly, it's just—"

"It's okay, I won't tell a living soul you're a softy on the inside." He half grinned and cupped his hand over mine, stroking the scars up my wrist with the pad of his thumb, rekindling that heat. That spark fluttered up my arms, across my chest, and up my face.

"Are you blushing, Desert Storm?"

My head tilted back as I laughed, holding my hat in the process.

I leaned an elbow onto the weathered wood of the bar and slightly side-eyed him, reaching out the only way I knew how, through darkness. A rope-like shadow wove in my hand. With a devious thought, it slipped behind his leather belt, sliding through each loop until it was completely wrapped around his waist. I manipulated his power of *Nai*, weaving it to my whim because his mind was being driven by his cock. I reined him in so quickly, with an effortless tug, he was wedged between my thighs so that only the two of us could see the magic I held over him.

An invisible tether wrapped around his neck, forcing him to lean down until my gloved hand was also wrapped around his throat. A faint tendril of darkness followed as it curled around him.

He took it as an invitation, grip tightening on the ledge of the bar, hanging over me as desire churned in his eyes. With a long, claiming lick, my tongue slid from his chin to the seam of his lips, finishing with a lustrous gaze, satisfied when his face turned red against his sun-kissed skin.

"Look who's blushing now," I whispered.

The crowd blurred around us the moment a song began to play. The sound of a guitar and piano pushed me to my feet. I never got to dance the way I wanted, in the middle of a room where nothing else seemed to matter. I wanted him to follow me, wanted to know how far he'd go, to see if he would chase and try to finish what had barely begun. I released him from my grip, the faint mist of shadows dissipating in my wake as I slipped into the crowd, leaving him where he stood. I didn't look back. I weaved through swaying arms and hips, moving past dancing bodies damp with sweat and clusters of smells. I felt the rise of freedom within every gentle push off the ground, closing my eyes as my head swayed to the beat. I glanced over at the bar to find an empty seat where Ryder had been.

His loss, I thought as I continued to move.

Suddenly, there was a second set of strings adding to the beat. The crowd parted at the right moment for me to see that Ryder was the second guitarist, watching me dance. His strumming became a siren's call to my darkness. I succumbed to every note, to the brush of his nails chiming against every string as my hips moved from side to side. Time itself vanished as I closed my eyes, losing myself to the song.

Just when I thought I couldn't feel any freer, a familiar arm wrapped around the cinch of my waist. A spark that could ignite any waning flame. I opened my eyes to find Ryder, leaning in as he gently moved me into his embrace. My breathing stilled, betraying my own heart in the way I was looking at him. It could match the fire churning in his eyes. He was enough to ruin me, careen me off a cliff, and in this moment, I didn't mind. I forgot where I was, in a world full of hatred, where people died every day. It all seemed to fade into the ash we were all destined to become. He was here for now. The hollowness inside my chest began to swell, the ghost of who I had been tapping on the inside to be let out, reminding me she was still here.

I felt less of a vessel in his presence, more alive than I'd ever allowed myself to be. I brought my palm to his chest, feeling his pulse thrum beneath my fingertips as he caressed the column of my neck. Time stilled as we moved to the beat, both our hearts racing. I sucked in a shuddered breath, removing my glove and exposing my hand. I didn't feel like the curse I was known to be. Shadows curled around us as I released them, blocking out the candle-lit room and those around us. I saw the threads of his power. The power of *Nai*.

"What are you doing?" He leaned down, whispering against my ear.

"I'm living."

I moved my lips against his as we danced. Glowing orbs returned as if summoned by my touch alone, weaving around the parts of me others saw as evil. It was his power latching on to mine for as long as this song lasted. He combed his fingers through my hair. His lips were supple and soft, the scruff of his beard an aching reminder of our time in the desert, and I found myself considering where else I'd like him to explore.

"This is dangerous," he exhaled in a heated breath. "So fucking dangerous." A strong, calloused hand slid down my waist as he leaned down, kissing along the column of my neck while our hips moved in synchronized motions.

I smiled, eyes closed as I danced on the edges, pushing to see how far I could take this. I would run to Earth's Fall if I could. That hidden space at the end of Blightstone Hollow that was only told in stories, a place I often hoped existed come the day I was done with this place.

"We are still here," I softly whispered into the shell of his ear. He turned his head ever so slightly, causing the scruff of his beard to rub against me. He dragged his lips to mine, hard and claiming—demanding in how he pulled me against his chest. I held my breath as the world slipped away, opening my mouth to his. We moved together as the darkness enveloped us until the song was over.

I opened my eyes in a soft flutter, caught beneath his penetrating stare. And I was still alive. Our magic waned as I looked around.

"I don't know how, but no one noticed," I said quietly into his ear, shocked that the room remained moving to the next song. But something caught the corner of my eye as another type of magic sent a vibration down my spine.

I turned to find Raven, hand extended, the remnants of his shadow receding back into his palm as sweat broke out across his face. He paled, fingertips shaking, and blood dripped from his nose. My jaw fell open. Shock and anger fused together as I rushed through the crowd.

"What the hell are you doing?" My voice shook, my mind still reeling to understand how he could have done *that*.

"Don't," is all he said.

He'd somehow strengthened his power of illusion, all so I could dan—

When the realization struck me, I brought a hand to my mouth. "Why?" My voice unexpectedly cracked. I was not worthy of such a thing.

He pulled a handkerchief from his back pocket and wiped the blood off his nose with a rendering force.

"Why do you think?" His eyes flashed with nothing but pain and frustration. "You mean more to me than a...*forced* bond. I—" He waved his hand, gritting his teeth with his jaw set in place. Whatever he had been about to say died on his tongue. "Seeing your smile is better than flying. I know where we stand, but it doesn't mean I won't go through great lengths to see you're still alive somewhere deep inside..."

He never looked at me; his gaze was far away.

"Good night, moon," he said, dissipating into the dark just as he always did when he was done. I watched him disappear into a shroud of nothing; only the stool remained where he'd just been.

Ryder came up behind me, secretly slipping me my glove. He was still confused.

"Are you okay?"

"I will be."

21
VESSA

Just as expected, Pa gently knocked at my door before dawn. I'd barely slept last night. Between that man still yelling at his wife two floors down, my dance with Ryder, and Raven extending his magic in ways I couldn't even begin to understand, I didn't think anyone had gotten any decent rest.

"Come in," I said, gathering my things.

Pa opened the door with a deep sigh, sadness brimming over.

"The pie was good, wasn't it?"

"Yup, too good."

"I know." I felt the burn in my eyes as I bit the inside of my cheek.

Not today, Vessa. Pull it back.

"This room is pretty nice," he observed, avoiding the looming presence of grief as he took a small tour. "Maybe on our way back, we can get you the same one and you can enjoy it for longer." There was a sense of foreboding in the air as he spoke, one I tried not to dissect. "I went ahead and filled your canteen with water. I'll meet you downstairs when you're ready."

That was his way of saying he was sorry.

"Thanks, Pa." I swung my satchel across my body.

He looked around and held his hands out. "Where's Raven?"

I sighed. "He never came to my window. I kept it unlocked just in case, but—" My mind reeled to what Raven had done for me last night, wondering if Pa knew.

"Men are too gods-damn complicated, Shadow. They're not worth plucking any worry strings over."

I smiled faintly, stepping into his space. I wanted him to reach out and hug me, show me some sort of emotion rather than stern advice. As the tears hung heavy under my eyes, threatening to release at any moment, I raised my brows, hoping the morning air would be cold enough to blot them away. I sucked in a deep breath. It came out as an unexpected whimper of a cry as my voice finally cracked. For some strange reason, I felt like we would never see this place again. Pa and I were saying goodbye to another piece of ourselves. I so desperately wanted to cling to him and never let him go. Why did this moment feel so gods-damn heavy? The back of my throat burned as I held my next breath, trying to rein in the raging storm swelling inside me. I missed who we had been back in Black Water Woods when it had been just the four of us. I missed fishing on the shores of The Nil Bend, talking with my sister all morning about what sweet pastry we would convince Ma to make to go along with our catch. She had been nearly two years younger than I. Maybe that was why I'd taken a liking to that boy downstairs. He reminded me of who I had been, and he still had his brother. I hoped he'd have an escape if things ever went south, because as I remembered the torrent of waves that had pulled me under, as I saw my sister's lifeless body, I didn't want him to ever feel that pain.

Now it was just the two of us, stuck in the past inside a world that seemed to want nothing to do with fae.

I stood before the only man who would ever be worthy of a tear. As one finally slipped free, I looked into his eyes. "I know, Pa," was all I could manage to say without falling apart. I patted his hand, and he cupped his other over it. We stood in silence, thinking about that damn pie. "I know."

)●(

DEEP IN THOUGHT, the tension set in my jaw was enough to remind me of my pulsating headache. I felt the need for release rising, the darkness coiling beneath my aching fingertips. It needed to go somewhere, an escape, one that could expel all the demons festering inside me. I walked down the stairs, past Ryder's room, the door now open with two women cleaning it. As I stepped onto the dimly lit hallway of the first floor, I heard that familiar grating sound that had kept me up most of the night. The door was slightly cracked. I paused, tilting my head just enough to peek through the gap. That same man who had been in the streets yesterday had his wife cornered, yelling about stale bread. The fucking asshole should be lucky he even got any today.

"I'm...I'm sorry. I—"

"You worthless bitch. You're going to be real sorry when I'm through with you." He stabbed a finger her way. She flinched in response. It was enough for me to grit my teeth. I couldn't stand seeing a woman flinch. I knew all too well what that meant.

I summoned the power of *Ano*, and with a gentle breath of air, the door opened ever so slightly. The woman now had matching black eyes. The anger rolled through me. Before I could take my next breath, he was closing the distance between them.

Hell-the-fuck-no.

I dropped my bag and kicked the door open, breaking off one of the hinges in the process. Both of them jumped as their expressions went wide-eyed. The man scowled as he balled his fists. He wanted to get physical with someone? Well, I was here for the taking. He charged me with a swinging fist, aiming for my face. With a palm out, I caught it. On contact, he felt the strength within my grip as I squeezed bones and muscle together. His eyes flashed with horror and anger as the information registered that I was far from human.

"That's right, asshole."

I reached for my revolver with the other hand. A silver flash of pure steel cleaved across his face, splattering blood onto the corner of his shirt. He flew back, stumbling into a table with a slit decorating the crest of his nose. I smirked, twirling the revolver around my trigger finger and slipping it back into its holster. It would have only taken a second to snap his neck from where I stood, but I was in the mood for a longer conversation.

"Is there a reason you made your wife flinch?" I sneered, grabbing his hand as I went straight for the saddle joint, pulling his thumb against the bend.

He wailed in response.

"I asked you a question."

He stared up at me with bloodshot eyes and whiskey on his breath. "Fuck you, cunt." He grimaced, crimson coating his teeth.

I smiled. "Wrong answer."

I slammed his face into my knee, feeling his bones shatter beneath the skin as I tossed him back.

"*Say it!*"

He was choking on his own blood. "Because I...I hit her." His voice was low, the sound barely coming out because his inner shame was rising.

"I want you to say it *louder*."

"Because I hit her!"

"I bet that makes you feel real good, doesn't it?" With the tip of my boot, I stepped onto his crotch slowly as I pulled harder on his thumb. Panic rolled through him as he writhed beneath my foot. The body had its limits. How easily things could change the moment our livelihood was at stake. And I had a thing for pushing those limits.

"No, no, no!" He shook his head again.

I bared my teeth as I felt every cord and muscle rip from his thumb until it snapped. Subtle, save for his screams.

I grabbed him by his shirt and hauled him up, tossing him across the room.

In a blind, manic rage, and as a final attempt, he came for me. I pulled out my revolver and shot him straight in the face. Blood and brain matter littered the wall and the expanse of the room behind him. The woman in the corner tensed, pushing herself against it.

I tossed her a sack of nara coins. She was no longer tied to this sorry excuse of a man, and that bag was enough to get her to her next saving grace if she chose to have one. Light brown hair clung to her fear-stricken face as her eyes bounced between me and her now-dead husband. Relief flashed in her eyes as she exhaled and loosened her shoulders.

"And *that's* how you leave a man," I said, turning to go, but the woman cried out.

"Wait!"

I paused near the doorway.

Shaken, her eyes darted to the sliver of hair that exposed

the tip of my ear, seeing me for who I really was. For a second, I thought she would scream again, having witnessed her husband killed by a fae. People began to gather behind us. Oddly, her eyes softened, and she motioned to her ear as if to tell me to quickly cover mine.

"Thank you...Thank you for saving me."

The kindness in her words was an echo, enough to make the back of my throat burn and pain tinge my nose.

"Thank you..."

A human not only thanking me but being kind enough to tell me to hide my ear.

"Thank you."

I simply nodded, a tilt of my hat before I turned and disappeared into the crowd.

I quickly pushed past them, catching the eyes of a few women, shock rolling down their faces as if astonished that a woman could have made such a mess. I kept my head down.

Just when I was about to move the curtain and exit the hall into the tavern, I was pulled into a room.

The boy from last night was strong enough to yank me into a pantry that led to the kitchen, his curls swaying back and forth as he made sure no one else was around.

"You don't want to go out that way," he warned in a hushed tone, cheeks tinged with red as if he'd been running.

"Why not," I asked, as my eyes quickly surveyed the room.

"There's a sheriff from Grand Dusk looking for you."

"Fuck..."

"Fuck indeed," he said.

I snorted. Such a cute kid.

"Well, what do you suggest we do then?" I smiled as sweat beaded above my brow.

He grabbed my hand again. "Boss ain't here yet. I'll lead

you out the back. Your family is already out there waiting for you."

I blinked back the confusion as he led me through the kitchen.

"Thank you for killing him. They were arguing for as long as they were here. And also, that was pretty badass." The excitement hummed in his chest. I could only imagine what that boy had heard out of that room all this time.

A smile quirked my mouth. "You're welcome. You got any idea what this sheriff's name is?"

"Sheriff Dawson. He looks as grumpy as your old Pa."

I snorted again, this time too loud because he turned around to shush me.

"Duly noted."

We stepped outside to bright azure skies as two yellow butterflies fluttered in my path. Oddly, it felt too sunny for a town like Ash Dunes, as if Mother Nature had cleared the way for our escape.

Ryder and Pa were already astride their stallions. As I mounted my mare, the boy ran up to give us a sack.

"Food for the road," he said, tossing the bag to Pa while stroking the neck of Ryder's stallion.

"What's your name, partner?" Pa asked.

The boy beamed at the gesture. "Even, not like getting even, but like...heaven. My younger brother's name is Daven. Same ending."

Pa blinked back with a chuckle as he tried to gather all he'd just heard.

With a gentle wave, Even summoned the power of *Ari*, smiling as the horse drank water from his hand. The gesture was so kind and selfless.

"He's special, just like you. In the right light, you will soar, and everyone else might want to get the hell out of the way for that," Even said looking up at Ryder.

"My my, little guy. You have quite the mouth on you." Pa cracked a smile, one so bright, it nearly stung my eyes.

Unsure how to respond, Ryder smirked and tilted his hat.

"Best be on your way."

Without saying another word, Even disappeared back into the shadows of the doorway, and in unison, we rode off.

22
RYDER

Before I broke the silence, more than half the day had gone by. End's Wrath and Vessa had been lost to their thoughts. I'd been left with mine; a place I often didn't want to stir. Whatever slept in the recesses of my mind needed to stay the fuck asleep.

"If we ride hard, we can make it to The City of Donia in less than two days, reaching the city in the late hours of the night."

End's Wrath responded with a nod, enough for me to gather it meant "*sounds good.*"

I clicked my tongue and nudged my stallion to ride beside Vessa. Her stone-cold gaze matched End's Wrath's. When I got no response from either of them, I knew not to pry. Last time, I'd said something ignorant, and I'd ended up paying for it.

Raven flew ahead, and it gave me sick joy knowing he and Vessa had tension. He needed to fuck off for as long as possible. There was something about him I didn't trust.

I was vexed by Vessa, by the siren of a storm that kept me in her range but rarely ever let me into her eye. In those moments when she'd let me in, searing me with those perfect lush lips, guilt had tried to take root around my jagged heart, attempting to tear me to shreds. Our magic danced in unison, and I couldn't help but allow my mind to wander back to those moments, of what all that could have meant. The way her waist had felt when I'd slipped my arm around it, wanting to commit such heinous crimes just to taste her on my lips again or even see her cast a glance my way. And as I watched her take off her hat and run a hand through her hair with the sun filtering through those long, soft locks, I wondered at how fucking magical she was in everything. Every time I stared at her, I was wrecked.

This was a job and nothing more, but my cock and heart were beginning to align, and it was starting to piss me the fuck off.

COME SUNDOWN, we built a small fire by the foot of a mountain that blended into rolling hills. It was a small bend that gave us cover with a fifteen-foot cliff at the mouth of it. The land was ever-changing and so was the air, feeling cooler than it had months ago when I'd passed through. It never snowed here, but the bite of this breeze was enough to make me think that maybe the world was acclimatizing to the way fae and humans were interacting.

I placed a rolled blanket between my back and a boulder, making my spot for the night as I eyed the crest of the hills.

For the first time today, Vessa spoke, her soft voice nearly ethereal, or maybe it was just the remedy I needed. My mind was playing tricks on me.

"There are a few lone trees at the top," she observed, the canopy's leaves a bright crimson. No doubt things in the land were changing, and that pretty little fae was so observant.

There was something about her and the connection she felt to her elements. Everything seemed to come naturally. She had to put her hands on something and always had some sort of observational words to follow.

"Those trees are a little too far from their home in Blightstone Hollow," End's Wrath replied.

Just then, a dark silhouette swept down, sending my nerves into a frenzy the moment the bird dissipated into a dark cloud, stepping onto the ground a man, this time with ease, as there had been no imminent threat. As he emerged from the shrouds, Vessa already had him in her line of sight.

He went straight for her with four rabbits tied in a withered rope, tossing them at her feet like some sort of peace offering or gift. She smirked. It looked like his way of saying he was sorry. For what? I still had no fucking clue. Maybe another silent fight I'd never know about.

A smile curved her full lips, and she took off her hat and gloves. He sat beside her, closer than he should have, as she leaned against him and patted the side of his face.

"My favorite," she said.

Raven groaned as he rolled his head from side to side and squared his shoulders, causing End's Wrath to look up from the brim of his hat.

"What's gotten into you, boy? Tough shifting back to a man?" He raised a peppered brow.

Vessa scoffed. "I can only assume it's from what he did last night." She darted a glare at Raven as she crossed her arms.

I sighed. *This* was my entertainment for the night? Umbra drama at its finest, and a front-row seat I hadn't asked for. I leaned further into my rolled-up blanket and pulled my hat over my face.

"You were being reckless. I had no choice," Raven snapped back.

"Elaborate, boy. I'm not too keen on riddles." End's Wrath's warning was enough to get me listening again.

Silence strangled the air.

"Well?" I gruffly said, popping off my hat just a few inches from my face. "Spit it out so we can all get some decent rest tonight."

Vessa snickered as her head tipped back, exposing the side of her neck, a place I'd love to lick again if given the chance. Her eyes narrowed back down toward me as her iridescent freckles shimmered against the flames.

Heaven's hell, she is beautiful when she's mad.

"*Ra-ven*"—she pronounced the "v" with a slice of attitude as she looked back to her father—"decided to butt into our dance last night and extended his power to shield me."

"What do you mean?" I placed my hat beside me. "Are you telling me Raven's magic was...dancing with mine?" My lips curved in disgust as I sat up and sneered his way. "Your...*magic* was all over my body?"

End's Wrath and Vessa laughed. The old man's deep bellow was so loud, it reverberated around our campsite. They were laughing so hard, I thought they'd lost their gods-damn minds.

"It's not funny," I growled and immediately stood, feeling violated when I'd thought it had been hers.

"Sit down, asshole. It was mine, but because we have a *forced* bond"—Vessa glared at End's Wrath—"sometimes our powers can merge when desperately needed, or depending on how strong the bond is. It can vary per situation."

"And you were too fucking desperate," Raven cut in, but he didn't find it any more humorous than I did.

End's Wrath was still laughing, not even phased by this bullshit. He sighed as he leaned back against the tree, covered his face with his hat, and crossed his arms.

"Fuck this." I took my blanket to seek shelter anywhere else but in the company of these fucking crazy western wood-landers.

)●(

I FOUND A SMALL, partially enclosed space far enough away to have some privacy. Not long after that, I heard light footsteps scraping against the gravel. With my legs bent at the knees, forearms resting on them, my hands remained clasped as I looked out into the desert night, watching the few tumble-weeds to see how long it would take for them to get enough kick from the wind to keep going. With the power of *Nai*, I gave them a gentle gale and watched them bounce away.

I felt like a mess, tangling myself up in something I didn't understand.

Vessa placed her blanket to her side and took a seat beside me. She was dressed down to just her top and pants. The black sleeve that covered her arm had been left behind. Her boots were never removed for long except at the end of the night, cloaked beneath the luminescence of the moon; she slept with them on.

"He's not like us," she finally said, watching the same tumbleweeds caught in the brush. "He was raised by the Umbra Fae, but we don't know exactly where he came from or which type of Elemental Fae he could be. We had suspicions he was from Emer Forest, the island north of Black Water Woods —our home. Yet he doesn't have the power of *Nan*, earth. I think a part of his earlier memories are missing, the life he had before us."

I guessed that explained a little more about him, why he had so many different powers. A male like me, who was stuck between two different worlds, only one of his was in the form of a bird.

I turned my head to look her way.

"He was a young boy who lived in a cage, waiting on the fate of an owner. I think this bond was a way out for Raven and a solution for Pa to try to tame my wild heart. If you can imagine, I was hard on the reins even back then."

I hummed. Any anger I'd held melted away as my lips curved into a half grin. "I find that hard to believe."

We shared a glance momentarily. She laughed, looking down at the soles of her boots, and began picking at a few stuck rocks.

"Pa said if I was bound, then I would have to think about the choices I made, and in return, he got a bodyguard for his daughter. Raven was chained in a cage and now to me. For the first portion of our lives together, he refused to shift back to our form. Not until we were older and, maybe, he was getting lonely. He has never been free, and we are all he's ever known. All was merry, until one day, it just wasn't."

There was a long pause.

"They came on boats from The Nil Bend." Her voice was a soft shudder.

"Who?" I asked.

Her brows hit her hairline as she struggled to keep the swell of tears from falling. Every shadow cast upon her face hid terrors. A part of me wished she didn't have any. I wanted to be angry with myself for feeling this way, for caring when this was just a job. I was no better than the ones who had betrayed them, but here I was.

"The humans," she whispered. "There was no warning, no sound. They came in the middle of the day when we couldn't call upon the power of the moon to summon our *ama* and *ano*."

With the pad of my thumb, I wiped a tear from her face. Grief was a crippling bitch. Some scars were loud and observable while others were kept hidden and preserved. No matter how one wore them, they were all the same. They were scars nonetheless, forever etched into their soul. She had both kinds, and my gods, she rode the fuck out of hers. She was braver than I could have ever been.

"We all lose in the end, Ryder. That's just how life goes."

My lips pressed thin as I tucked a strand of hair away from her face. "Ain't that the truth," I replied. Every word she spoke was an echo of my own thoughts.

"Even when you think you have something you want to hold on to, it will always be a breath away from slipping from your grasp," she said. "There will always be that voice to remind me every time I want to latch on to anything that brings a sliver of happiness my way, things could change in the blink of an eye."

"It is the ebb and flow of being caught in the middle of a changing world when we are still hanging on to our pasts," I said as our eyes locked.

Though she and I were different people, I felt our souls were the same.

She leaned into my shoulder and nestled into my warmth as a comfortable silence bloomed. I allowed it to grow, just a little, enough to wrap my arm around her.

"The fact that I can get this close to you and still be alive is worth holding on to." My heart fluttered inside the vessel of cobwebs and dusty corners.

She hummed faintly, a sleepy tone that had me gently leaning us back until we were against the rolled blanket. She nestled into the crook of my neck, and I felt her eyelashes against my skin as she closed her eyes. "You're nice and warm, so I'll let you live for now."

I chuckled, closing my eyes as I placed my hat over my face. Soon, we fell asleep under the stars.

23

VESSA

The blanket was a welcome comfort this strange, frosty morning. Sometime in the night, I had draped it over us. Well, mostly over me. My palm remained on his chest, and beneath, his heart was a resting pulse. I could ruin and crush his heart within the same breath and, by the next, be ready to douse myself in whatever magic he would cast my way. I was on opposite sides of my own spectrum, hating the way he made me feel. He was a warning and a desire, rough with a simple touch that could unravel me, and here I was with my legs intertwined with his.

With Ryder still asleep, I was left with nothing but reeling thoughts. He lazily moaned at the sudden drag of my leg as I shifted. He turned onto his side, facing me with warm, muscled arms caging me in. My face was buried between his pecs, halting my next breath. His rich scent enveloped me. How could such a rough, rugged man smell so good? Indecisive about what to do, I closed my eyes and hoped to drift back to sleep and forget about any of this, but there was something hard nestled between us, right below my stomach.

My eyes widened as I felt his length throb against me.

Fucking hells.

There was a deep warmth pooling just below my belly as his bulge pushed against my center, the angle pressing just right. It pulsed in response as the rest of me stilled. The sensation grew to a need. I moved slightly against him, feeling the pressure build, coaxing me ever so slightly to thrust my hips. Heat flushed across my face and chest as my pulse pounded in my ears. Before I knew it, another thrust of my hips, and I was quietly grinding against him. The pleasure grew to a wild, untamed need as another carefully taken breath escaped me. I pressed down a little harder, allowing more pressure to build between the apex of my thighs, with my center clenching and aching for what was not inside me.

What am I doing?

His body was so massive beside mine. Just his length alone could tear me apart. My heart pummeled against my chest, and I found it hard to breathe.

"Vessa." Ryder's length twitched in response to what I'd been doing. I could have sworn it grew bigger once his thoughts connected. I exhaled a shaky breath at how he said my name, deep and husky. It was a relief to know he was awake, because my heart and lungs couldn't have handled much more. He groaned, another throb, and his hand was in my hair, cupping the back of my head. With surprising force, his lips came crashing down, our tongues clashing in a mangled mess as his hips pushed against mine. His tongue was a warm welcome inside my mouth. I moaned against him as he rolled onto his back, aligning me right back where I belonged. I straddled his thighs as I rocked against his length with the shame still blushing my cheeks.

Oh gods.

His hands trailed up my waist, and with a simple pull, I

lifted my arms and my top was off. He groaned, eyes hazed with lust as he took in the sight of my breasts, nipples hardening against the cool morning air.

"Fuck," he exhaled on a bated breath, and by the end of it, he was kissing the center of my chest, moving down toward the mark of the moon. His tongue slid over that flesh, eliciting a spark deep within my core. Whatever was brewing there felt like banked embers blooming back to life, and he was here to fan the flames.

"Ryder," I softly moaned. I had never allowed anyone to touch that space before, and I wanted more of it. He began to move his head upward, but I nudged him right back to the very center. He licked me there again, this time ending in a little bite. A soft whimper escaped me. He enjoyed exploring my body with his tongue, taking his time as if it didn't exist around us.

He brought his lips to my nipple, sucking and flicking the hardened flesh. I moaned, moving my body against his, core clenching nothing but air as heat pooled below my belly.

I needed more.

"I should torment you for starting without me," he finally said, gliding his lips across my chest before taking the other nipple into his mouth. My head tipped back. I was so hot and crazed, but it wasn't fair I was exposed and he wasn't. My nails dug into his chest, and with a simple grab, his shirt split down the middle. I tore his sleeves off next, tossing the fabric somewhere behind me.

"Just to keep it fair." I smirked.

A primal sound raptured through his throat, and he suddenly grabbed me by my waist and hauled me onto my back. My dark hair splayed across the blanket.

"I think I like this game," he said, positioning himself between my thighs. He studied me for a moment, leaning his weight on one arm, half caging me in while his other hand explored the peaks of my breasts. "Maybe this time, we can finish what we started."

Ryder's fingertips trailed over every curve of my body, featherlight in the way he explored me. His eyes flicked to mine; a pale and cooling warmth of blue reminding me of a calming sea. A look that could surely undo me. His hand hovered over my pants, tracing the seam until he slipped beneath, and I felt his bare flesh on mine. I was left waiting on another heavy exhale, eyes drenched in desire as he rested just above my wet entrance.

"Do you remember when I said I was far from a gentleman?" His gaze darkened.

He moved faster than I could respond, gliding his finger the rest of the way, down my bundle of nerves, and plunged his middle finger inside me. I gasped, arching into him, gripping his arms as he caught my moan with his mouth, kissing me with a ferocious passion. I felt his muscles strain against my hold while he slid in and out.

My gods, he is the devil.

Thanks to the fucking curves of these mountains, we were far from sight and sound as another moan ripped out of me.

"You're so tight, Desert Storm," he said into the shell of my ear, pulling out to roll his middle finger over my bundle of nerves. "And so very wet."

I moaned. "Don't stop or I'll kill you." The only words I could manage to say.

He darkly chuckled. With every penetrating stroke of his finger, heat flushed my face, but it wasn't enough. I wanted more. I wanted to see what he would look like gazing up at me with his head buried between my thighs. It was hard to pull away with his thick finger already filling me, going so deep as if he knew exactly where to hit. I was chasing that high.

"I have another game I'd like to play," I said, but I let him plunge into me a few times more before reaching down to slide my pants past my hips. I was halfway there when he leaned back onto his knees. The blanket fell down around him, exposing his pitched cock inside his pants. A dark, wet spot had formed above the tip as the morning light filtered behind him. With his bare chest exposed, his dark, tousled hair brushed the edges of his shoulders. I held a hand above my brow to block out the sun. My gods, the devil was awfully tempting.

He slowly leaned down, gently tugging the hem of my pants the rest of the way with his gaze never leaving mine. He smiled, a grin so wide, I caught a flash of shyness flush his cheeks when I bent my legs and fully opened for him.

"Are you blushing, cowboy?"

He grabbed the blanket and hung it behind his body, blocking out the sun to get a better view. I lowered my hand now that he'd given me shade, my eyes roaming over every muscle on his body.

"I cannot confirm nor deny such accusations," he said, his voice a soothing calm. "But when I'm done with you, it will be you who's blushing."

Slowly, with every tantalizing second that passed by, he lowered his head, kissing my inner thigh first before linking both his arms around my hips. The torment was driving me mad. He made his way down, kissing and stroking his tongue against the soft flesh before he gently grazed his lips over my bundle of nerves. With a hard, languid lick, his tongue slid up my core, igniting a wildfire inside me. He then kissed my other inner thigh. A groan rumbled in his chest, roused by the power I allowed him to have in this moment. He was exploring how my body reacted to his. And then, with a sudden thrust, he yanked me onto his mouth and slid his tongue in. I sucked in a sharp breath as he began to work my center. My gods, a mouth like that could make me hate and need him at the same time. Another soft whimper escaped me.

"You taste so divine," he rasped. He looked ravishing himself, so breathtaking the way his eyes seemed to penetrate my soul as they narrowed in on me, as if he knew how deep to go and what spots to hit. Our bodies were syncing as the mark on my sternum thrummed. I chased the wave, longing for a release that I knew would leave me throbbing hours after. He was giving me what I desired, what I yearned for, a taste of how it would feel to forget the world around us as I allowed myself to get lost in this.

My power moved in wispy shadows, curling in the air and giving shade from the rising sun.

"Fuck, don't stop." The words fell from my lips in a darkly coated demand. He moaned into my sex, a song to his soul as he succumbed to my desire. Every stroke of his tongue rode me to ecstasy. His sweet, sexy mouth and the scruff of his beard seared into me with every tantalizing touch. He speared his tongue endlessly, so continuous that I wondered how he could even breathe, but greed eradicated any more of those concerns. He reached up, cupping a breast and barely getting a handful. My core clenched, my pulse growing with a tempest's speed. My chest was tight as I grabbed onto his shoulders, thrusting harder onto his tongue as his arms pulled my hips into a deeper embrace.

He moaned as the pleasure coursed through him. The sound so deep, it vibrated over my clit, creating that final push to spur me over the ledge, and I crested that wave. The release came crashing through me in a dance of pulsating throbs around him. I cried out in ecstasy, riding the fuck out of his tongue as if the sun would never rise again. I gasped and moaned as if the mountains would come tumbling down. He thrusted again and again, driving his tongue so deep, I nearly saw stars when everything around me blurred. And when my release began to slow, we flowed into a soft rhythm until the waves were calm. With both our hearts still thrumming, he slowly slid his tongue out, giving me one gentle lick before he collapsed beside me.

I was spent. We were left a heaving mess with only our panting, misted breaths to fill the silence of a serene morning.

When my heart was a resting calm, I pulled the blanket back over us.

"You are way too damn pretty," I observed, staring at his swollen lips and his sliver of a pearly smile that seemed to peek out every time I spoke.

He chuckled, turning onto his side as he rested his head on his hand. A few strands of hair lay slick against his neck. "Well that doesn't seem like much of a problem," he said, gaze devouring me within the same breath.

"It could be. I guess we will have to see how it goes," I teased, not minding the distraction at all. His hair was tousled, a sheen of sweat glistening beneath his eyes.

"I don't think I've ever seen anyone as enchanting as you." He plucked a lock of hair from my face and tossed it over my shoulder.

My heart beat wildly against my chest as he seemed to map out every freckle across my face. I didn't have to hide who I was with him. As if he could sense my thoughts, he brought my hand to his lips, hands that didn't need to be gloved in his presence, and he kissed every single finger.

"These hands are dangerous," I warned him, smirking in the process. I pointed two fingers, aiming for his heart, and curled my ring and pinky, gesturing the form of a pistol. He smirked at the motion when I cocked my thumb. "Bang, bang, cowboy. You're dead." I slightly jerked my hand up.

He brought my hand to his chest, tucking my middle finger back in so that there was only one pointing at him. "You only need one bullet to kill." A wicked grin formed on his face. "But it would take a whole lot more to kill me, Desert Storm."

"It takes one bullet to kill, two because I'm a spiteful bitch."

"Maybe that's why I'm so drawn to you. I have a thing for danger," he said.

"Is being a guide always dangerous? I'm sure it's not every day you have clients like us."

Something flashed in his eyes, but it was gone so damn quick, it was hard to grasp.

"There will always be danger at every corner, no matter what side you're on or what you do. We are living in a time when nothing is safe anymore. I'm sure your father thanks the gods for blessing you with such a gift." He gestured to my magic-honed hands with a stroke of his thumb. "You are quite the storm: dangerous but worth the risk."

24
RYDER

"*It would take a whole lot more to kill me, Desert Storm.*"

I'd nearly given myself away. My heart had lurched in my chest the moment I'd felt her power thrum against it. I'd almost slipped; my own fucking words were a constant, growing reminder of the job that had to be done.

We spent the rest of our day stealing glances at one another and occasionally going over the plan. Every so often, End's Wrath would ask me to run through it again, as if he were looking for any cracks in my façade. I felt a sliver of him trying to slip through as I was snagged by Vessa's gaze, but I worked the walls of my mind so well that nothing could get in.

Every time Vessa looked my way, it sent a whip of guilt striking across my thoughts. I was starting to feel like a damn failure, a constant rise and fall, trying to define where the lines were being crossed. My thoughts wandered to her slick heat against my tongue, to her luscious, soft lips on mine, to the flash of horrors etched behind her piercing purple eyes. She said she was the devil, but so was I. Two souls caught in a world of two biomes, where there was only space for one.

"Bang, bang, cowboy. You're dead."

Her words would grow to haunt me. I would have to carry her death as a shadow of my own amongst the rest of the souls I'd taken. I was crossing every fucking line with the two most dangerous fae.

The stars began to stroke the sky as the sun descended upon the horizon. It was less than an hour's ride until we reached the walls of The City of Donia. I was locked inside an hourglass, feeling every grain of sand pelt against my face.

With my hands on the reins, leather creasing at the grip, I reminded myself I had a job to do. I needed to get my fucking head straight and leave my heart and cock in the Desert of Miera.

"Raven needs to shift so we can pass through the gates without suspicion. It's not every day you see a woman with a large bird as a companion," I said. Raven responded with a caw that sounded more like a protest as he beat his wings. She caught my glare and laughed.

"Anything worth sharing?" I asked, all humor drained from my face.

There was a long pause as if their conversation continued.

I scoffed, resting an elbow on my thigh. "Well, Sunshine?" I drawled, looking straight at her.

She slowed her mare until she rode beside me. "Looks like I'll be riding with you." She smirked before veering off to the side. End's Wrath and I followed suit. We all rode in silence as the clamor of the horses' hooves galloped against the ground.

"Raven has never ridden a horse before, and he's too big to sit with me. I trust my mare will be a better mount. They are familiar with one another."

Raven drifted down into a plume of dark shadow and

appeared on Vessa's horse in his male form. The bastard was too tall. He shifted uncomfortably in the saddle as Vessa handed him the reins. "She knows where to go. You don't need to worry about giving her any commands. I'll do them for you."

He gave a simple nod. I chuckled. Far from being a cowboy as I watched him gain balance, gripping the saddle horn for dear life. He was dressed far too clean for these parts of the land.

"I have a lot more respect for riders," Raven said.

Vessa chuckled as she mounted my stallion, hauling a firm leg over the saddle.

With a flashy smile, she looked back and jerked her chin. "Come on, cowboy. We have a city to see."

I smirked, slipping the toe of my boot into the stirrup, and mounted behind her. I slid my arms around her waist, and the space between us was no more. Her look alone was enough to kill me, but as soon as we took off riding, it confirmed she rode hard and fast with everything she did. My cock might have twitched at the thought.

The excitement in her voice was like being tossed into the middle of a burning forest. The sense of foreboding bloomed in the pit of my stomach, flaring into the sky—a heat so intense that I should have already been digging my own grave, digging hers right alongside mine.

25

VESSA

Ryder and I rode together ahead of Pa and Raven, spending my last moments of freedom with my hat off, ears exposed to the wind.

I couldn't have ridden any faster into the dark, ignoring all sense of warning as Pa's words echoed in the back of my mind. I knew what I was getting into, I knew everything about this part of the world was dangerous, and I was ready to face it head-on.

That glimmer of a perfect life had never had enough water to bloom nor soil to grow. It'd been snipped before it ever had a chance to thrive in these dry lands, but I still happened to be breathing this air. Surviving all of this had to have been for a greater purpose. I'd felt the world shift beneath my feet when the stone of Eternal had been removed, just as everyone around me had been sent aflame. Beyond the walls of The City of Donia lay a fate that only the hidden spaces of my soul could recognize. I'd allowed myself to align with all elements given to me, harnessing the power of *Ano*, using light to guide the way. Having been born on a blue moon, my soul was tethered to both sides, fueling the boundless dark of *ama*, the power my sister once had. That piece of her would always remain within the shell I had become, and I embraced all that she'd never had a chance to be through the eyes that told me, for some crazy reason, she could still see. I was the light to her dark. This was when I felt her most, when all else was gone and the luminescence of my power beamed beneath the rising moon upon my hands, ears, and soul.

In the vast expanse of the desert, this feeling ended beyond those city walls. This was one final release before I headed into the belly of the beast.

I needed to discover everything on my own terms, all the evil that dwelled in Donia, and deal with it my way.

We slowed to a trot as we crested the hill, revealing the city's glow and plains around a dark horizon. This was one of the biggest cities I had ever seen. It was surrounded by an impressive stone wall, which only opened on two ends, allowing twin rivers to feed the city. Narrowing my eyes up ahead, I put on my hat as Ryder handed me my gloves. Pa and Raven stopped beside us with dark eyes as they took in what was ahead.

There would be no souls to save once we breached those gates.

Little did they know, hell was coming.

)●(

There was a glow cast over the city from an unknown source. No amount of candles could have created such a light. It was as if someone had fallen in love with the moon, pulled her off her throne to become a prisoner, and kept her bound behind thick, fortified walls. The sight was nearly unfathomable. Beyond that was a darkness I could only assume was the ocean.

A city that has no place to turn will only drown.

My power thrummed against my arm as an unsettling warmth bloomed. Ma came to me like an echo of emotion, a message that had no sound, only feeling, and today, her energy was loud. I turned to my left, as if she were there, only to find Pa wearing the same expression as I. Awestruck with sadness, as if we had been chosen to be left behind because of who we were. I sensed his mind drift to a place mine so often did, reminiscing about all the "what ifs" and daydreaming about a future we could never have because we'd watched the other halves of our souls die. Simultaneously, we nodded at one another, understanding this wasn't the time to stay there.

As we looked into the darkness, others moved toward the city either by horse, wagon, or on foot. They were caught in the lure of The City of Donia, like bees to honey.

"These walls remind me of the chains I will *never* wear," I said, eyes hardening as I nudged Ryder's stallion forward.

"I'm right there with you on that one, Shadow. Remember what I told you." With a few clicks of Pa's tongue, he moved to ride closer beside me while my mare instinctively did the same, creating some sort of barrier around me. Raven understood the unspoken mission, and with darkening eyes, he sent me a reassuring nod that somehow eased the tension fighting to rise within me.

We shuffled in with the crowd like slow-moving livestock, feeling suddenly confined. I preferred a drunken room full of people over this any day. Raven reached out, squeezing my hand as I grasped the reins, and brushed his thumb across the top. His eyes held a look of knowing comfort, ignoring Ryder's staking claim as he entered our space. Ryder remained like a dog guarding his favorite delicacy.

The moment Raven withdrew his hand, Pa's words repeated in the back of my mind.

"Remember what I told you."

My pulse rose as my eyes trailed up the wall to find lawmen strapped with pistols and rifles as they surveyed the incoming crowd. There was something off about a few of them. I swallowed as my heart hammered against my ribs while anger rolled through me.

Suddenly, Ryder leaned into the shell of my ear, easily pulling my attention away the moment his big strong hands gently squeezed my sides.

"You'll want to keep your head down, Desert Storm. They see a pretty face like yours, all shiny, and they might ask questions."

I couldn't help the way he made my heart flutter.

"You are not like other fae, my moon," Ma would say.

His hands remained relaxed, but his thumbs caressed my hips, causing my next breath to shudder. I slightly turned back, caught beneath his stare as he smirked.

My jaw clenched as we neared the entrance and didn't relax until we were inside the walls of Donia. My brows knit, seeing the bustle of life beyond. There were merchants lining the streets, selling a plethora of goods from dyed linen to spices and food. Above were two-and three-story homes, all made of smooth, beige sandstone. The streets were bricked, with the sand dusting between the cracks.

A magical hum filtered through the streets, sending a throbbing pulse to my temples. I looked at Pa, wondering if he could hear it too, but his expression remained the same.

"They sure know how to shine a turd," he murmured.

"No kidding," Raven chimed in as he adjusted himself on the saddle once more. I chuckled. The bird was made to fly, not ride a horse. He'd be glad to get off.

"I know you like to lead, but I'll take it from here," Ryder said. I sensed his smirk as he slowly moved his hands along the top of mine until he slipped the reins from my grip, leaving me with nothing but a warmth building between my thighs.

We veered off the main roads into smaller alleyways, where the houses grew increasingly in size. A few more three-story buildings shared a line as their clothes hung to dry. The further we rode in, the nicer the buildings became.

"This is where we will be staying tonight," Ryder said as we neared the tallest building in the area. Four stories high.

Pa looked reluctant and arched a thick brow in Ryder's direction. We were far too gritty for a place like this.

"She only gets the best, right, End's Wrath?" Ryder flashed him a mocking half grin as he dismounted.

I followed suit, landing beside Ryder, the height difference vast.

Up ahead, two young boys and a girl approached us, taking the reins from Pa and Ryder.

"Where will you be taking them?" I asked, stepping forward, ignoring the sounds of Raven struggling to dismount. I sensed his irritation. He wanted to say "fuck it" and shift, but he relented. They took a step back, as if my stride was too aggressive.

One stuttered before he spoke. "Out back, Miss. It's where we accommodate all the guests' horses." He jerked a thumb behind him, where a smaller structure was attached to the side of the building. My lips pressed thin as I nodded. I heard a heavy thud as Raven finally dismounted. Turning, I found him straightening his shoulders, rolling his head from side to side, tired of being in his male form. There was a light sheen of sweat on the column of his smooth, pale neck.

"Is there anything else you need, ma'am?" the girl asked behind me.

"No," I said, eyes still on Raven, drawing my attention to the length of his broad shoulders. As if he sensed my stare, he looked up, mouth curling into a half grin with narrowing eyes in challenge to open our bond and hear what he was thinking.

"Let's get inside," Pa said.

"Right." I released the tension in my jaw and turned to see Ryder already gathering the rest of our things.

Before I knew it, we were walking into a large entryway with pillars rising to the ceiling. I stood back, examining the structure as Ryder got the keys to our rooms from a woman behind a dark mahogany desk. I overheard him saying we would be here over the course of a few days as he handed her a sizable pouch of nara coins.

"Looks like we're on the top floor," Ryder said, handing a key to Pa, but he paused when he got to mine and dangled it above my palm. He closed the distance between us, slightly leaning down so his pale-blue eyes could see me beneath my hat. "Desert Storm always gets the best," he said, lust-coated, sending another wave of heat down my body.

That look alone was enough to transcend me, but he reeled it in so quickly, hiding behind that veil he often clung to every time I tried to see past the palpable desire. Something was lost within him, a struggle that became more evident as he turned, walking toward the hall that lead to our rooms. We followed, our spurs chiming in an unsynchronized clamor as we went up the stairs. I wondered if he was thinking about where Raven would sleep tonight, wondering if he would shift into a bird and fuck off, or stay. There were only three keys. Nonetheless, he could not lick his claim on me no matter how talented his tongue was.

We made it to the fourth floor. The four of us took deep breaths as we silently went to our rooms. Pa's was at the end of the hall; he left first, giving me a silent nod with a look that said to stay out of trouble before he closed the door behind him. As expected, he did not lock it. He had been eager in his strides, eager to open up a deck of cards. Knowing he would be content in his little corner of the world made me smile.

On the opposite end of the hall was my room. Ryder led the rest of the way, stopping by the door before it.

"I guess this is good night. I'll see you at dawn." His voice was smooth and husky. He was a lure in my existence and a temptation as I studied the seam of his lips as they curved into a smirk.

"Well...*bye*," Raven said, slightly leaning over my shoulder to dissipate the coiling heat.

"Good night, Ryder."

Raven walked in first, immediately going toward the balcony as I hovered by the door. I paused momentarily, allowing the thrum of my pulse to vibrate through my magic. I closed the door and clicked it shut, and within a few seconds, I heard Ryder close his.

I turned to find Raven, unfazed by the luxuries this room had to offer as he looked out over The City of Donia. Smooth marble floors filled the space with a massive bed against an ivory-painted headboard gilt in gold. I tossed my satchel, hat, and gloves onto the mattress, watching remnants of dust puff out on impact while I made my way toward the washroom. It was off to the side, surprisingly with no doors. I peeked in to find a marble clawfoot tub already filled with water and its steam curling into the air. Beside it, a pile of dark, fresh linen had been placed onto an ivory side table.

I went for the note that lay atop it.

You said I owed you new clothes. Enjoy. From the cowboy demon.

I scoffed under my breath, feeling my cheeks warm the moment I raised the sheer, pale-blue fabric into the air. Wearing this would leave nothing to the imagination, save for the button clasp at the back. There was a matching undergarment. After having more than a handful of my breasts, I couldn't be too shocked he would know what size to get.

"Flustered, Vessa?"

I nearly jumped, placing the garments down onto the pile as I casually covered them far from reach. I spun on my heels, finding Raven leaning against the opening with his arms casually crossed, looking a little too tense for the circumstance. There was no playful smirk displayed.

I stepped into his space until we shared the same air. My eyes narrowed in on him as that tether called to open my side of the bond.

"Would it bother you if I was?" I bit out.

His jaw tensed, but he remained poised as he towered over me. "We are not romantically bound, Vessa. You are free to do what you want with any untrustworthy cowboy you see."

And there it is. I laughed, throwing my hands into the air.

"You don't even *know* him," I snapped, crossing my arms as I shifted my weight to one side.

"Do *you?*" he questioned.

I went to speak, but my mouth was left agape as words evaded me. I quickly closed it.

Seconds passed as his deep-brown eyes narrowed on me.

"I'm starting to," I finally said.

He huffed a laugh; his breath, feather-light, fanned across my face. Spearmint. Always spearmint. Never a hint of whiskey or herbed smoke. He was always too clean, deadly without calloused hands, but something snagged my attention. *He* was hiding something.

"Is there something you want to tell me, bird?" I opened up my senses. A copper scent tinged my nose, sending my shadows on full alert.

"There is nothing to be said." His eyes hardened.

"Lies." Tendrils of shadow unfurled from the tips of my

fingers, curling around my arms until they drifted beneath his shirt, sliding up the hard plains of his abdomen, a second pair of eyes to see something I couldn't.

"What are you hiding?" I whispered, slightly tilting my head in observation as a wicked smile curved my lips, seeing how my touch easily undid him. It was a void he was so easily drawn to, a place he could never reach. I was his temptation. Whatever he was hiding would be in vain, because the shadows found his lie, tearing his shirt at the sleeves.

My eyes widened at black veins spreading across his shoulders under remnants of dried blood. His body must have been trying to shift while riding into the city.

"You need to shift, Raven."

"No shit," he said dryly before stepping back into the bedroom and toward the balcony.

"Then why are you still here?" I yelled, my voice strained as I followed right behind him. His height eclipsed the light. Sure, we were always battling one another, but I still cared for him. He turned quickly, stepping into my space, but I stood my ground despite every fiber of my being wanting to rest.

"You think it's easy to be me? That being in the form of a male comes naturally? This right here"—he pounded both hands on his chest—"is my second skin. The longer I'm in it, the more I realize how much I hate it. I cannot stand to be in this form."

"You don't have to do anyth—"

"*Yes,* I do, and that's what you don't understand." Raven combed a hand through his hair and clenched his fists. "You think it's easy watching other men live a normal life while I'm stuck in this space between two different worlds? And now it's an even more constant, looming reminder with *him* around." His breathing deepened. Silence hung in the air as he desperately searched my eyes. My mouth fell open slightly, unable to find the words, but I knew I couldn't tie myself down to anyone.

"We are not romantically bound, and I belong to no—"

"No one. It's what you always say when avoiding your own shit. But you know what I think about that?" His gaze darkened.

I took a step back, but he moved forward until my heels hit the edge of the bed and my ass sank into the mattress. He leaned closer, caging me between his arms as his knuckles pressed against the bed. A few loose strands of his hair hung forward, barely brushing against his thick, dark brows.

"Lies. Because it's pretty obvious you want to be his. I don't need this fucking bond to smell your arousal."

Moments passed, and there was nothing I could say as tears lined our eyes. I wanted to say I was sorry, yet in the same breath, I wasn't, because we both understood our arrangement. We would always be a fucking mess. He had his life, and I had mine, and somehow, we would always meet in the middle to help each other. It seemed like he had been helping me more than I had been returning the favor. I cupped the side of his face, allowing the faintest thread of power to open the bond so I could feel what sort of pain he was in. A tear fell from his eye the moment he felt it, felt *me* slipping in.

This is just the bond, nothing more, I said to myself as we held one another's stares.

"Is it?" Raven said aloud. I sucked in a deep breath, my pulse heaving itself to a racing speed as his eyes trailed down my face, lingering on the seam of my lips before flicking his gaze back to mine. *"We were never given a chance to find out."*

His voice penetrated my mind, my soul, feeling the thick, heavy beat of my heart at the intensity of our bond once it was fully aligned. I quickly closed the connection.

He huffed out a laugh, watching the heat flush across my

face while he held me caged between his arms. "All we have is time, Vessa, no matter how fast the world is changing around us."

Drawn to the truth of his words, I swallowed the lump forming in my throat.

"You always had the choices I didn't," he whispered, his nose gently grazing the side of my face.

I opened my mouth to speak, but a knock at the door seized my next words.

Raven chuckled darkly, the sound reverberating against my chest as we remained frozen. I looked back at the door, knowing who stood on the other side of it.

"Be careful who you run to when you're lost." Raven's whisper fanned down the column of my neck.

When I turned to meet his eyes, he was gone. Nothing but a fading shroud of misted shadows left in his wake, and my sight narrowed on the faint silhouette flying off into the city.

For the first time, I didn't just see a bird, I saw a raven, flying into the night, looking for

his next hunt.

I opened the door to find Ryder in a fresh pair of clothes—a dark gray shirt that clung to his muscular form, matching his pants. His hair was freshly brushed under his cowboy hat, which he removed with a slight wiggle of his brows. A smile quirked those soft lips, ones that I was drawn to. I liked this side of him, the softer side, as he stood in the doorway, leaning into the frame with piercing blue eyes.

"Ma'am," he teased, tilting his head. When he put his hat back on, he plucked something hanging from his back pocket. "A rose for a desert rose."

It was a short-stemmed hybrid of some sort, gleaming with magic. "I've never seen anything like this before," I said, taking it in my hands.

"They call it a moon pearl rose. It's a beautiful thing at first sight, but beneath the luminescence of the moon, she comes alive for all to see. The thorns represent a beauty one could never touch, but every once in a while, some stupid bastard will try."

I chuckled. "Are you the stupid bastard?"

Ryder stepped into my space in answer as I held the rose between us. An awareness raked through me, one that stilled my breath at the truth of his words. No matter what storm I threw his way, he was called to it. His gaze confirmed such thoughts as he studied my face.

"Pain never scared me," he said, cupping a hand against my cheek, brushing his lips across mine as if searing them to memory before he kissed me. This time, it was slow and calculated, as if he'd been imagining this moment since the last time we'd been alone, and maybe I had too. He backed me into the room, kicking the door shut behind him in the process. I smiled faintly against his mouth, running a hand through his long, dark hair, tasting the hint of whiskey that was always on his breath. He was rugged with soft lips. His grip confirmed a deep desire that was hard for me to ignore. I felt the power in his touch every time we were near. He was a storm himself, and we were two tornadoes with an undeniable pull to collide as one. The arousal was palpable as he groaned into my mouth, and I felt my power stroking along my fingertips. I set the rose down on the dresser beside the table as he laid me onto the mattress, but my mind halted.

"Wait," I breathed as he nestled his face in the crook of my neck.

"Vessa." He groaned. A sound that rumbled in his chest like an ache, sending my heart to flutter. I'd never known two syllables could undo me in one breath, yet he did it so effortlessly.

I moved up onto the bed.

He exhaled deeply, sighing, as he knew he had to stop. "Fuck," he grunted, resting his forehead against mine. Moments passed before we spoke, and he sat back onto his knees.

I slid out of place, lying horizontally as I turned to see him still kneeling, the moon casting light onto his body.

"As much as I love seeing a man like you kneel before me, I think it's best we try to get as much rest as possible. We have a long day ahead of us tomorrow." I briefly smiled as we held one another's gazes. He would get his last payment tomorrow, and I would have my endless supply of tonic. I didn't want to think about anything beyond that—what would happen once his job was over, or the fact that I hadn't been taking the tonic. I was stuck between a rock and a hard place, and my insides felt like they were on fire. I was playing too many reckless games.

"You're right. We do." He moved to get off the bed, but I caught his hand. He studied the way mine glowed in the moonlight, shimmering with its own faint light. I still knew sleep wouldn't come. As much as I tried to take charge of my own body, it had its own ideas.

"Tell me something about you I don't know," I said, yawning in the process as Raven's words came back to haunt me.

Something flashed in his eyes as he lay beside me, gone within the next breath as his weight brought down the mattress.

He hummed, looking past me, scratching the scruff of his beard as his eyes shone in the light.

"No lies," I teased, but it made him glance my way.

I sensed something in him had snagged while he chewed on his bottom lip. He huffed a faint laugh, then stared into the space between us. "'No lies.'" He thought long and hard for a moment, leaning onto his elbow. He combed his fingers through his hair and took a deep breath before his gaze flicked back to mine. The shadows hid so many stories he would likely never tell.

"That rose is from Blightstone Hollow, and it sells here for a lot of money."

I arched my brow and rolled my eyes. "The only reason your pockets are lined with nara coins is because they were given to you by Pa. Try again."

He laughed. "Gods-damn, hold your horses, woman. There's more."

With a speculative look, I snickered.

"While the lands are constantly changing, and while the trees in Blightstone Hollow are spreading, a moon pearl rose will always remain the same. No matter the curse or blood that taints the lands. Like the moon, its existence will always be. You can try to burn it, stomp it to pieces, but by the time the moon rises once more, its glow is as strong as ever." He cupped the side of my face, dragging the pad of his thumb across my bottom lip with a never-ending desire. "It's a story my mother used to tell me before she died—how magical Blightstone Hollow was, and the stories that came out of it were endless. It was just a rose to me until I saw it tonight right outside this place. It reminded me of you, Desert Rose. Always so strong."

"'Desert Rose.'" I smiled faintly, brushing away the locks of hair splayed down the side of his face, gently tucking it behind his ear. He didn't shudder when my fingertips brushed the sharp edges of his scars. He closed his eyes, as if my touch were a remedy.

"Always so bright," he said, bringing my hand to his lips as he closed his eyes, kissing each finger. The magic within my palm illuminated his face; a halo of soft lavender and faint starlight glinted in the irises of his eyes. He was caught in my aura, my light, and as I felt the world slip away into a dream that beckoned my name, his last words fell into a void as I was whisked away to sleep.

"LITTLE SHADOW. Is that your name? Here, have this..."

26

RYDER

A sharp, searing pain in my side pulled me away from a dream that was forgotten the moment I opened my eyes. I nearly shot up before I jerked back, peering into a beady black eye. The raven canted his head before cawing in my face.

Vessa's rich laughter rang in my ears as she seemed to say something through their bond before lazily rising up onto her elbows. Her hair was tousled, and her top was slightly misaligned—another slight shift and her breast would pop out. She caught my stare as I hoped to the heavens for it to happen, and she smirked, setting her top back in place.

A crimson blotch caught my sight, and I looked down to see the remnants of blood. "Did this asshole just clean his beak on my shirt?"

"It's far better than what he was about to do." Vessa smirked.

My lips curled in disgust before Raven beat his wings and flew off my chest. He perched on the ledge of the balcony and did his morning business.

Fucking gross.

I dragged my legs over my side of the bed. In one swift motion, I reached back and pulled my shirt over my head, tossing it into a corner. I felt Vessa's lavender eyes roam over the corded muscles of my back. By the time I turned around, she was watching every move I made while the silhouette of her raven watched hers.

"I want to say I owe you a shirt," she mocked, "but I kind of like this view."

I scoffed. "Thank your bird for that." I shot a daggered glare in his direction.

I had a feeling he would stay in that form for as long as possible, but as the sun crept out from the depths of its dark, there was a whole new day ahead of us. I felt the weight of today already making jagged roots atop my chest.

"I'm going to change and then I'll see you downstairs," was all I said before I left Vessa's room.

)●(

Time was pressing as I quietly sat on the edge of my bed, my mind pulling into a thousand places at once. Fang already knew we were here. I'd seen a few of his henchmen strapped as lawmen, stalking our arrival on the rise. One of them had thrown me a silent nod as we'd entered the city. His stone-cold glare had sent a warning down my spine the moment I'd seen his eyes linger on my arms wrapped around Vessa's waist. The small notion told me he might have done more than tell Fang we'd arrived. Fire Fae were untrustworthy fucking pricks. Yet here I was, fighting myself off because I was no better than them.

In the same stroke of power, my yearning for Vessa beckoned at her door, wanting to be let in. I was supposed to ravage her body, mind, and soul, pull on the edges of her mind and see what made her so special, but every time my heart was near her, all I wanted to do was kiss her smooth, bronze skin and bask in the aura of her light that she allowed me to be in. She was a killer, a legend, and a call to every fiber that made me who I was. As rotten as my heart pulsed with tainted dark blood, it wanted to beat for her.

This was my only fucking job, and I was slipping. This was what I was supposed to do, but every time I needed to lie about who I was, I couldn't. Lies came easier when not in her presence.

"Fuck." I grunted, hunched over on the side of the bed, forearms resting on my thighs as I leaned my forehead into my palm. Looking away, I waved a hand in the air with my two pointer fingers and summoned Fang. Sighing, I ran it through my hair and waited for the apparition of his disgusting face to appear.

"Seems like your hands have been quite busy." Fang's words caused my jaw to clench. As expected, the Fire Fae were nefarious fuckers. As much as I wanted to punch through the apparition and grab Fang by the throat, my clenching fists remained out of sight, digging crescent moons into my palms, allowing the pain to keep me focused.

"It's what you paid me to do, right? A handsome bastard like myself had an easy way in."

Fang curved a thick brow and ever so slightly held a specu-lative grin. "I was told she's a beauty, a rarity indeed."

There was a long pause as we stared at one another. The hard lines in my face hid the malice burning in my fingers at the way he spoke of her. He searched for any cracks, anything that might indicate things might have changed, but when he found none, he nodded.

"You know what to do. If she isn't delivered at my feet by

the time the sun sets tomorrow, it'll be your head on a pike." His lips curved into a wicked grin. "I'm sure it will make a lovely new display at the Scarlet Gallows."

I waved away the apparition. Fang's face disappeared, unearthing a rage inside me that had my blood boiling. I pressed my chin into my balled fist and took a deep breath. My next thought was interrupted by a heavy knock on my door. It wasn't an angry pound nor a light tap. There could only be one person who would make a knock sound so heavy and calm at the same time.

End's Wrath stood in the doorway. Cowboy hat tipped forward, clad in a black trench coat, hands gloved. The old man was strapped more than usual today, which struck me as odd, being he did not need bullets to end a life. I had witnessed what he'd done in the Desert of Miera—removing the flesh off the bones of bandits through the power of *Ama*. He was a man with plans, always keeping an extra ace up his sleeve, and I knew he had many.

"Time is ticking, cowboy," End's Wrath said. The creases in his eyes held a hardened glare as a toothpick hung from the corner of his mouth.

"Don't worry, old man. You'll be back in time to enjoy a quiet game of cards before you know it. Your rooms are paid in full for the next few days."

He said nothing as he stood in the doorway, watching me from beneath the brim of his hat as he picked at his teeth. I finished gathering my things and stepped into his space as he blocked the door. He sized me up even though I still had a few inches over him. Being six-three had advantages, as my attention suddenly shifted over his shoulder to the beauty standing in the hallway. Vessa waited with the strap of her satchel pressed firmly between her breasts. And gods-damn, she could quench any hunger I'd ever felt. Words evaded me as she stared into my eyes. The looming presence of Raven came into view, wearing a dark, slim-brimmed hat, a beige, rolled-up long-sleeve shirt with suspenders, and a pair of black trousers. He looked like a bodyguard for hire, only, he was dragged by the strings of his heart. I despised the bond they shared with every muscle in my body.

Drawing another breath, I tipped my hat in greeting, staring into Vessa's eyes. That drew out a mischievous little smirk that made her nose scrunch up, and another stone plunked into the pit of my stomach.

WE HEADED to the east side of Donia. The light that illuminated the city waned the further away we went from the capital of Fang's palace. We were entering a poorer side of town, where it was normal for the alleyways to reek of copper and be full of questionable slumped-over bodies. This was a nesting ground for the lost, in-between spaces where taverns filled every crevice with heinous acts. This was a place where bandits did their business and where those with guilt went to hide. I'd never forget the way those cries had echoed throughout the night, the way it'd made my skin crawl as fights broke out in the alleyways below until the last sounds had been of a fading life. I'd spent most of my mine in this shithole, bouncing between here and the library until I'd become a bounty hunter. I'd never wanted to step into this area of my past again, but here I was, greed snuffing out most of the memories, because the more money that lined my pockets, the closer I was to never thinking about this place again.

We tied our horses to a post outside a slim, three-story building. A human male leaned up against the wall with his hat tipped down, as if he were resting his mind. I nudged him out of his thoughts, and he jolted back as if we'd appeared from a shroud of smoke. I saw the desperation in his eyes and hunger brushing against the hollow of his cheeks. I handed him a small pouch of nara coins.

With a seething glare, I whispered in his ear, "You better count every breath as a blessing while I'm away, because if anything happens to our rides, those will be the last ones you ever take." My words were laced with warning.

"Yes, sir." With a fear-stricken expression, he nodded, dusting himself off as if he had been magically turned into a businessman, and straightened his spine along with his hat. His eyes wandered to Vessa, and I could tell before the scumbag even moved that his gaze would linger on the swells of her breasts. I grabbed him by the throat and slammed him up against the wall. He gasped as his eyes went wide.

"Look her way, and I will snap your neck where you stand," I growled.

He nodded best he could within my grip.

I didn't notice how bright his eyes were until they were emeralds drowning in a sea of a sprawling, bloodshot gaze. When I felt satisfied, I released him.

We entered a tavern, where patrons were scattered in their own private booths; dim blue light filled each space. It was half empty, showing we'd come at the perfect time.

End's Wrath arched a brow, already surveying and most likely planning.

When the bartender saw who strode in beside me, he gave me a quick nod and jerked his chin to the staircase on his right. We went down a dingy flight of stairs made of stone. Every few feet were oil-filled lanterns. There was no evidence of using the blightstone to light the way, which struck me as odd, considering what went on down here.

It was the main source of light for most of the city. The

stones were melted down into the same liquid as Vessa's tonic, only, they made a portion of it into candles so they'd burn longer.

As we descended, the air became thin, stagnant, and I wondered how anyone could live or do business in a place that smelled like this, but I already knew how deep desperation could run.

We made it to the end of the stairs, entering a large basement that was set up like a lair. To the naked eye, it looked like a bunch of metal crates, but the contents were valuable and stacked by size, depending on how many nara coins one had to offer.

As the last Umbra Fae stepped into the space, I felt the shock course through them both, invoking a power that caused the hair on the back of my neck to rise. The only one who was hard to read was Raven, which was a shocker, given End's Wrath always held a poker face. As he plucked the toothpick from the corner of his mouth and surveyed the vast room, a look of relief and worry etched his face. I would have given a left nut to know what he was thinking.

"The contents of those boxes are the fuel behind the motives of every greedy villain lurking within the shadows of this city," I said as we walked past them.

I'm a bastard, knowing I'm one of them.

Vials upon vials filled wooden tables. Half-made constructs and some mid-experiments littered the space as the honey-amber glow of the blightstone rested on top of several small candles.

This was the largest stash of tonic one could ever dream of getting their hands on. I looked over my shoulder, watching Vessa's eyes widen, an angry, grief-stricken expression crossing her face as her eyes trailed over the room. This whole operation went against fae nature and beliefs, especially the

Umbra's. It seemed like seeing the Eternal being used, melted down, and sold did something deeper to her. The flutter in her jaw was enough for me to want to say End's Wrath warned her, but I reached back and squeezed her hand. She blinked, tears stinging her eyes, as if I had snapped her into the now, as if she somehow needed to place the blame somewhere. Here I was, in her range. Her brows slammed together as she locked eyes on me.

"I wish I could unsee all this." Her faint whisper echoed throughout the space, striking another pang of guilt inside me.

"This is what's needed," End's Wrath reminded her. I could tell she was indifferent, as if she had somehow changed how she felt about the tonics.

"It's what you paid me for, End's Wrath. You're finally here," I said. Vessa shot me a look that could have ended me, but I turned as the hair rose on the back of my neck.

At the end of the room was a man who was like me—half man, half fae—a being who could walk both worlds yet didn't belong, and he was staring straight at us.

27

VESSA

There was a distant hum in the air, a slight shift in the breeze that had sent an awareness down my back the moment we'd entered this room. All at once, the center of my chest burned where the mark of the moon carved my path, a call to my very own power. Though I stood in the entrance of a place that held so much greed, by some inclination, I knew I was destined to be here. I felt it beneath my footsteps, and as I pressed my palm onto one of the stacked metal crates, the vibration grew. There was a small basket with a handful of blightstone in such strange shapes. I picked one up and held it in my palm. Raven's arm brushed against mine, his body heat dragging my glare away for him and I to share a look. I opened the bond.

He reached out, examining the stone closely before saying, *"What the fuck have we walked into?"*

"I don't know, but something isn't right," I replied through the bond. These stones had been melted down only to be hardened once more. As I looked at some above a low-lit candle, I realized they were being melted...again.

Now I knew the city was not humming, it was wailing—the Eternal was hidden somewhere in the city walls. Stones were known for having energy, and somehow, I was able to *hear* it.

At the end of the room, a man stood behind a table with his sleeves rolled up and shirt slightly untucked. He looked to be in his sixties, but his rich, tan skin had a glow—no doubt using the power of longevity from these stones.

"Ah, there you are," the man said, moving his attention to Ryder.

Within a few strides, Ryder sauntered over to the table, dragging a hand along the metal crates in examination as we trailed slowly behind. "I'm always on time, Sergil."

Now getting a closer look, I studied the artificial firmness of Sergil's face. It was unnatural for humans to use this; the sheer wanton effects of the tonic had made every fading line and wrinkle look like a waning façade.

"My, my, she has the brightest of curious eyes," Sergil drawled as he slightly tipped his glasses for another look. His almond-shaped eyes roamed over my face, as if he was piecing something together, observing me like I was another specimen to be pulled apart in his shit-festering lair. While he had me under his glare, I had a feeling he wasn't fully human nor was he the main maker. He was trained, because there was no fucking way he could have learned this on his own.

"Keep looking at me like that, and I'll drain every ounce of that tonic from your veins." I smirked, leaning into the table until I was inches from his face. "And I promise you'll feel every ounce of it leaving your body." He was part of the problem as to why this shit kept being sold on the black market. "This whole fucking place should be burned to the ground," I said, glancing over at Pa, who had resumed his poker face.

Ryder pressed a firm hand over the top of my stomach,

gently nudging me back. "This is all just a transaction. We are only here to get what you need," he warned before turning to Sergil. "Then we will be on our way." Ryder's stilted conversation had me on edge as something unsettling raked down my spine.

I gritted my teeth, turning to look at Pa for some sort of response, maybe fucking backup? He returned my daggered stare with a warning as he walked up to Sergil. "Business is business until you cross this table. Count your blessings—this transaction is the only reason I haven't slit your fucking throat." He tossed a bag of nara coins onto the table, slowly pulling out another.

One, two, three... My eyes went wide. I knew each pouch had over a thousand. He was giving away almost everything we had.

"I am not worth any of this," I stated. *Four, five...* I couldn't stay here any longer.

"I'm out of here." I couldn't stop my heart from pounding, feeling the betrayal as I realized we were only feeding into the problem. We could have stormed this place and took what we wanted, but I knew Pa. He never shared all the details of his plans. I could only assume he was complying because we were in the enemy's territory. There would be more nara coins to come, but it still didn't make this transaction any easier.

I hadn't realized I had left the connection open until Raven called my name.

"Vessa, wait."

"Don't follow me."

Raven's cursed growl echoed throughout the room.

Before I reached the stairs, the final bag thumped onto the table, causing my next step to seize. "She only gets the best."

I shuddered at the words before ascending the stairs.

Walking out the tavern doors was all I could do for now. I

had an idea of how to get back to my room, but if my assumptions were right, Ryder's stallion would guide me the rest of the way. I approached his horse too abruptly, sending him to stomp his hooves as I reached to untie the reins, stirring the human male in the process.

"Hey, where are your other frien—"

A thick tendril of darkness unfurled and went for his throat. "I'd shut the fuck up if I were you." I mounted the horse and shot him a seething glare.

He choked on his next words before I released him.

"Gods-damn. You're just as violent as your lover," he said, rubbing his throat.

I scoffed.

Lover?

I spat in his direction. Those words held too many obligations and responsibilities that I had no time to consider. Raven was already up my ass, and to have another male tied to me?

"I belong to no one," I snapped before riding away.

RAVEN'S CALL came through faint threads of magic, scratching at the edges of our bond. I knew he was being careful where he shifted. I was surprised he had followed my order to remain with Pa and Ryder to finish off the transaction, but I knew as soon as he was able to, he'd be in his raven form to come find me. But none of that mattered. Things would always be tense between us as long as this bond was forced. Pa had paved our path to hell, and I was tired being a part of it.

Riding through the streets of Donia felt like a betrayal of the very values and peace our lands once had. No matter where I looked, I couldn't help this numbing feeling that I didn't belong here, no matter how easy this place made life seem with its cozy bookshops and places to eat. The merchants outside some of these small businesses were thriving, but I knew most of their success was made from the working hands of fae. I knew what lay beyond their accomplishments. Fae would never be welcomed in their true forms, having to glamor their ears, scarred or pointed. Some were still being sold and enslaved. Not every fae who hid among the humans had a choice. This entire place was a prison.

It wasn't long before I found our building, as if Ryder's stallion had been here many times before. I rode up to the stables and dismounted once I saw one of the boys walking my way from the barn doors.

Without saying much, I handed him the reins and went back to my room.

I plopped down onto the bed, warring over the complexities of this situation as the weight of it all pushed against my chest. I closed my eyes and took deep breaths, trying to calm myself before it got out of hand. The muscles in my body ached. A tear slipped free as I finally gave in to the tonic's call, popping the top off and swallowing the contents in the last vial Ryder had given Pa for this journey. It wasn't long until I succumbed to the effects, overcome by fatigue, and with it, my sorrows drifted me to sleep.

I must have slept for an hour before I was awakened by a clamor of boots and the deep bass of Pa's voice in the hall. I got out of bed and placed my ear to the door. I heard Pa invite Ryder into his room, and I peeked out to catch a glimpse of Ryder entering before the door closed behind them. Raven was nowhere in sight, which told me he was already roaming the skies. In haste, I removed my boots and quietly tiptoed down the hall to eavesdrop.

"Well, looks like your job is done here, cowboy," Pa said. A few heavy bags of nara coins thudded on top of the table. Ryder's last payment.

"Keep it," Ryder said as the coins made a slight ring—what I assumed was him pushing the bags back toward Pa. My next breath stalled as confusion fell across my face.

What is he doing?

"I don't want any more of your money. I think what you and Vessa have gone through is enough."

My heart pounded against my chest as my cheeks heated.

"She struck you that bad, huh?" Pa's gruff voice ended in a sigh as he drummed his fingers against the wood. "I don't blame you a damn bit, but you need to understand what you're getting into. She might be pretty to look at, but she loves just like gold, hard or cold. You cross her the wrong way once, and your fate is sealed."

There was a long pause before either of them spoke again. A chair grated against the floor. Someone sat down. I could only assume it was Ryder in the way he groaned when he leaned back.

"This is just a job, End's Wrath. One where people die every day where I'm from."

"Does she know this was just a job for you? Or is that what you keep telling yourself because you're just that stupid?"

Ryder laughed as I heard his hand drag across the scruff of his face. "Heaven's hell, you are bold, old man."

"Ain't nothing funny, boy. You'll walk away, expecting her to chase you down. Let me tell you right now, Vessa doesn't chase. She hunts. You leave this city tonight, and she won't ever go looking for you."

"I beg to differ," Ryder drawled in challenge. "You'll see."

My pulse pounded in my ears. I'd known Ryder was arrogant, but I couldn't help the stone dropping into the pit of my stomach at the thought of him just up and leaving.

This is his job, Vessa. Rein your shit in.

With bated breath, I waited to hear what they would say next.

Suddenly, I heard the chair grate across the floor again. I took that as my sign to leave as I spun on my heels and slipped back into my room just as the door opened. Ryder's boots thudded against the ground, the sound of his spurs clanking until he stopped right outside my door. I held my breath, hearing him exhale faintly on the other side. The hesitation clung to the air as a simple piece of wood stood between us. I could somehow sense the strain of thoughts that brushed against his mind; they came in a blazing heat whenever he was near me. As I waited for a knock, seconds went by, and my pulse throbbed in my ears as heat flushed across my face and chest. But then I heard the sound of his door closing.

I exhaled as a swell of emotions bled through me. I didn't know how to feel about that. My thoughts were reeling. I started to feel the confinement of the city's walls as they barreled toward me, straining every muscle in my body until the thoughts consumed me. My heart pounded against my chest, drowning out all sounds until there was a knock at my door. I paused, allowing myself to take a deep breath before I opened it to find Ryder leaning against the frame, already scouring my face as the tension in his brows lifted.

"Are you surprised to find me here?" I asked, looking up at him as a ghost of a smile appeared.

He tossed his head from side to side, weighing the options, and shrugged.

"Hmm, maybe."

Though my heart was fluttering, my mind was reeling. This place was so loud, and I didn't mean to share inner thoughts, but it slipped out. "Are you just going to stare me in the face, or ask me for some company in your room?"

He bit out a laugh as he combed a hand through his hair. His gaze lowered to my lips briefly, calculatingly, before he leaned down, curling an arm around my waist. With one forceful tug, as if he were roping me into his body, he leaned into the shell of my ear. "Desert Storm, I thought you'd never ask."

28

RYDER

I hadn't fully grasped what I'd been doing when I'd pushed away the last payment from End's Wrath, but seeing how much he valued Vessa had broken me a little. I'd never seen End's Wrath show any sign of desperation, but the amount of nara coins he'd been willing to pay was enough. For all I knew, maybe this was one of his tests, one I wasn't sure if I'd failed, but as I strode toward Vessa's door, I felt like I had won the biggest prize of all.

I saw what the city was doing to her. All the sounds, the people, the reality of how fast the world was changing around us; she was drowning in the center of it. Like her, I wanted to escape. It was strange that every time my mind drifted, all I wanted was to be in her arms and hold her in mine.

I hesitated for a moment as I stood outside her door. I should have just left and slipped out of sight, never to be seen again, but I was a stupid fucking bastard.

Finish the job.

My heart was trying to shred apart my plans, and I was still walking the finest line, knowing there were flames chasing at my heels.

If I did leave, I would always have someone on my trail. I would never really be at peace.

When she opened the door, I somehow found that in her. I deliberately yanked her against my body to hear that little yelp I'd hoped she'd make when her hips pressed against mine. She did just that. The sound sent my cock swelling, and it did more as she reacted to the sound of my voice.

We both wanted to forget, and we were both running out of time. Between passionate kisses, I wanted to learn as much about her as I could, because there was this never-ending, overshadowing awareness that this could all end at any moment.

Fuck this city and this life. I wanted to get lost in her enchanting lavender eyes and kiss each luminous freckle across her face. To taste the magic of her darkness and lick it off her body like honey until the two of us were one. Then I would consume every part of her and drive her to the brink of madness with my cock.

She took my hand in hers and led me to my room. Like the desperate dog I was, I followed. She strode in as if she owned it, tossing her hat and gloves onto a settee and noticing my balcony had doors.

"Nice." She threw me a wink before disappearing into the washroom. I assumed she'd pieced together that I'd made sure her balcony had no doors or windows, just a stoned balustrade so her *feathered bodyguard* could perch. I might not have liked the pasty prick in his male form, but he was bound to her.

I heard her shuffling around, which made me raise a brow. I waited a few moments, assuming she might have to relieve herself, but my heart nearly melted out of my chest when she walked out with the top few buttons of her shirt undone, exposing a sliver of the pale-blue undergarments I had surprised her with. She draped her leather vest over the knob of a chair and noticed the bag of black licorice ropes on the table. She smirked, plucking one from the sack, and took a small bite. Her eyes closed in a soft flutter as she moaned, casting a hooded gaze my way with a smile, knowing I watched her every move. A soft chuckle hummed in her chest as she closed the distance.

The roped candy hung from her mouth like a cigar, and her hair cascaded in soft waves. With every stride, they swayed with the curve of her hips.

"I'm starting to believe you're truly the devil, looking the way you do," I said, feeling the hollowness inside my chest swell. "Here you are, striding into my life, stealing away every breath I take along with my candy."

The corner of her mouth twitched in amusement, maybe satisfaction.

"A man willing to give his last breath to me?" She took another small bite. "Sounds intriguing," she teased, draping an arm over my shoulder.

"Don't get too ahead of yourself, darlin'. Who said I'd let you get away with it?" I grinned, draping her other hand over me as I plucked the licorice from her soft, supple lips and stuck it in my mouth with the other. I couldn't help but wonder at the thought of those perfect lips wrapped around my cock and how they'd feel as she sucked me into oblivion.

We saw each other as something we wanted to claim. That was the side of her I strived to chase. No matter how far or dark it got, I was ready for that ride.

My hands had killed, but so had hers. For the time being, maybe they both could be tender for one another. As I slid one around her waist, the other slowly roamed down her thigh until she lifted her leg, allowing me to grip the back of her knee. Another yank, and her body was flush against mine.

I lifted her up, taking a firm hold as my hands cupped her ass. Her legs straddled my hips as she took my hat and placed it on her head.

"Looks like your hands are tied, cowboy. What are you going to do now?" She then stole back the roped licorice and tossed it behind herself onto the bed.

I couldn't give two fucks about the tug of war with that rope anymore, because now she was in my range.

"The very thing I've been wanting to do since the moment I first laid eyes on you." The vow I'd made pushed to the front of my mind. The one where I would cross every line with her until I could claim her as mine.

The anticipation hung in her eyes, a hooded stare as I moved us over to the edge of the bed. I gently placed her onto the mattress, watching the way her dark hair fell away behind her shoulders, making those soft streaks of highlights disappear.

"You have been a disturbance in my mind, invading my every thought since I met you," I confessed, slipping my hat off her head and placing it somewhere to the side. Then I removed her boots, massaging her legs and ankles. I knew she had been sore, and alleviating some pain was the least I could do.

The tips of my fingers trailed the hollow of her neck and brushed away a rogue strand of hair. With a light touch, I traced her arm along her scars, loving the way her bronze skin slipped into a star-filled darkness as my hands linked with hers. A touch that was made of shadow and light. She clasped my hands, biting her lower lip as the anticipation hung in her eyes. I leaned down and tilted my head, licking the column of her neck as my hair brushed against her collarbone. She moaned, rolling her body, a move that drained all thought and flowed straight to the swell of my cock.

I kissed and nibbled on the soft flesh just beneath her ear, eliciting another moan from those perfect lips. I caught her moan with my mouth, stroking my tongue inside in abrasive perusal. We became nothing but clashing tongues and teeth.

"I'm going to take your breath as mine, Desert Rose. When I'm done with you and we are both spent from expelling every power that makes us the monsters we've become, you're going to be mine. I don't think any forced bond could take that away from us."

She pulled away, staring at me long and hard with burning desire. I knew it was a bold move. I was ready to take a dagger to my heart for wanting to claim such a thing, but the way darkness ignited in her eyes as she grabbed a fistful of my shirt and pulled me down for another bruising kiss, it was enough for me to know that, by the end of the night, she would truly belong to me. She was not gentle about it, meeting me with the same abrasiveness as her tongue swept across my lips, deepening the kiss, and gods-damn, she was wickedly talented. I was ready to take everything she had to offer me and more. She was the remedy for my deprivation.

Time didn't exist with her, and I nearly lost track of how long we stayed in that position, though a subconscious part of me knew it must have been nearly midday. I ran a greedy palm down the length of her thigh as she linked her legs around my back. I groaned, exhaling her name and something else— words that fell away as she pulled me in for a deeper embrace. My hand dragged across her top and pulled it down, circling my thumb around her nipples that were firmly pressed against the mesh fabric of her undergarment.

"All I've been thinking about is who I'd have to kill to see you in this color, and here I am, wanting to rip your clothes to shreds." I licked against the fabric in desperation, cupping my mouth around her breast because it simply wasn't enough. She gently nudged herself up and removed her top. I sat back on my knees to watch her every move. My length bulged and throbbed against my pants. When her top fell away, the sight was nearly painful.

I tugged my shirt off, tossing it far from reach. Her eyes went to the plains of my chest. She slowly reached forward. She seemed to like the chest hair as she ran her fingers through it, gliding her thumbs along the raised flesh of my nipples. Her gaze flicked to mine. With a flirtatious smirk, she gently pinched them. My heart nearly leaped as she dipped her head, running her warm, soft tongue over them, licking and biting. I exhaled deeply and tipped my head back as I combed a hand through her hair, caressing her working jaw with the pad of my thumb. My fucking heavens, the things she could do with it.

Vessa kissed her way down, swirling her tongue along each ab before those perfect hands began to unfasten my belt. I watched the curve of her back as she worked the latch with her ass sticking in the air. It was a shame she was still wearing pants. She could see my desire leaking through the fabric, and with a smile, she tugged them down.

My heart thrummed like a feral beast when my entire length flung out, hard and beaded with pleasure. Her cheeks heated seeing my desire for her. The thought of her pretty little mouth wrapped around it caused an ache. I wanted to be inside her more than ever.

As she leaned down, I stopped her midway, pulling her back a little with a gentle caress across her shoulder. "Naughty girl, you still have your pants on. If you're going to wrap those lips around my cock, the least you could do is grace me with the sight of that beautiful ass, nice and arched."

She gnawed on her bottom lip and smiled.

My heart thundered as she leaned back and removed those pants. I sat back on the mattress and watched as she clumsily took them off, discarding them to the side. A rush of hunger surged through me seeing that little bush of hair atop her mound as the memory of my nose buried against it flashed across my mind.

She leaned down, and that beautiful face was inches from my cock. She inhaled my scent and moaned. Something I hadn't been expecting her to do. I chuckled, probably sounding a little insecure, and thanked the fucking heavens I'd bathed this morning. While her lips brushed along my length, I soon forgot that feeling, because in the next breath, they were wrapped around the tip, then she slid her mouth down.

A feral moan rumbled in my chest as I bit my lower lip, holding back another untamed sound that wanted to escape. I leaned back onto my heels, gripped the sheets, and tilted my head back as my eyes widened when I felt her slide down to the base.

Gods-damn. She was everything I could have asked for.

I fell into her snare as she worked my cock and bobbed her head. I felt the power of wind emerge from my flesh in warm, calming orbs. It was a call for hers, touching on the edges of a bond that wanted to be formed.

Sure, this could have been any one-night stand—most fae could fuck without any strings attached—but this felt different; it was a calling only she could quell. One I couldn't have fully understood until I'd kissed her for the very first time. While the power of *Nai*, my wind, drifted in the space around us, the constant flutter down my arms sensed her opening that thread.

She loosened her grip around my hilt and lifted her head. Lips swollen, she took in the magical sight while she gasped for air. "Blue, just like your eyes."

She took my hand in hers and pulled me up until we were knee-to-knee on the mattress. Naked and bare with my magic weaving around us.

"I wouldn't have expected a cowboy so rugged and brash to have a touch so soft."

I felt the same about her. A double-edged sword, and I was a mindless fool for pulling myself into her blade.

Shadows twined around her hands, a darkness matching my own that was a reflection of the horrors and pain she hid behind her eyes. She reached out, cupping her hand against my face as if she were cradling everything that made me wretched. I closed my eyes unexpectedly, as I exhaled a deeper breath.

"So this is what it feels like to be less broken," I whispered, opening my eyes to find her already lost in mine. I wasn't entirely sure how I felt about a woman having such a powerful effect on me, but the threads of my magic weaved with hers, responding to its call with a soft, shimmering light, moving with us as she led me down on top of her.

"You don't have to hide from me, cowboy. I see all your demons. Let them reign while we enjoy this moment."

I had so much I didn't want her to know as panic rushed down my spine in a lick of cold sweat. With all the power I had, I locked it all up, tucked it far away, and fucking destroyed the key.

As I wedged myself between her thighs, my length rested between us.

"Who we were before won't matter if you will have me for who I'll try to be from here forward," I whispered. The unexpected vow sounded more like a longing plea as I looked into her eyes, studying each luminous speckle atop the bridge of her nose.

She caressed the back of my neck and pressed her lips

against mine, searing in the answer. My hips gently moved, and she opened her legs wider as I nudged at her entrance.

Every moment that passed was an eternity as she seemed to sift through every thought.

Without warning, I slid inside her, all the way to the hilt.

She gasped.

Suddenly, the most beautiful light appeared around us from the shrouds of her darkness. A bond, one that shimmered like the essence of the moon with threads across a night sky.

She blossomed, and my gods, it nearly ended me. We stayed in this position for a few moments, allowing her to adjust to my size. Her slick heat was warm and welcoming as both our hearts thundered against our chests. I brought her hand to my lips.

"You are the perfect storm. One I'd gladly chase into the night," I said, kissing her palm. I had yearned to enter the eye of her storm, to find a quiet calm within the madness that was to be me. As I began to slowly move inside her, I was finding that quiet place.

The weight of my body pressed her into the bed, and she welcomed it by running her nails down my back. I leaned my weight on an elbow, watching the way her hips rose to meet mine. It was a struggle not to lose it all when I felt her clench around my cock; the gentle throb nearly sent me to move deeper with every stroke.

"I told you being pretty was going to be a problem," she said, casting a mischievous smirk my way as she gently brushed her hands along the scars on my ears.

I leaned my forehead against hers, half grinning. "I'm pretty, and you're the devil. It's quite an interesting match."

Her laughter caused her to squeeze around my hilt once more.

"Fuck," I grunted. "Keep clenching that pretty pussy of

yours, and you might nearly end me right here and now." I thrusted deeper, cock throbbing before I pulled back out, causing her to whimper.

I kept my pace, moving inside her as desire burned in our eyes. The light surrounding us intensified the deeper I dove through her center and mind. The gravitating force pulled me through every thick-ass wall, one by one, in flashes of light.

It was maddening.

I saw the beat of her heart at the very center of my thoughts. This kind of feverous love could make anyone lose their gods-damn mind, and I would gladly lose it all for her.

She was not only the last of the Umbra, but she was everything around us at once. I couldn't explain it. All I understood was that, as my mind moved forward, every thrust inside her body brought me closer to her. She was revealing parts of herself I didn't think she knew she was exposing.

My heart nearly stopped seeing Vessa connected to the Eternal stone. This was the reason Fang wanted her.

She was the secret who harnessed the power to enter Earth's Fall, the hidden realm that lay at the edge of Blight-stone Hollow.

He wanted to kill her. She could not only restore the lands but stop the blight from spreading.

My breath stilled until I felt her touch startle me back into her gaze.

"Are you alright?" she asked.

Words evaded me momentarily as I realized I would never let Fang have her as long as I was breathing.

I smiled faintly before nestling into the crook of her neck, my body moving with hers as I kissed her soft bronze skin. "Yes," I said, thrusting harder, "my Desert Storm."

I whispered against her mouth, curving a hand beneath her

lower back. Without leaving the warmth of being inside her, in a quick motion, I moved our bodies so she straddled me.

"Now, show me how you like to ride."

She lifted herself off my body, hovering inches above the slick and wet surface of my cock. She was on full display, a dark angel in the midst of our bond across a night sky. A wicked grin curled her lips as she slid all the way down, claiming me with such a vibrant, deviant gaze, I thought I was flying.

"Do you want to know something?" I asked, thrusting my hips as I enthralled her into my essence.

She pulled me up until our chests were touching. Her voice was nothing more than a low murmur, as she was purely hypnotized and hanging on my every word. Darkness swirled around our hips, a shadow slithering around my waist, over our thighs, and the swell of her ass.

"When we are one, as we are now, I can manipulate your power, Desert Storm," I said as it solidified into a lasso, her body tied and bound to mine.

Her eyes narrowed in on me as she bit her lower lip. In a whisper, she called upon my *nai*, and it kneeled to her every whim as I continued to stare in a daze. The scent of licorice filled the air. She summoned the piece of candy into her mouth and sucked on the remaining length before pulling it out and slipping it into my mouth. I chuckled as I bit off the end piece.

This was pure ecstasy.

"I have a little secret too," she said, honing my gift as hers as she wrapped a thread of my power around my neck, tightening it around my throat.

"I want every part of you, Ryder." She tugged on the rope. "Give it to me," she demanded, slowly riding the length of my cock. Her eyes churned like lavender-honey magic, starlight in the way she made my own fucking power bow to her.

"I am yours, Desert Storm. Take everything from me as I will from you."

She pressed her palms against my chest, gripping me and riding at such a punishing pace that every ounce of my power was a star caught in her orbit. She took the reins and rode the fuck out of me with the same pace as she lived her life.

Hard and fast.

We watched the bond form before our eyes, the both of us riding a dangerous path, not knowing where it would lead us. I felt her pussy clench around the base of my cock as I moved my hips with hers. Together, we chased that high, searching for the brightest star, uncaring if we burned in the process. She gasped, leaning down and burying her hands in my hair. I had a firm hold on her hips, helping her keep that pace.

"Ryder, please don't stop," she moaned.

I loved hearing her beg. "Say that again, and this time, look at me."

"Don't stop or I'll kill you." She smirked before deepening the kiss.

I plunged deeper. "You are so perfect in every fucking way," I said, making sure every thrust rubbed against her bundle of nerves. Another groan rumbled in my chest, rendering my next thoughts useless as her moaning intensified.

She found her orgasm at the end of my words, and it all came crashing around us as I followed right behind her. Those sweet moans calling my name unleashed a primal growl within me. I grabbed onto her, holding her against my chest as my swollen, throbbing cock slammed and came inside her. With every thrust, I felt her clenching and pulsating around me, and together, we rode that high until it slowed.

She collapsed onto the bed, nestling herself into the crook of my body as I pulled her into my embrace, trailing my fingers against the scars on her arm. Her palm rested against my beating heart.

We were spent, and I was nearly gone.

"I told you I would make you mine," I said, still trying to catch my breath.

)●(

VESSA and I spent the rest of the day exploring one another's bodies, weaving our magic together and smoking the blended herb she'd gotten from End's Wrath's pouch from her pipe made of bone. She was a killer with grace as she sat in the center of the bed, naked and tucking a loose lock behind her hair before wrapping her lips around the pipe's ivory tip, inhaling until she felt the burn. Everything she did was beautiful. We ascended upon that high together, clothes no longer a necessity as I sat on the edge of the bed, strumming a faint melody on my guitar while we spoke about our pasts between drinks, peeling back the layers we'd kept hidden within ourselves. The memories hurt less in one another's presence. She watched the strain of my forearms as I plucked every string. Before I knew it, I was placing the guitar off to the side and moving inside her again.

In the back of my mind, I wondered what bone she would rip from my body if she ever caught wind of who I really was. And as her nails dragged down my back, I realized something...

I was less of a villain *with* her, but I would become any monster *for* her.

She might be the devil, but she was also dancing with one.

Nighttime fell. I didn't hear the last words she spoke as sleep claimed her, but I knew I would be haunted by what was to follow.

"If she isn't delivered at my feet by the time the sun sets tomor-

row..." Fang's words echoed in my thoughts as I dozed in and out of sleep for the rest of the night. It was a blended sense of worry as Vessa's threats seared deeper. Every time I watched her sleep, the more of a bastard I felt.

My thoughts roamed over different scenarios of what to do.

I woke before dawn. Hell, I didn't think I'd ever slept. I had to kill Fang before he got to her.

Vessa would be safe as long as she stayed here; I had paid a great deal to hide our presence. This was the one place in Donia I could trust. The place was family owned, and they never cared to dabble in the politics or the quarrels of warring differences. Nara coins would always have a sway, and so would I as long as enough lined my pockets.

Watching the rise and fall of her chest, a peace was settled in her expression. I draped the sheets over her naked body, pressed a kiss to her temple, quietly got ready, and slipped out the door.

29

VESSA

I'd spent enough time out in the wild to know the sound of a single-action revolver cocking back. A magnum holds a powerful sound for a human, but it was nothing more than a mild inconvenience for someone like me. Waking up to it pissed me off outright.

I knew as soon as I opened my eyes I would be staring down the barrel of a gun. As heavy as it sounded, no bullet was powerful enough to stop me. Still, its familiarity didn't cease the wave of cold sweat sweeping down my spine.

My eyes flicked open. My vision remained obscured as I struggled to get ahold of my whiskey-drenched senses. The muzzle of the gun blurred into two as I felt the world spinning.

I followed the slick lines of steel, trailing up the barrel to a pair of icy-gray eyes peeking out above a thick, gritty, rusted beard—I wasn't sure if the rust was the natural color or days' worth of filth. A smile crept over his mouth as his eyes darted to the sheet barely covering the swells of my breasts.

A pungent, acrid scent filled my nose when he opened his mouth. "Damn, what a fine-looking treat."

I growled. It didn't register that he had his other hand wrapped around my throat until I felt a growing heat emanating from his palm.

Fucking Fire Fae.

Shadows unfurled in the wake of the threat as I gritted my teeth. A darkness solidified into sharp claws as my nails dug deeper into his flesh, causing his grip to loosen and his gun to fall to the floor. A round fired off, whizzing by my face. Someone had surely heard the sound.

I silently thanked the gods for sparing someone like me, because all hell was about to break loose.

I gripped his forearms, grimacing beneath him as his burning hold intensified. The two of us elevated our power, engaged in a struggle of who would take the lead. This asshole was about to meet his end. Did he know who the fuck I was?

Apparently not.

Fire held no bounds with me. I felt the power of *Lam*, finding that thread of fire as my claws became a wielded heat.

My nails seared into his flesh, feeling every layer of his skin burning at the seams. A growl ruptured in his throat, and he released me.

He stumbled back with a heavy thud, and I moved off the bed in haste.

The sheets fell away, exposing my naked body.

Fuck modesty; what was mine was mine, and he was in *my room*.

I'd slept without my boots for the first time in forever, and now I fully regretted it as I slammed my heel into his face. I did not want any part of my flesh touching him.

He quickly rose to his feet, taking a heavy swing at my face. I pivoted beneath his arm and kicked him in the kidney. He flew headfirst toward the wall, but a tendril of shadow whipped into a lasso and roped around his neck, contorting his body into an unnatural position.

"Huh, well, that's interesting," I murmured, observing my handiwork as I effortlessly wielded a sliver of Ryder's onyx lasso.

I wrangled the Fire Fae and flipped him onto his back to find panic in his eyes. His desperate call upon the power of *Lam* was laughable.

"Aw, looks like you're coming up empty," I mocked, pouting my lips as I studied his bloodshot eyes and desperate attempts to try to loosen the rope.

I tied the lasso around his wrists and then to the edge of the bed before casually sauntering over to Ryder's discarded shirt. The ivory fabric hung over my frame just enough to cover my ass.

I searched the Fire Fae's pockets for anything—ammo, nara coins, clues—ignoring the sounds of him choking.

Just then, Pa and Raven burst through the door.

"What in the gods-damn name of hells is going on here?" Pa said.

I ignored him, too distracted as I pulled out a newer version of a WANTED sign, one that portrayed my eyes a little too far apart. I scoffed.

"See, asshole? It says, 'VERY DANGEROUS,'" I said, but the Fire Fae only appeared to be half listening.

A shudder swept down my back as Raven stood behind me, his anger sending a tremor through our frayed and forced bond. I clenched my teeth and lifted my chin, eyes still on the fire bastard on the floor.

Don't fuck with me today, bird.

I handed Raven the WANTED sign over my shoulder. When I turned to face him, his eyes were full of weighted thoughts.

Its gravity hung in the silence between us. He smirked, flashing a dimple before his gaze fell to the paper.

"Are you fucking kidding me?" He slapped the corner and leaned against the wall before passing it to Pa. "I'm not a fucking blue jay."

Pa sighed and removed his hat, combing a gloved hand through his hair.

The Fire Fae tried to speak. To ease the tension in the room, I decided to loosen the lasso.

"Tell me who sent you." I grabbed a fistful of his shirt.

He gurgled a nervous laugh that rumbled in his chest. "You have more than a WANTED sign on your head, pretty little Umbra Fae. You don't think Ryder is after the same thing as the rest of us?"

My breath stilled. "How do you know Ryder?" My voice fluctuated in confusion.

He laughed again. "How does anyone not know who the land's best bounty hunter is? Where is he now?"

A chill swept down my spine. From behind me, Pa's leather gloves creased.

I blinked back as a stone dunked into the pit of my stomach, registering that Ryder's things were missing.

"You're worried about these measly little WANTED signs when you should be worried about why Fang hired Ryder to bring you to his palace. Word on the street is you're kind of special...worth more nara coins than any heist I've ever seen. Looks like Ryder's done his biggest one yet." The Fire Fae smiled, inhaling the smell of sex and Ryder's licorice and spice coating my skin. His eyes roamed over my body as if he could still see the flesh beneath the shirt.

I grabbed him by the throat. "You're lying," I growled, nostrils flaring as tears stung my eyes.

"You got that all wrong, sugar. It's the pretty boys who always lie," he drawled.

I hadn't realized how hard I'd gritted down on my teeth until copper tinged my mouth. I bit my cheek as anger consumed my hold. My grasp crushed his muscles, bones, and trachea, cutting short his gasps and pleas. This fae just fed my inner beast by sending my thoughts brimming. I watched life leave his body. I released the shadowed lasso around his neck upon a final breath he would never feel as his body slumped down into a quiet, endless sleep.

No words formed, only menacing thoughts as I grabbed my belongings and stepped into the washroom.

I felt Raven's looming presence moments after as he stood in the doorway with his arms crossed, likely catching a side view of my breasts as I pulled a clean top over my chest. I tugged my riding pants up my hips and geared up.

"So, you belong to no one, huh?" he mocked. I slipped my leather vest on as my head whipped in his direction. Bloodshot anger swelled in our eyes.

Forcing a half smile, I grabbed him by the chin, pulling his head down until he met my seething glare, seeing the effect my simple touch had over him.

"He said pretty boys lie...You're kind of pretty yourself, bird. So where does that leave us?"

"Us?" He grinned, that dimple reappearing. His hand curled around mine, the size difference evident as he placed it over my heart. I took one step back as he moved into my space. I took in the slant of his nose, knit brows, chiseled face...He was tugging at the thread of our bond as his rich brown eyes narrowed in on me. The fucker knew what he was doing. I felt his presence with more force than before. My back hit the wall as he placed two heavy palms on each side of my head and leaned forward, caging me within. I pressed my palms against his firm chest as the dark linen clung to his muscular form, but it didn't stop him from getting closer.

"He might be on your lips for now, Vessa, but when the day is gone and all is still, remember my touch along the chain you think is around your neck," he said, leaning into the shell of my ear and stroking the thread that bound us together. As frayed as it was, I felt the flutter along the edges. I sucked in a shuddered breath. He smiled in satisfaction as his warmth enveloped me. "And I haven't even touched you. Imagine how *flustered* you'll be then."

His jaw tensed in strangled silence, enough to hear me swallow the lump in my throat.

I found my bearings as I lifted my chin, gaze hardening into something fierce as I shoved past him. "I don't have time for this. I have a cowboy to hunt."

PA SAID nothing as I stormed out of the room and descended the stairs. He knew there was no turning back once I had my mind set. He could either stay behind or join me. Of course, he chose the latter.

I tossed two hefty pouches of nara coins onto the desk downstairs. The older woman's eyes widened as they bounced between me and the sacks.

"A stupid cowboy once told me nara coins talk in this shit-hole of a city, so I'll cut to the chase. Tell me where Fang's hideout is, and you will get to keep your life and some coins."

The woman leaned in, eyes skimming over my face as if she were analyzing how I knew Ryder, and smirked. "You cannot be serious?" She leaned back into her chair, tending to her nails as if they were more important. I stood in silence and clenched my jaw. Her gaze flicked up as she mulled over the bag of coins and then me.

"Fang owns this city like he does the Eternal stone. That greedy fuck lives in the palace north. If the three of you can manage to sneak past his gang of bandits and lawmen, then *good luck.*"

Anger coursed through me as I ground my teeth.

"Two birds, one stone," Pa said, slowly turning for the door as he cracked his neck. Raven's eyes darkened as if this was the fuel he'd been waiting for.

"Oh, and you'll want to enter through the eastern cliffs so you aren't spotted," she said, reaching for the bags and tucking them somewhere beneath the desk. Her glare skimmed my face, studying the strain in my jaw.

I smirked, flicking my hat with my middle finger in farewell. "Oh, no need for sneaking around. We know how to make an entrance."

30

RYDER

This was the calm before the storm. I could feel it in my bones, almost hear it if I tried. The hiss in the air and wind that seemed to whisper words from a far-off place. It's as if the soul of my future self was telling me to prepare and listen.

The power of *Nai* was my wind, the air in my lungs. We didn't have a home like most fae; we went wherever the wind took us. That was what my mother had told me, a human who was once so beautiful. She had rarely spoken about my father. He was a Wind Fae—something I'd learned over time as I'd honed my gift—nothing more. I often thought up stories about what had happened to him. I used to believe he'd followed the winds so far, he'd gotten lost. As I'd grown a little older, I'd recognized the anger hiding behind my mother's eyes, and I'd assumed from then on out, he was just a piece of shit. I'd spent most of my life alone since she'd died, with nothing but my thoughts to accompany me until I got my guitar and horse. As my horse's hooves echoed down the alleyways and streets, I thought about the way Vessa had looked when she'd watched me play. I wanted to spend more time outside my head... with her.

I continued north. The smell of freshly baked bread seeped out from the homes of those who were up before dawn. I knew every pebble and crack engraved in these roads and every distinct smell from certain homes whose inhabitants' lives I'd never know. I knew this city more than I understood myself. I knew when the cobblestone streets turned to white granite, we were at the edges of Fang's lavish lair.

Looking ahead, I saw his lawmen strapped and guarding the entrance.

I dismounted, rolling my head from side to side, and cracked my neck. The sound drew a few stares my way. I straightened my long, dark trench coat. With a tip of my hat, I flashed them a pearly smile and started up the path.

A grin curved my lips as I walked past them. As always, I was reminded of the monster I'd become—I knew by the end of this, one way or another, all those men would die. It wasn't a hunch or whisper of the wind; it was a vow.

There was an eerie, quiet calm as I entered Fang's palace.

Stonewashed pillars lined the foyer, branching off down the halls to different parts of the palace as the bottom of the stairs opened up to the space ahead, leading to a second floor —such a foolish way to squander nara coins. At the top step, I saw the crack on the marble railing, the bloodstain still visible from years ago, a memory forever etched in my mind: the night I'd bashed a man's face in because it had been time for him to leave. Fang's extravagant palace hid the stories I could never tell. I was just as heinous as him.

"You're a little early, Ryder." Fang's voice echoed in the expanse of the grand room as I entered.

I strode in, pretending to be complacent within our roles. I did my job, he did his. Criminals finding common ground to mind our own fucking business. But little did he know that things had changed.

Cascading water filled the silence, a fountain Fang had installed years ago. Though it was off to the side, wedged between crystal-clear windows, it was always the focal point of parties.

"Early bird gets the worm," I drawled, my voice a low echo as I sauntered in, seeing a few more pieces of armor adorning his wall.

Fang had bled me for the boy I'd been until it'd made me a man. He was the same monster he had been years ago. He sat on his throne with a setup that looked more like a raised patio with two long settees running parallel. Empty bottles littered the small table in the center, and the aroma of women's perfume still clung to the air. His grip tensed around the cane made from the bones of fae. His slender, sweaty palms remained clasped around the skull of a large bird at the top. Every time I heard it drag across the stone floors, I remembered the day it had been made. Bile worked its way up my throat— even for someone like me, that memory was far too disturbing.

"Is that what you're calling your cock these days?" he said, playing with the tip of his carefully crafted mustache that was more of an aristocratic statement. He looked a little thinner than the last time I'd seen him but still wore his signature, crimson, long-sleeve shirt tucked inside a black vest. His dark robe hid the rest of his lavish outfit, seemingly from the night before.

Those beady, dark eyes narrowed on me from beneath the brim of his hat, sending the small row of rings pierced into the edge to chime with every subtle motion. His grip tensed as I ascended the few steps to his dais. I took a seat on one of the settees, trying not to be disturbed by the scent of sex wafting in the air. The fucker was a wrinkle in time, constantly doused by the tonic of the Eternal stone. I instantly noticed the effects of mass consumption. I could surmise he hadn't slept the night before, knowing his prize had set foot in Donia. He must have partied all night long to remedy his overactive mind.

"You look like shit, Fang. The Eternal must not be working well with you these days. Those bags under your eyes look like a sack of balls."

"All the more reason why we need that Umbra Fae. There are rumors she has something to do with it. With the power of the Eternal stone waning, the tonics are becoming less effective, which means less nara coins coming in."

"What about your sweet little candle business? 'The flame that burns thrice as long,'" I mocked, reaching for the unopened bottle of whiskey that had somehow managed to survive the night.

"Always with the jokes," Fang said, leaning forward with a scowl. "My reign will not be known for *fucking candles*."

I ignored the splash of spit that flung onto my pants. Getting under his skin was far too satisfying. "I like candles, and so does every other woman when she bathes," I drawled, flashing a smirk before I took a swig of liquor.

"Which is why we need that Umbra *bitch*. Sergil cannot wait to get his hands on her."

My grip tightened around the bottle as my jaw tensed. I saw how Fang looked at me as I thought about the way Sergil had eyed Vessa. No doubt she would be an experiment to him.

"When your cock was buried inside her, did you find out how she's connected?"

I laughed, imagining punching through his face as I focused on the way it intensified his stare. Deploying facetiousness, a wicked grin curved my mouth as I said, "Why? Who wants to know?"

On my next breath, he lunged for me, but I would always

be too quick for him. I parried his attack, moving out of reach. The clumsy fuck landed with his face buried right where my ass had sat. I grabbed him by the back of his robe and tossed him to the side, sending the table and other settee off the dais.

"I won't mince my words, Fang." I gritted my teeth. "The deal is off, and I just came to say farewell."

The animosity finally hit the air. I saw the betrayal flare in his eyes, and in a blazing heap, he gripped me by the coat as we engaged in a tussle that flung us down the steps.

His strikes were hard as they'd always been, packing a punch just to show his role, but today, I was here to prove a fucking point.

"You fucking traitor. After all I've done for you." He growled before I introduced my fist to his jaw and his head whipped to the side, sending blood splattering across the floor.

I growled, pulling him off his feet, and slammed his body against a pillar. The stone cracked on impact, deepening the fissure as it vined up to the ceiling. I swung too wide, and he caught my fist in his hand and punched me in the gut with the other. I lurched forward as he swerved a heavy uppercut into my jaw. He grabbed me by the coat and threw me against the same pillar.

I spit to the side, welcoming the bit of pain with a blood-coated grin, knowing I'd keep fighting for her until he took his last breath.

"Come on, Fang." I seethed. "Show me who you really are." A darkness hung around us as I pulled on the tail of an angry bull. I wanted to see him become the very thing he despised. "You can use glamor all you want, but I know who you have always been."

I was looking into a mirror, an eye for an eye, soul for a soul. He had taken mine long ago, so it was only fair I took what remained of his. He was a Water Fae. I knew the power of

Ari mocked him every day while he hid in his city surrounded by twin rivers with an ocean for a backside. It was a reminder of everyone he'd killed. I'd heard them on the nights I'd stood in the palace. Ripples in the water had floated on a gust of wind and into my room. Maybe subconsciously, the fountain reminded him of a power he refused to touch.

"The power of *Ari* calls you like a siren," I said—words of a distant language unbeknownst to me; maybe the cries of the fallen.

"You might have a way with words around women, but they will not work with me. Your desultory plans have always been your demise, Ryder. Unlike you, I'm always a step ahead."

My brow arched.

"I received a little tip from someone about where you were, and I decided to do a wellness check. You know, in case you had a change of heart," Fang said.

Silence hung in the air. My jaw clenched as panic threatened to spill over, but I quickly reined it in, eyes darkening.

"Judging by the look on your face, I see I was correct. By the way, where is your little Umbra half-light now?"

A growl tore through me as I sent his body flying, the force so strong, his body broke the next pillar.

He was unearthing a demon I hadn't felt in quite some time—a darkness that would ravage this city until she was safe in my arms. Just then, a calamity of gunshots and cries wrung out outside the palace. As I diverted my stare toward the entryway of the grand room, Fang was at my back.

There was no time to form my next thoughts; they exploded in a white haze as he used his power of *Ari*, summoning a blow against my temple and knocking me to the ground. I landed on my side. Without a doubt, I knew the clamor of destruction outside was Vessa, but when I reached through the bond, I felt the sharp, jagged edges of the dark;

one that might as well have said *fuck you*. I cursed under my breath and slowly rose to my feet, licking the blood off my bottom lip before I spat.

I grinned, seeing Fang in his true form. His fae ears took shape in a shade of blue that mirrored the azure sea surrounding the city. His hands, ones I had spent far too many years sparring with, reminded me of their crashing waves.

"There you are," I whispered. Water swirled in crystal orbs around his fists. "I admit, blue doesn't suit you." I pulled a dagger from its sheath and stalked his way. "But maybe red will."

The electricity that coiled down my spine faltered my next step.

I knew the moment she entered the room and felt the darkness she brought with her. Before I could turn my head, she unfurled her power, then clamped it around my neck. I felt the fevered chill of betrayal against my skin; I felt *her* in my next breath.

Fang's laughter bellowed at the threat of a woman who had every right to end me. My dagger clamored against the ground as I tried breaking from her grip.

She spun me on my knees until I was face-to-face with her. I remembered when she'd said she was the devil, and for the first time, I felt it.

Moonlight-silver eyes stared back, an emptiness in them as the ground shook beneath my legs. The wall behind her cracked, splitting in a thousand fissures up the wall. Pieces of rubble fell from the ceiling and crumbled to the ground.

She did not move.

She did not blink.

She only tilted her head as she bore a daggered stare, as if she were trying to piece together who I had been before all of this.

End's Wrath stood in the foyer as Fang's lawmen flanked him. From beyond, the garden encircling Fang's palace caught my eye. The Umbra Fae had torn down every wall that had stood in their path. A gale of wind stirred, unearthing everything in his way. I saw End's Wrath for the legend he was, the monster from the stories. He was a man carved out of stone, who had lost so much. A man who would end it all for her. The cries that ruptured through the lawmen's throats was proof. He carved a calamity of destruction as a searing reminder of how far he would go. He tore through their minds and fears. I felt it in their screams as a chill swept down my back. His force was a gravitational draw to him, until their flesh was stolen from their bodies, becoming nothing but a mist of blood and chunks of meat in his wake amidst the rubble.

Light broke through, and she was nothing but a shadow cast in its rays.

They were the Umbra.

The woman who was staring down at me wasn't Vessa.

She was death.

The moment she'd brought me to my knees, I'd known I only had seconds to act before she'd snap my neck. I wanted to escape the way she was looking at me, and in the same thought, if these were my final moments, at least I'd had a chance to look at her once more.

From the corner of my eye, I saw one of Fang's rogue survivors rush her. She did not move as he closed the distance. Not until he was at arm's length did she punch her fist through his chest and pull out a beating heart. Shadow curled around her hands, a darkness that bled into the air, bending to her whim. It was wicked and cruel, and gods-damn, I was a bastard for still finding it a turn-on.

The man's body collapsed, leaving behind a vessel and a

heart thrumming in her grip. She observed it for a moment before she slowly turned to me.

"Where could I begin that doesn't end with me taking your life?" she finally said, a swell of anger brimming her eyes. Again, she did not blink; a silver glare remained.

"Vessa..." I deeply exhaled the moment she released her shadowed hold. "Let me explain."

She squeezed the pulsing heart in her palm until it burst into a mist of blood, spraying the both of us.

"Imperfect souls can live a thousand lives. I cannot live another if you're not in mine," I said, damning myself for... *fucking hells*...for everything I'd done wrong.

Within the edges of my mind, I used the power against her hold, pushing to my feet against her shadows that bound me to the ground. She wanted me at arm's length while I wanted her by my side. I hated this feeling. I remembered moving inside her, how easy it had been to rein in her power and wield it with mine. Though I remained a few feet from her, the temptation to test that newly-formed thread only grew in desperation.

I swallowed when I saw that her end of the bond still had starlight. In the blink of an eye, the inky swells of her darkness solidified into an onyx lasso. It slithered around her waist, and like cracking a whip, I thrust her body against mine.

I caught her in a hard crash, landing in a bruising kiss, as I couldn't stand the way she was looking at me. Both our powers fell away as we became just two beings in the middle of a crumbling palace. At first, her body tensed against my lips, but they soon softened, and she ran her hands along my neck.

"I'm sorry, Desert Rose. Please forgive me. I couldn't do it, not after knowing who you were." *Fuck, who was I kidding?* I leaned my forehead against hers. "Not after knowing what you meant to me." We both shared the same air, exhaling deeply. "I couldn't..." I rasped, shaking my head as I caressed the back of her neck. She pulled away, staring into my silver-lined gaze full of regret. A flame of betrayal flickered on the edges of her eyes, but the silver moonlight drifted away. Like a break in the clouds, I saw her lavender stare, honey-magic like the stars. The anger still held within as she heaved.

She pushed up onto her toes to kiss me. The rogue tear that slipped down her face felt like guilt whipping against already open wounds. Her lips moved against mine as if for the very last time.

The grin on her face was almost as haunting as her next words. "Your knife or mine."

31

VESSA

He tensed at the whisper leaving my lips as I unsheathed my dagger. I bared my teeth and went for him. He pivoted and took a few steps back as shock raked through the bond. In the same breath, he grinned, expecting nothing less of me.

"I will always love dancing with you, Desert Storm, even one as dangerous as this."

So this was what wild love felt like; it was untamed and turbulent. Nameless and unexpected. Like a storm without warning, he'd come into my life with the force of his wind and pulled me onto his path. Like any unexpected storm, destined to leave mass devastation, one never had a name until it reminded you of the loss.

"*Ryder,*" I whispered, a word that nearly wrecked him through the bond as his jaw clenched.

All I saw was red and all I heard were words that drifted upon an echo of promises we had made.

"*You're going to be mine. I don't think any forced bond could take that away from us.*"

"You don't have to hide from me, cowboy. I see all your demons."
But I'd missed this one.

"Who we were before won't matter if you will have me for who I'll try to be from here forward."

This was him trying? He had been hours from handing me over to Fang. Even if the woman behind that desk hadn't told me where he was, all I would have had to do was follow his thread of betrayal and the faint wailing sound of the Eternal stone. Its cries only grew the closer we got.

I went into a stance, dagger at eye level, and kept my shadows lurking in my grip.

I saw the ring dangling against his chest, the one I'd given to him the night I'd decided to share a piece of myself with a reckless cowboy who had been on his way to stealing my heart, so I went for his.

He whipped his lasso around my waist, but I caught it pulling him forward. I tried to cut the rope with my dagger, realizing the bond we shared wouldn't allow it.

Ryder tsked as he closed the space between us. "It cannot be done so easily." I growled as he blocked every attempt. "We don't have time for this; there are bigger things at stake here," he said.

He somehow wrapped the lasso around my arms and yanked me toward him. With my arms pinned, he held a firm, warm grip on my sides. The subtle drag of his thumbs along my flesh fluttered my heart. Damn him.

He searched my face, finding that flicker of desire still burning for him.

"Gods-damn, woman. Your essence is everywhere, and I cannot escape you even if I tried. Your scent is in the wind, and your touch remains an imprint on my tarnished heart."

"Go to hell," I said.

He grinned. "Only if you sit beside me."

Out of the corner of my eye, I saw Fang's satisfied glare enamored at the sight of me. It quaked down my spine sending my upper lip twitching into a snarl. I'd seen him before. Though he was clearly a Water Fae, something else stuck out. My mind reeled, trying to place where our eyes had met before as the two men stared at me from two distances—wanting me in different ways.

One with a loss of logic because his cock and heart were hand in hand, and the other with flat-out greed. I saw the look in Fang's eyes; he wanted me dead.

I was done being seen as something to kill.

Ryder loosened his grip, and the lasso fell to the ground in a plume of smoke. I narrowed my eyes on Fang, taking a few steps forward, observing the contrast between his blue-tipped ears and terrible crimson shirt. "Blue is a shitty color on you," I scoffed, feeling a flutter of darkness curl up my wrist.

"That's what I said." Ryder's voice interrupted my following thoughts.

"I'd shut the fuck up if I were you," I snapped.

The weapons on the wall behind Fang rattled from the water leaking through the cracks of its broken surface, gathering over pikes and axes. Some appeared to have been rusted over time; they must have belonged to beasts not of this world. No man or fae could hold such a weapon and remain standing.

"Still wild and free. It's been a very long time since I've seen you, *little shadow*. But now that you're all grown up, you remind me less of a shadow and more of a *death comet*." Fang's words swept a chill down my spine as my vision blurred, tunneling into a swarm of memories of the masked man Pa had traded with upon our shores.

"Little shadow. Is that your name? Here, have this…"

"We trusted you," I whispered, shaking my head in disbelief with vengeance swirling around my hands. The more I looked into those eyes, the better I recalled the man who had mimicked my nickname the moment he'd heard Pa say it. The man who had made me feel we were a spectacle every time his boats had docked our shores. He hadn't been there to trade with the Umbra Fae, he had come to scope us out.

Before I could spit out another word, his power of *Ari* forged a hold around the weapons. They broke from the shackles of the wall, shooting straight for us.

Ryder turned, pushing my body behind him as he summoned his power in a forceful gale. His wind parted the weapons, which speared past us into rubble. As I felt the rush of metal whiz by, the call of the Eternal stone was a hiss sending goosebumps along my arms.

The urgency to end Fang curled around my fists, but the call of the stone was louder.

This is not my fight.

The words sent an understanding, knowing the fight belonged to the man who stood behind me in what was once the doorway.

Pa strode forward, releasing a tremor under the ground that rippled like a whip, sending the stones beneath our feet rolling through the expanse of the room, splitting marble in its wake until a large boulder flung up and clipped Fang on the side.

The Umbra Fae knew how to make an entrance that showed the city this wouldn't be tolerated any longer. Take it for what it was. The stone didn't belong here, and neither did any of us.

"Look who it is. The devil himself." Fang grinned, wiping the blood off his face.

"How does it feel to be so close to death?" Pa said, arching a salt-and-pepper brow. He plucked the toothpick from his mouth and flicked it away.

"I guess you'll have to ask your wife and the rest of your village yourself." Fang's grin widened, satisfied to see the truth rake down my spine. A cold lick of sweat swept over me before heat coursed through my body. "The looks on your faces are as priceless as the blood in your veins, but now that I think of it, seeing your people die still takes the cake."

There was nothing more to lose as we stood before the one who betrayed us.

Pa stalked forward, staking claim as he challenged Fang to a duel. The air was charged as the two faced off. Fang's fingers twitched as they hovered above the holster while the other hand churned with power. I'd seen Pa in many showdowns but none that would avenge the years of grief and pent of rage we'd endured. The darkest shadows spun around his fingertips. I knew only one man would leave this room standing, and as Pa cracked his neck and squared his shoulders, my bet was on him. I felt his power surge. There was nothing that could quell the loss, only the vacant look in Pa's moonlit eyes as End's Wrath fully awakened.

I backed away, but Pa looked straight ahead with words that would forever haunt me. "Whatever you do, Vessa. Never look back."

I paused, not realizing the effect it had on me until tears lined my lashes. The ground shook once more, causing the walls behind Fang to swell with water. Pa refused to look at me, but I caught sight of the anger brimming in his eyes as silence hung between us.

"Go," he said, jaw fluttering as he darted a glance at Ryder, giving him a nod. I felt Ryder's firm hold on my bicep as he pulled me away. I nearly stumbled, but my eyes remained on Pa, always on Pa, until the wall broke free behind Fang and he siphoned every drop to bend around him. Another quake shook the ground, and Pa sealed himself in. The rubble became an impenetrable wall as his silhouette disappeared into a cloud of dust. We were back in the foyer, a room of ruin, save for the few statues of faces and limbs that had survived his wrath.

"I didn't know Fang was responsible," Ryder said, full of devastation.

Shock still consumed me as his words echoed. There was no time to process anything.

The sound of muscles and bones meshing together made me turn. I caught sight of a limb being torn off a man as Raven so effortlessly ripped it from its socket. His shirt was torn, exposing his left pectoral. His hair disheveled as the muscles in his forearms glistened beneath a fresh layer of blood. Somewhere amidst the chaos, he'd lost his hat, exposing a sliver of pointed ears. He was in his element. Blood coated his lips and the tip of his nose. I felt like I was seeing how he hunted for the first time but as a blood-lusted fae. As I looked behind him into the city, plumes of smoke rose from homes and buildings. The smell of gunpowder filled the air while shots rang out in the distance. My lips parted slightly, unable to grasp what was unfolding before my eyes.

"This can't be," I murmured, taking a few more steps toward the chaos. I saw Elemental Fae with no more chains of glamor. There were more pointed ears and powers than I had seen in years, and they were fighting back. "How?" I whispered.

"Apparently, we started a revolt against Fang's reign. They kept saying, 'The Umbra is here,'" Raven said.

I looked over my shoulder at the wall, knowing Pa was getting revenge on the other side. Raven placed knowing hands onto my shoulders, dragging his thumbs in comfort. Anger swept down Ryder's spine, ricocheting through the bond where I'd shut him out. I could tie off the threads that bound us all I wanted, but the truth was, that shimmering light would keep bleeding through the cracks toward him.

"I told you your day would come. Now, what do you need?" Raven said, searching my eyes; my bond with him was different. Before I allowed my thoughts to roam over how the fuck *this* would work, I cleared my throat and took a deep breath.

"We need to find where Fang is holding the stone," I said, turning my attention toward the long-haired, brute cowboy who still elicited a burning desire in me. I stabbed a finger into his chest. Ryder grinned in response, sensing the effect it brought. "And you're the asshole who's going to take me to it."

THE SOUND of a civil war muffled the cries of the Eternal stone. Between Ryder and me, I knew we would somehow find the way. He led us down a narrow hall that veined east of Fang's palace. The muscles in Ryder's neck and forearms pulled taut as he walked the halls. An awkward silence loomed while emotions from the three of us were left to fester. I didn't realize how deep in thought we had all been until Ryder spoke.

"So are we going to talk about why Raven has a mouth rimmed with blood, or is it going to be something we never mention?"

I growled, quickening my pace as the sounds of gunfire faded behind us. I listened for the hum that felt like unspoken words, waiting for the gentle flutter along my arms to pull me into the Eternal's unseen path. Whether it was fate or the stone itself, I listened. Ryder scratched the scruff of his beard as we came to a halt.

"Wait," he said. I quickly turned, slamming my brows together, not realizing I had stepped into his space. "It won't be long until more of Fang's lawmen come after us. I know the stone could be in two areas, but we don't have time to search both." He looked down, searching my eyes as he pressed a hand on my arm—a plea in his gaze. With a subtle nod, I let him in. His end of the bond broke through those barriers, putting my thoughts at ease. I felt him, his voice, his aura, smooth and sultry as those piercing blue eyes stared back at me between a frame of wavy dark hair. He moved through my thoughts as wind, a warmth that settled over my body.

"You are connected to the Eternal as I am now with you. With my wind, the power of Nai will show its path," he said through the bond.

From the corner of my eye, I saw Raven lean against the wall and look away, frustrated. I couldn't go there now.

I gave Ryder a nod. He softly exhaled as he pressed a palm over my sternum where the mark was. The threads of our bond fused with power, creating a soft, glowing light between us. He closed his eyes as a rush of energy blew past us in a breeze. My shadows unfurled, giving sight to the wind glittering like the stars on the path to the Eternal stone. When he opened his eyes, a smile curved the corner of his mouth.

In a calm tone, he said, "Let's go."

It wasn't long until it led us down a few more narrow halls. Around every turn, the ground gradually sloped deeper into the palace.

Ominously, the marble faded to old cobblestone walls as water dripped from the ceiling. Candles lit the path to a room with no doors. Through it, I heard the Eternal stone's soft cry. I looked up at Ryder, whose stare remained on the entrance. Adrenaline coursed through me as I stepped forward, leaving the two men behind. Heat immediately wafted from the room, and I summoned shadows to curl around my hands. I kept my darkness at my fingertips, clenching my jaw as I stormed in.

Upon entering, the smell of fire filled the air, and the

crackle of popping lava churned in a three-tier fountain made of lava stone. Its onyx structure encircled the palm-sized Eternal stone that was placed upon an altar. Behind it were three stained-glass windows depicting a man and a woman in medieval armor, warriors kneeling with swords for a dark-haired woman in the center. She was garbed in white and appeared to be in midair. Their eyes were closed with sullen expressions, magic etched into the glass above them with wind on one side and snow on the other. The windows looked out to an ocean view, indicating we were on the cliffside.

"What is this place?" I said, staring at the stone as something deep within my soul ached.

My jaw fell open.

"They are bleeding out the Eternal, keeping it under constant flame. This explains what the Fire Fae do for Fang. He's been using them...for this," Raven said.

"Fang mentioned the power was waning." Ryder darted a look of concern my way as his lips slightly parted.

"It is... *dying*." Anger stung my eyes. I looked at my hands, but the illness coursing through my body was always a constant ache. *If I am connected to the stone, then...*I gasped. "I am dying." I took a few steps back as my eyes bounced between the Eternal stone and the two men with the same worried expression.

This is why I've needed more tonic lately.

"This is fucking crazy," Raven said as he walked toward the middle window facing the ocean. He dragged a hand through his hair and groaned. As he turned my way, his gaze was glossed over. Between the falling lava, determination soon found its way to the surface. "Vessa, what are you going to do about it?" he asked, not in a desperate plea, but with resolve.

A grin curved my lips. "These assholes are done fucking around."

I looked at Ryder, who was beaming with pride as I stepped onto the fountain's ledge. Now at eye level with the Eternal stone, I held out a hand, calling upon the power of *Ano* and *Ama*. I was a gods-damn half-light for a reason. The truth had bound me to harness both sides of the moon, the light and the dark. Born on a blue moon, chosen by the goddesses. This power that made me a prize and a curse coursed through my veins until it unveiled itself in my palm. I called upon the Eternal stone through my mind, searching for the threads of gravitation until I felt the connection to the stone. I screamed as pain spread across my chest, feeling the Eternal stone's agony under fire. Sweat beaded down my face, and my pulse rose to a racing speed. I pushed forward, gritting my teeth against the hold. The moment I lassoed the bond, the ground rumbled beneath our feet. Lava swirled and lapped against the fountain. I moved my foot just in time.

Fuck...

I glanced at Ryder, who was seconds from pulling me off the ledge in case more toppled over.

"Come on," he whispered, watching my every move. He nodded and licked his bottom lip in anticipation.

Another scream tore through my throat as the stone loosened from its hold, sending fissures to vein up the walls around us.

The Eternal stone lifted. Upon release, a calm washed over me as it cooled before dropping onto my hand. With just a touch, the glow melted into my palm and up my arm, a temporary rejuvenation, enough to get me through this.

My eyes bounced between Ryder and Raven as tremors still shook the ground. "I'm going through Blightstone Hollow to Earth's Fall, and from there, I will place the stone far from reach."

"At dusk we ride." Pa's voice sent me spinning on my heels,

a sound that brought me much comfort. He stood in the doorway with a toothpick hanging from his mouth. "I ain't dying in this shithole. Let's get the hell out of here."

)●(

IT DIDN'T TAKE LONG for Raven to scout where our horses had run off to. While we followed Raven to our mounts, Pa dragged Fang's body by a rope binding his hands and legs. The monster was hardly recognizable, having been nearly beaten to death.

"Better him than me," Ryder scoffed.

Pa turned, looking him dead in the eye. "I don't involve myself with the melancholy of love." He glanced my way. "She's your problem now," he said with a wink.

Pa was more than a man. He was a predator who knew how to keep his prey barely alive long enough to torment them. The city dwellers stared upon End's Wrath, getting a taste of their fate if they dared to step in his way.

"Who we were before won't matter if you will have me for who I'll try to be from here forward." Ryder's words echoed in my mind. He looked out into the city as sweat beaded above his brow with a few strands of hair clinging to his neck. Beneath the exterior of this beautiful man was no hero—he was the villain just trying to survive the monster he'd become. I knew that now. We all had a side of ourselves we kept hidden. I didn't forgive him, and I certainly wouldn't forget it either. Still, I couldn't help feeling we were on borrowed time. Once we reached Earth's Fall, I was uncertain what would come next. I stepped into Ryder's space, catching a faint smile beneath his stare. He leaned down and linked an arm around my waist. Wind drifted between us as he brushed a few strands of hair behind my ears, exposing them in broad daylight.

"Look at what you've done, Desert Rose," he whispered. There was a warmth that spread across my chest as I turned to see Elemental Fae stepping into the light, no glamor, no gloves. I could finally take a moment to truly soak in a sight that nearly brought me to tears.

"We've made quite the mess," I said. "I wish my Ma and Lia—"

Pa whistled loud enough for his stallion to hear.

I chuckled faintly, linking my arms around Ryder's neck. "I see all your demons, every single one."

A sliver of that pearly smile peeked out from the corner of his mouth.

"And I see you," Ryder said through the bond. I was reminded of how he'd felt, his scent, and the way his body had rolled against mine as he'd buried himself inside me.

I pressed up onto my toes, brushing my lips along his dark, shadowed jawline, loving the way his scruff felt against my lips before they found his.

I deepened the kiss in a serene surrender. "I'm in search of a guide who can accompany us through Blightstone Hollow. Extra points if he has the skills of a bounty hunter."

Ryder's eyes roamed over my lips as if he were still starved. He took my chin in his hand, chest pressing against mine. "As long as I'm breathing, anyone who steps in your way will be slain at your feet."

"Is that a promise?" I drawled. He smiled, the sharp edges of his canines peeking out. "Your promises seem painful," I said.

"Are you afraid of pain?"

"Are you?" I pressed my palm against his chest, shadows unfurling to claws that slipped between the fabric of his shirt, caressing his chest hair.

"I asked first," he challenged, sweeping his gaze across my

face. Silence hung in the air as I mischievously grinned. "You're staring at me like I'm a prize," he claimed.

I smiled. In some ways, he was. A dangerous one at that.

Raven's silhouette flew above us, drawing my stare to the sky as he scoured the area.

One by one, we quickly reined in our horses and rode east, away from Fang's crumbling palace with his body strapped across a riderless horse. We weaved through brawl after brawl between humans and fae. The Eternal stone was tucked inside a small pouch hidden in my vest pocket. Ryder led us to the east side gates as fast as our horses could carry us.

When two worlds collide.

The words of our ancestors echoed through my mind. I felt the power of amber and bloodstone that made the Eternal what it was.

I felt its yearning for Earth's Fall.

Home.

The word descended upon my thoughts.

I glanced over my shoulder, seeing Pa's look of satisfaction as Fang's body rode beside him. Fire scorched several areas of the city we left behind.

They said you had to forget who you were in order to survive these lands. Behind those walls had been a future built off greed. No one should be forced to forget where they came from.

I was the equalizer.

The half-light who had carved a path for them to decide how their own futures would pan out.

As we headed east for Scarlet Gallows, destiny would lead us down the Serpent's Path in Crimson Valley and into Blight-stone Hollow, where fate patiently awaited.

32

VESSA

hile we rode into the Scarlet Gallows, we saw how quickly the word of war had spread. For the first time, the horrors heinous enough to make it far west bled before my very eyes. All those stories of the massacres told beside a campfire were now up in flames, with every noose to go with it. Emotions stormed through me, outraged that a place like this had existed all this time. I'd never realized how far Fang's grip had reached, but now the remaining Elemental Fae were bringing justice to those who had stood on his side, regardless if they were fae or not. We were riding so fast, I only caught glimpses of Fire Fae taking their stances against them. Their souls be damned when they embarked on the Vale.

Fang was barely hanging by a thread when Pa tossed his body onto the ground, left to be ripped apart by those who sought revenge. Karmic justice was what I called it. All that had been lost would never be replaced; the peace our home once brought would never be the same again, but hearing Fang's final cry before his life came to an end was more than a blessing. It was a calm that offered a small gift, enough for me to know the fight had been worth it. The Scarlet Gallows would now harness the blood of fae and humans—tainted with another horror that I hoped would be a reminder to anyone who dared to stake a claim upon this land again.

Our horses slowed to a trot as we followed the Serpent's Path through Crimson Valley. It wasn't long until we were further south, at the entrance of Blightstone Hollow.

Ryder had kept his vow—he'd ended anyone who had stood in our path.

The call to a divine place fluttered along my arms, sending the hairs on my neck to rise. Crimson birch trees lined the path as fog curled around the horses' hooves.

The three of us rode side by side beneath the canopy of trees that arched the entrance above us.

"Raven." I opened the bond. He coasted down with the next beat of his wings, vanishing into a shroud of shadow. He landed in the form of a male, casually walking alongside my mare, keeping his hand beneath her chin as he narrowed his eyes on the terrain ahead.

"Four able bodies are better," I said.

This place was warm, as if hell itself was seeping through the cracks of the forest floor, creating a fog that felt more like steam. It still did not cease the chill that fluttered down my arms being in such a sacred place. The crimson leaves varied from shades of bright red to a deep maroon. The bark reminded me of bones with fear-stricken faces. The overgrown knots on the trunks were rough and jagged—haunting if I stared too long. But it was Ryder's gaze I felt the most.

"Are you spooked, Desert Storm?" He smirked, eyeing me from beneath the brim of his cowboy hat, a pale-blue glow within its shadow.

I scoffed, but his words still tugged at my core.

"You can ride with me if you need a distraction."

I watched the way his hips moved astride the horse, remembering his length pressed against my center when we'd been in the city. He knew exactly how to eradicate my negative thoughts with just a simple motion. He was a tease, and I wanted a taste. Warmth spread across my chest as I looked at this wicked and shameless cowboy. I—

I felt the power of *Nan* before the release of an arrow as it whizzed by, but there was no time to act. It missed my head by inches. The rustling in the brush came from all directions as heavy footsteps charged from different locations. Time stilled as my mind reeled back to when our homes had been ambushed in Black Water Woods; back when I'd been defense-less and raised in a world without fear. I remembered what it had felt like to be stalked and hunted as I struggled to survive. It was all coming down around us. The only difference between the past and now was that there was no fear, only death awaiting those who dared to play with it. From the shrouds of fog, screams tore through the enemies' throats, proof that karma would always have a place in the dark as Pa summoned the power of *Ama*. His shadows unfurled, and with them, he disappeared into the brush to become them.

Several more arrows flew into the air, coming out of the thick mist that hid most of the terrain. My mare bucked before she reared, and in the next breath, I was flying. Raven growled, the sound so shattering that pain broke through our bond as he shifted too quickly, not entirely, as he moved beneath my body to soften the landing. My head flew back against his chest, and my jaw slammed shut, biting my cheek in the process. He wrapped a firm arm around me. I caught sight of the top of his shoulders, barbed with long, stiff feathers. Their glossy, iridescent shine had blood beaded at the tips. I felt the length of his body, large beneath mine. I grabbed his forearms as my shadows reacted of their own accord against his hold, solidifying my nails into claws. They dug into his flesh, sending Raven to growl as the tendons in his forearms flexed until he loosened his grip.

"Fucking hell, Vessa," Raven cursed, his voice heated raw. I wordlessly jumped to my feet, watching my mare take off as Ryder reared, turning back to get me. He held out his hand, reaching for me. His hold was strong, but his *Nai* was the extra pull to haul me up behind him. I grabbed onto his sides and held on, catching sight of the arrows protruding from the ground with steam curling up through the broken soil.

I'd seen these arrows before. "The arrows are tipped with poison," I called out, seeing Raven's silhouette flying above us in his full bird form. I sensed the heaviness within each beat of his wings; his heart was beating erratically. Something felt off, but Ryder's words pulled me from thought.

"I need to get you to Earth's Fall," Ryder said, calling out to his horse to ride faster.

"No!" I yelled, squeezing his sides. "I'm not leaving Pa."

"He told you to never look back."

But I did, and he was nowhere in sight. Pain seared my eyes. I blinked back the tears that fogged my vision as the urgency for me to go back swelled in my chest. "We need to go back. My gods, Ryder, if you don't turn back, I will end you," I said.

I felt the hesitation in his thoughts, racing through a thousand scenarios before he finally bit out a curse. Raven disappeared between the trees as Ryder and I veered off the path and disappeared into the haze.

)●(

IN THE DISTANCE, I heard the blunt force of arrows blasting into the tree trunks. As we drew near, shards of bark littered the ground in passing.

"These arrows belong to the Earth Fae," I said. We braced ourselves as Ryder's stallion jumped a fallen log.

"Friends of yours?" he called out, gripping the reins.

Once upon a time, maybe. I couldn't remember, but now, seeing their arrows doused in poison aiming for us, "No."

I knew they could kill from a distance. Their arrows could surpass my shadows' reach. With a call to the power of *Ano*, I held on to Ryder as I leaned down, reaching for a satchel full of arrows and a lost bow as tendrils lifted it to my grip. I strapped the satchel to my back as he leaned forward. I saw an Earth Fae garbed in emerald green but wearing a hat like men in the city, which told me they worked for Fang. They weren't known for being a part of society. Like us, they kept to their own territory, the island north of Black Water Woods. Now, it was evident they wanted to die.

Upon an exhale, I released the arrow, followed by a cry cut short as it protruded between the eyes of the enemy. One by one, I shot them down. Ryder's lasso pulled them out of their hiding places. The onyx rope yanked them from the brush and into my line of sight. I inflicted them with their own venom, reveling in the sight of their bodies littering the ground, but my heart nearly stopped at what lay ahead.

In the clearing, the silhouette of a man was on his knees, salt-and-pepper hair matted with blood that clung to his neck.

"Vessa, stay back," Pa yelled in a futile attempt to protect his kin.

I dismounted Ryder's stallion, feet landing in a plume of fog curling up as shadows coiled around me. Fear jolted down my spine seeing Pa handcuffed with a lawman beside him. I tossed the satchel off my back and narrowed in on the older man. He wore a gambler's press to his hat, but the silver star pinned to his dark blue coat drew my attention.

The sheriff.

My heart sank to the pit of my stomach, and I paled. The tie around the sheriff's neck was loosened. His brows sagged as he scowled. Those deep eyes had a claiming look as he glanced down at Pa. His beard was a dark blonde, and he looked like a miserable, grumpy bastard.

"The Umbra herself has finally emerged from the shadows," the sheriff said. "It looks like somebody just pissed on your grave." His voice coiled like a snake.

"Well, asshole, I'm about to piss on yours," I retorted, feeling the sensation of darkness drifting up my wrists. His men stepped into sight, aiming guns and other weapons at us as they chuckled.

The sheriff tsked. "My, my, you have a mouth on you. The name is Sheriff Dawson. You're under arrest for...Well, let's see here." He smirked, giving me a final look before he pulled out a paper marred with blood. His eyes narrowed on the words as he read aloud.

"'Wanted for the murder of forty-five harmless civilians and counting at Grand Dusk's Tavern. Wanted for shooting an unarmed man, point blank, in the face. Wanted for larceny, murder, arson, carrying unregistered weapons...' The list goes on. 'Last seen heading west in the company of an old man and a pet...*blue jay.*'" He laughed, flicking the paper before tucking it back into his coat pocket.

"Sounds like someone you shouldn't be fucking with," I bit out.

The sheriff's presence brought a sense of betrayal, one I couldn't place until I saw Raven step from the shroud of fog behind them. He strolled up to the man on his knees—the one who had raised him as his own—with a malicious grin on his face. My next breath left my soul as the air around me thinned.

"More of a raven, if you haven't noticed," the prick said, squaring his shoulders as sharp feathers still sprawled across them.

Raven looked my way, the truth suddenly unveiling the reason I had always rejected the bond and why my shadows had reacted so violently when he'd caught me falling off my horse.

"Flustered, Vessa?"

My jaw clenched. I couldn't breathe as my eyes bounced between him and Pa. I felt the heat of Ryder's body as he stood beside me with a lasso of shadow in his hand.

"An Umbra with Donia's most wanted bounty hunter. This is going to go down in history," Sheriff Dawson said.

"Fuck you all," I spat.

"End's Wrath needed no guns, arrows, or magic to bring him to his knees. It's funny when you think about it," Raven interrupted, sticking his hands into his pockets. "A man can love so hard that it's the one thing that fails him in the end."

"Why?" My voice broke while something silent flashed behind Raven's eyes as the betrayal carved a line between us.

"I want out. I'm done being your fucking pet." The muscles in his arms flexed as his jaw fluttered. Hurt and pain hid behind his eyes. We'd never needed a bond to know how one another felt.

I reached out through the connection as unseen hands stroked his face. "Lies," I whispered, sending both our eyes to gloss through the threads that bound us. He closed his eyes as his next breath stilled at my touch. Still affected, still the same man beneath this beast he'd been forced to become.

"Don't do this to us," I said.

"US?" His eyes flicked open—a daggered glare toward the cowboy who stood beside me. Then Raven looked my way.

Caged. Trapped, is what his eyes read. He closed his end of the bond cold, nearly sending me to blink back.

How many times had we looked at one another, feeling confined within the spaces we'd been forced to live in? The eyes of the one I trusted with the entirety of my soul had now betrayed it. A swell of tears lined my lashes, but now I finally knew.

"As soon as End's Wrath heard an ambush was waiting at Earth's Fall, he bucked so quickly, it was almost embarrassing for how legendary he is. I thought it would be enough to take him in, but now with the three of you..." Sheriff Dawson just laughed.

"You have a shitty way of fucking with fate. Now here you are, desperate to see how the Umbra Fae can get out of this one," Raven spat in anger, probably because I'd come back when I wasn't supposed to.

There were no questions or other thoughts that formed in my mind. I reached into my vest pocket, ready to throw the Eternal stone at their feet in exchange for the only one in this world who could keep my chaos at bay.

"Vessa, no!" Pa gritted out, his plea so loud, it nearly shook me.

"Fuck this stone. It means nothing to me without you." My voice cracked with the last words as tears stung my eyes. "Nothing is worth *any* of this." I was tired of fighting. Tired of sleeping with one eye open. I remembered the quiet mornings when Pa would play cards. I was afraid to face another day of silence without him in it.

He'd given himself up for me, and I'd come back. I'd always come back to any hell for him. Damned be the ones who ever tried to take him from me.

Though the sun was setting above the trees, I felt the faint energy of the moon barely breaking sight. The center of my mark thrummed as the air around us constricted. I willed the darkness to come, the same one that often felt like it was at my throat; now, it was wrapped tightly around theirs. Only this time, they knew where it was coming from. Black, inky swells of shadow snaked around their necks. My fingers curled into tight fists, clenching as the pain bit into my palms while their eyes bulged from their skulls. Bows and pistols fell to the ground with the sound of gasps breaking out. Pain tinged my eyes as the moonlight silver took over. I was harnessing too much of the Umbra. A crimson tear brimmed the corner of my eye. My evil was unyielding, unbending, a true power rushing through my body.

Here I was again, death chasing at their heels. But weapons were always wrongfully drawn, pointed at one another, magic or guns. There would never be any peace. They were not going to survive this, not while the very last of my blood was shackled to the ground. I was so consumed by the fear of losing him that I didn't see Raven's arm flying up, unaffected by my force because we were bound, a bond forced by the very man who was on his knees. From the corner of my eye, I watched as Ryder moved, but time nearly slowed.

We were not quick enough.

The cutting edge of the knife slammed into Pa's lower back. He coughed, a slew of blood spilling down his chin and onto the ground. Raven rammed the dagger so deep, it cut clean through, tearing the front of Pa's shirt.

A cry seared my throat, snapping all their necks at once—a blast that swept through the surrounding trees, splitting them in half. I fell to my knees as a strangled sob expelled from my throat.

Raven stood in place, watching the way Pa's body slumped

forward. I could have sworn regret flashed in his eyes, watching me break. The same person who had counted the stars with me in the early morning hours. The one who had stood by my side when night terrors consumed my dreams. But in front of me wasn't the man I'd thought I'd known. His eyes shifted into someone I could no longer see. A numbness swept down my body, but I somehow managed to rush forward toward Pa.

Ryder went for Raven, but the traitor disappeared into a shroud of shadow, only to reappear as a raven flying off.

"End's Wrath never told you that his death would free me. As I said, Vessa, you would always be my demise." He spoke to me one last time before I felt the end of his bond cut clean and run cold, void like the death pool of darkness I had always given him.

I pulled Pa onto my lap, shaking him until I saw those deep-set eyes look up.

"My Vessa...my daughter, I have always known my fate. I knew this was where I'd take my last breath. It was a nightmare chasing me for so long, but after your mother died, I couldn't run any faster to this moment. I was destined to die here to save you and give you the life you always deserved to have."

I hung my head between my shoulders and sobbed. My gods, his words were so unveiling. For the first time, I didn't want any of this to make sense, but it did. It really did.

"Take the Eternal stone to its resting place. There, you will find your peace."

"There is no peace without you." My voice was raw and ragged, begging. He had known all this time and never told me.

How could he?

"Don't do this to me."

"This was our last ride, Vessa. Never lose that freedom you

have when you ride into the night. That's how I will always remember you. Wild...and free. My Shadow."

I shook my head, fighting for the tears to stop falling so I could see his face one more time. The warmth of his blood bled onto my clothes and dripped down the sides of my legs.

"You must fight for what's left. Don't look back. Ride fast. Your life depends on it... To Earth's Fall..."

I saw the moment his sight vanished into a void, a vacant expression that saw beyond what my lavender eyes could.

Silence had never been so earth-shattering. My breathing stilled. The air no longer existed in the space that left us empty. The ringing in my ears grew to a throbbing pulse. Before I could fully grasp what was happening, I heard the most terrifying of sounds, ones that ripped my soul to shreds. I didn't realize at first that it was me screaming out in anguish. The life had left his eyes, and he gazed into a void, into nothing, nothing as I shook his body. My world had blurred and ended in one breath. I could bend the dark, manipulate power, and harness the moon's energy, but I couldn't bring him back. I was powerless to the otherworldly things that bound me here. For the first time, I felt useless. My mind fell into despair as I leaned over his body.

Still warm.

Maybe he will breathe again. Maybe we can save him.

I waited for that subtle rise of his chest, the thrumming beat of his heart against my ear as I rested my head against him. I waited, praying to the stars my heart would still so I could *hear him.*

Breathe...breathe, breathe, I begged.

Voices sounded off with gunfire in the distance. The clamor of horses' hooves rumbled through the ground, an echo in the sway of my entire world shifting.

I strained against the strong arms that wrapped around my

waist. My shadows unfurled in all directions, losing sight of where to go. I was trapped inside my racing mind as every muscle tensed.

He was gone, he was gone.

The thoughts rang out until they were screams for all to hear.

"Come back!" My cry ripped from my throat as I looked to the canopy of the trees, screaming for his soul to return. A curse tore from me as I thrashed in Ryder's arms.

"We are running out of time," Ryder pleaded.

We always had been.

I didn't know how I moved, but I managed. Every step heavy until I placed my foot into the stirrup and mounted Ryder's horse. He got behind me, reached between my arms, and gripped the reins.

I turned back one last time, watching Pa's lifeless body until he disappeared from sight.

33

RYDER

We never had any time to process a gods-damn thing. We could be gone in the next breath, no time to strain against reason.

Survive. Live. Fuck. Laugh. Repeat.

End's Wrath died, and I didn't even know if he'd had a name beyond the legend. Vessa was the only extension of the man he had been, a father who had tried his best. I bit back the sting of tears trying to form—holding them in, but they were a force on their own.

I'd failed Vessa.

I'd failed End's Wrath. I'd failed him no matter what he had said to Vessa.

In the beginning, all I'd cared about was saving my soul. Now, here I was, wishing I could have traded places to save his.

I hadn't been fast enough, and I would have to carry the shadows of that moment for the rest of my fucking days. Her cries would become a darkness shrouding my heart.

There was no ambush waiting at Earth's Fall; they must have assumed we'd all been taken by that Sheriff Dawson. I knew we'd reached Blightstone Hollow's end when a thick wall of haze lined the entrance of the forest.

"Don't stop. Keep riding," Vessa said along the bond.

I wanted to say I was sorry, but if I spoke, I knew she would end me. I briefly peeked down to see the vacancy in her eyes. I'd made a promise. I would get her to Earth's Fall even if it killed me.

I squeezed the horses' sides to ride faster, holding my breath as my stallion leaped into the thick, steamy fog, exhaling when we landed on terrain no different from Blightstone Hollow's. It was the chill that suddenly swept across the land that snared me. The climate changed within the blink of an eye as a cool breeze grazed our skin. My stallion slowed to a trot. We rode up to a fountain filled with crystalline waters. The fountain of the Eternal. Giant stone statues of unknown warriors whose tales had been forgotten surrounded it. We dismounted.

"Wait here," she said, briefly glancing my way. A heaviness settled onto my chest as she spoke those words, but I watched her leave with my head tilted in observation. She confidently walked the path as if her soul had been here before. To my surprise, she walked past the fountain to a waterfall I hadn't seen until she stood on its ledge. Beside it were statues of gods who each of our powers belonged to.

Moments passed in silence. I thought I heard Vessa's voice carry through the wind. I could call upon my *nai* to listen, but I was done prying. She had many things to sort through, and I hoped, by the end of it, she would still see me in the same light she had when I'd first met her in the saloon.

The ground furiously shook before my next thought could form, throwing me off balance. The fountain of the Eternal and everything around it rose, unearthing the entire expanse from where the Earth's Fall truly began. My eyes desperately narrowed on Vessa. I'd never seen a light so luminous in all my life, none as blinding as hers. Shadow and light surrounded her the same way nebulas brushed the night sky.

Lavender, like the freckles that glittered across her face.

I dropped to my knees as Vessa expelled every ounce of power from her chest. Her loud cry cleaved a deeper mark on my soul than ever before as she destroyed the stone within a simple breath. Panic swept down my spine in fear that she could end herself in the process. The winds picked up. I gritted my teeth, sensing the heaviness taking residence in my heart as a gale force pushed me back. The fucking hells would open up before I ever let anything take her away from me, even death itself. For the first time in a very long time, I felt the recesses of my mind tearing apart, revealing a feeling I'd kept hidden for so long.

Loss.

I was afraid to lose her the same way I'd lost my mother. I was afraid to be alone again.

Flashes of Vessa were engraved into my mind, from the way she looked down as she smiled, to the simplicity of her touch that could undo me every time, to the stoic strength she held in a world that was always at her heels.

This was how she'd chosen to live her life.

Hard and fast.

Another deep breath.

A roar tore through me as I mounted my stallion without question. I was out of my fucking mind riding toward an unearthing mass of destruction. Wind Fae had no home, but I saw one possible with her, and I would go wherever the wind carried her. I called upon the power of *Nai*, begging it not to fail me now as my horse jumped into the air. In desperation, I sent a silent prayer into this sacred place to carry me to her. My soul reached into our bond.

In the final leap grew a blinding light that swallowed me and my stallion whole.

34
VESSA

"*Keep to the shadows and low-lit taverns.*"

"Here, my fate awaits," I whispered into the quake of truth that rumbled beneath my feet. I saw it all.

I was not here to return the stone; I was here to end it.

The Eternal stone held a power over our land, and it was now torn with pain. I'd seen what its existence could do to those who were weakened by greed.

I was the last of the Umbra, dying and always on the run. A war between two worlds who couldn't figure their shit out, and I so happened to be caught in it. There was no peace. I had seen battle and famine for far too long. All I knew was how to fight and survive another day just to wake up and do it all over again.

I saw the sun through the Eternal in a blinding, white light. No matter how fast we rode, I was destined to end up here.

No longer under the wing of Pa, I stood alone in the vast expanse of this space as I was surrounded by serenity.

Peace.

This was where I had chosen to be.

Within the power of the Umbra, darkness coiled up my arm, brushing along my skin. I had always known this distant part of me, the other side of the moon. It was the other half of what I'd lost, affirming what I had to do. The power of *Ama* was a familiarity that gently wrapped around my hand and the Eternal stone as light broke out from between my fingers. I was a reckoning force, cast in light with the power of *Ano*. I was the Umbra, willing the end of the Eternal stone. It split in two as more fissures veined across its golden amber glow, dispersing into a thousand shimmering pieces of blinding light that lulled me into a vacant space. Darkness followed bright rays, appearing as stars upon an open night sky. My soul was whisked away as my mind flashed through a lifetime of memories—the ebb and flow of my existence. Running barefoot in the woods with my sister, nothing but soot on our feet and hungry bellies craving pastries. Her voice was a calm throughout the woods. I followed it until I caught sight of her bright violet eyes with azure drops around them, child-like until I blinked again and caught a glimpse of what she would have been if she had survived. Tears stung my eyes. She was beautiful, surrounded by lush, wild terrain. I saw Raven smiling for the first time when I'd offered him a gift in a place where he had felt so alone. The smile that Pa had worn even on days when Ma was being wicked. It was the sound of *her* voice that stilled my next breath. A call to the divine as a silhouette took shape, causing me to run as fast as my legs would carry me, only to discover I didn't have to run. The gravitational pull brought us together. Rich brown eyes greeted me as familiar hands touched my soul. I couldn't stop the tears from falling when I saw the woman who smiled back.

"Hello, my moon. Home so soon?"

Home...

Words so foreign on my lips, they nearly broke me. I'd never felt I belonged in a world that was vastly changing. But there was one thing I knew for sure as I studied the shape of her face and curve of her high cheekbones with bronze skin and dark hair matching my own.

I belonged to her.

Every word I'd ever dreamt of saying to Ma evaded me. Only tears fell in heavy waves, cascading down my face; I could barely see.

She held me in her arms. A phantom touch, recalling what her warmth had once felt like on cold winter nights. The way her soft skin felt inside her arms.

"Always so swift." Ma chuckled. *"But you have flown too far from where you need to be. It is not your time."*

I tried to speak, but words here were sent with emotions. I nodded as she stroked my long, dark hair and took my face in her hands, wiping away my tears with her thumbs.

"It is not your time," she whispered again, taking me in her arms, but I felt her slipping out of reach. Looking past her, my chest nearly cracked once more as I sucked in a shaky breath. Pa's silhouette, an Umbra in a waning light as he tipped his hat one last time and turned with Ma following after.

)●(

DESERT ROSE...

"Desert Rose..."

My eyes fluttered open to find Ryder caught in the sun's rays, light filtering through his hair as he looked down.

He helped me sit up and handed me a flask of water. Still stunned, I splashed it over my face as I reeled over what had happened. Looking around, we were sitting by the fountain.

The birds were chirping somewhere hidden within the trees. The weather was a touch of a warm spring.

"What happened?" I asked.

"I don't know. I woke up and found you lying beside me."

He took my chin in his hand, overcome by emotions as he shook his head.

"Desert Rose, you scared the shit out of me." He gave me a bruising kiss, one that seemed to be the beginning of a salve that would heal my new inner wounds.

He pulled away and looked at me again, probably wondering how we could have survived as he enveloped me in an embrace. We stayed this way for quite some time.

"I'm surprised you're still here," I finally said.

"You can run me into the ground, and I'll still be dumb enough to be here at the end of it."

I laughed, resting my head against his hardened chest. I didn't know what would happen after this, but I remembered the ring that hung around his neck. Somewhere between then and now, I had fallen for this foolish cowboy. As I took it in my hand and studied the small circle that resembled a half-lit moon, I realized something fierce.

"You are mine, cowboy. There isn't anyone in any realm that could take you away from me."

A warm chuckle hummed in his chest.

"Damn them all to hells if they tried," I said.

He leaned forward and cupped my cheek, dragging the pad of his thumb against my mouth as he flashed a pearly smile. "Damn them all to hells."

Looking past Ryder, I saw his stallion with the chest full of tonic—the last card Pa had played—strapped to its side. I smiled faintly.

Arching a brow, Ryder seemed to notice.

"Whatever challenges come our way, we will manage it," he said.

A warmth bloomed, knowing Pa was finally with the woman he loved. I'd have to think about that whenever I felt myself slipping into the dark.

Besides, a new vendetta was on the rise.

I'd let the bird live for now, let him get a taste of what freedom felt like while I enjoyed some of my own.

But when he woke to the sound of a hammer cocking back, he'd meet his fate. It would take one bullet to kill, two because I was a spiteful bitch. I knew my path.

May the ancestors send whatever darkness or light we need to guide us.

The End

Vessa,

My beautiful daughter, only those who truly sit in the dark can see the world for what it is. Sometimes it's scary, other times, it's a gods-damn ride. I'm honored to have my last one with you, to see you grow into the warrior I raised you to be. I think your Ma would be proud you stayed wild like her, giving every man in sight a hard time.

You gave me life, you gave me reason.

I can't go with you on your next adventure. If I defy the path I've seen, I'm afraid I'd be disrupting what's to come. You won't understand any of this right now, but I reckon you will. I can only hope I will be able to guide you when you really need me. I know we never had that talk about "fated mates," but if Ryder is the one, your bond should make it so you won't need to take the tonic as often.

Your condition will never leave you, but you'll manage.

Though this chest is enough to last you for quite some time, for your old man's sake, use it sparingly. Save my special blend of herbed smoke for celebrations. If my visions are right, by the time you drink your last tonic, you'll be where you're supposed to be. Now I can already hear you questioning how. You'll know when you know. I just wish I could be there when that day comes. Until then, when your mind is messy, pull out my deck of cards and sort through your thoughts.

Remember you are the Umbra. Stay free.

Love you,

Your Pa

Vessa

35
RAVEN

Epilogue

Upon Eternal

Once upon a time, a raven fell in love with the moon. He looked upon her every night, enamored with how bright she'd shine in the darkness he was cursed to live in. She became his opium, his safe place. She was powerful enough to move the seas, powerful enough to bend the light. But it was what he saw inside her that moved him most. The moon was stronger than the Eternal stone, more than any tale had said her to be. She was more than an Umbra, she would be his way out someday. This bond wasn't forever, though love could last eternal; it would be the very thing that would save her in the end.

I'd had a choice to make: to live with the Umbra Fae and remain in the very cage that held my real name along with all my memories, or to fly free, never seeing Vessa again. I chose the latter. I chose me.

I was lost between male and raven, finding it was quieter soaring through the clouds. Less messy, though the bloodlust remained no matter what form I was in. My life had been stolen, but as we'd grown older, the thread of curiosity had arisen. I'd felt her pluck that string as her mind had wandered to the what ifs, finding myself lost in it, pushing those boundaries more and more.

There'd been a time where my soul had lived for hers, but as much as her presence grounded me, I had known that I would always be trapped.

Caged.

Bound to a woman who had been tempted to touch me yet afraid of how hard she would fall if she kept going. I would rapture her soul in a simple breath. I had always known when she'd pull along the threads of our bond. On those late nights when her bed had lain empty, I'd seen her imagine where she wanted my tongue to slide, always afraid of that loss of control; it had scared her more than lust.

Freedom always came with a cost. Now, I saw it for what it truly was. One could never really be free. The echoes of her voice would always be in the back of my mind.

Somewhere beneath that bond was a love that had never been given a chance. It was a noose hanging around my neck, pulling taut the more I saw her with him. As I craved to be in her shadowed grip, that cool mist upon my flesh, she would always be unobtainable on the other side of it, as her hand slipped away when we were made to come together just to fall apart again. Destiny held a tighter hold, a truth the moment I had seen Ryder. Watching her slowly slip away from me made me realize how much of a possession I had always been. The heart and desire were the most destructive of things. While I had caught those brief moments when she might have given me her heart, when I had done more to her with a simple touch, I was not her path. I had seen it in her eyes, the betrayal cutting like knives. She wasn't ready to let me go, but I had to.

What would the moon want with a bird when she had the sun to cast her gaze upon?

I was alone in a world with no time to understand; I'd learned it by fault, rebellion, and by fate, leading me by the heart while she had fallen in love with a cowboy led by his cock, destiny or not.

I'll cherish the times she made me smile, when we'd looked upon the stars on nights she couldn't sleep, and when she had looked at me the few times she would have kissed me.

I would rather have her hate me forever than to watch her die. A realization as I'd driven the knife into End's Wrath. He had known it was coming. *"The great loss Vessa will have to face before she finds her peace."* Something greater awaited her. He was meant to die there, by my hand, and I was meant to be free. It was the only thing I could have done that would be a deep enough cut to have her end Sheriff Dawson and his men in an instant. To save her life and to free mine.

She wasn't supposed to come back. Fucking hells, she was not supposed to come back.

Tears stung my eyes.

I'm sorry, Vessa, my eyes had pleaded. For a breath, I knew she'd seen it, felt it before the last remnants of our bond were torn by the fray.

Her catatonic stare had been enough to know that she would never forgive me.

I'd looked at her one last time as I'd flown away, for I knew, if our eyes ever met again, there would be the barrel of a gun between us.

"Goodbye, Moon."

AFTERWORD

Thank you for reading *Last Ride of the Umbra Fae*. For all future bonus chapters, character art, audiobook announcements, and more, follow me on my social media pages and sign up for my newsletter.

ABOUT VESSA

Though this is a fantasy story, there are things we read in books that are very parallel to our world. The FMC has a disorder similar to an autoimmune disease. Autoimmune diseases cannot be cured, but their chronic symptoms can be managed. I want to thank Jenn T. for educating and fact-checking me on this as well as being a sensitivity reader for my FMC.

For more info, please go to:

autoimmune.org

Did you enjoy the book? Please consider leaving a review on:

Amazon, Goodreads, Storygraph and wherever you can. Reviews help authors reach their audience and give other readers a chance to discover our books. <3

Also by Monica Amore

A Flame Under the Moon
Darkness of Fate Series

"Do not fear me, Princess. I just came to collect what's mine."

Acknowledgments

Granni, my desert angel, and the other half of my soul. I know you have been moving the stars for me with this career. I see it, I hear it. This was a story I had no idea needed to be told until I lost you. You had always embraced me for who I was and never shamed me for how I felt. I dream deeper now because I know it's where I'll find you. Until we meet again on those cerulean shores, I'll keep searching for your trails of stardust. Love you to the moon and back.

Poppy, I was never a daddy's princess; I had always been a grandpa's warrior. I take great pride in that because you have always been my hero, my home when things get too dark. We've had a wild ride together. Now that the dust has settled, I still enjoy our quiet mornings full of endless coffee, talking about everything we will do tomorrow. I am so grateful for you. This book would not have been possible without you.

My husband, my partner in crime, you let me talk about my books all damn day and still share the same enthusiasm. You're always striving for more ways for me to be seen, and the dedication and countless hours you've put into my projects speak volumes. I am eternally grateful. I still don't think I deserve you, but I know you will keep trying to prove me wrong anyway.

My daughter, my powerhouse. You keep me humble, and your witty responses remind me to embrace these moments, have fun, and enjoy life. You are the break in the clouds on my dark days and the sunshine my spirit needs. You are my fierce little warrior.

My mother, when I showed you Vessa, I felt your smile over the phone. You said she looks like the women in our family and that we don't often see a beautiful brown-skinned woman on the frontline of these stories. Vessa was already special to me, but you affirmed how special she would be to others. Thank you for riding out this summer's storm with me.

My sister Z, you are meant to do great things in this world. Do not let anyone stop you from reaching for the stars.

My editor, Rachel, I love our dynamic. I am forever grateful for the time and dedication you put into my books. It's always an honor! Thank you Chelsey, and Cait.

I am beyond grateful for my Alpha & Beta team. Annika, LaKeishia, Salina, Karrie, Sara (tairen_soul), Laura, and Courtney. Thank you for reading this in its rawest form. LaKeishia, you didn't know it then, how meaningful your words had been in a time of darkness. You gave me the courage to write this book. Salina, you have been a pillar of strength for many of us; you continue to inspire me every day, I love you. My beta readers Ashley, Sara B., Jasmine, and Brittany, you are all amazing! Jasmine, words cannot express how grateful I am for you. Thank you and Darby Jo for being here for me.

Jenn T., Amaya, and Jenn A., thank you for being a sensitivity reader for Vessa. Your time and dedication to her and this story mean the world to me! Jenn T., my warrior, I love you and I am truly honored.

To these amazing women who also remind me this is not a competition. There is room at the table for us all. Brea Lamb, Tara N. Gabrys, Lindsey N. Rhoden, Nova Nox, and everyone in the Author Support Group.

Under the Moon Baddies Street Team! Thank you for reminding me and everyone else how amazing my books are and that it's okay to go at my own pace. Your love for my characters keeps me going. I am forever grateful for you all. I love you baddies! And thank you, Jessica, for helping me with this release! Betty, you're my local baddie. Can't wait for the summer.

To all my amazing readers, you give me life and give my writing reason. These stories are for you and anyone who needs an escape. Thank you for every message, tag, review, and like/share you give on my books. It means more to me than you will ever know! I will continue to strive to take my books to the next level and spoil you all with more character art, bonus chapters and other fun announcements along the way. All of this would not be possible without you! I am forever grateful.

ABOUT THE AUTHOR

MONICA AMORE is an author who has west coast roots—born and raised in the City of Angels and the Mojave Desert. She now lives in a hidden forest with her husband, daughter, and cats somewhere in the Midwest. When she was young, she wanted the hero, but now she wants the villains. When she's not writing fantasy romance, she's somewhere barefoot in the woods or tucked away in her haunted little library reading more books. She loves iced coffee, spending time with her family, and enjoys being outdoors.

Follow her on IG @authormonicaamore
Website: www.authormonicaamore.com